Sealing the Deal

Also by Sandy James

The Ladies Who Lunch Series

The Bottom Line

Signed, Sealed, Delivered

Sealing the Deal

SANDY JAMES

New York Boston

This book is a work of fiction. Names, characters, places, and incidents are the product of the author's imagination or are used fictitiously. Any resemblance to actual events, locales, or persons, living or dead, is coincidental.

Forever Yours
Hachette Book Group
1290 Avenue of the Americas
New York, NY 10104
www.hachettebookgroup.com
www.twitter.com/foreverromance

First published as an ebook and as a print on demand edition: November 2014

Forever Yours is an imprint of Grand Central Publishing.
The Forever Yours name and logo are trademarks of Hachette Book Group, Inc.

The publisher is not responsible for websites (or their content) that are not owned by the publisher.

The Hachette Speakers Bureau provides a wide range of authors for speaking events. To find out more, go to www.hachettespeakersbureau.com or call (866) 376-6591.

ISBN: 978-1-4555-5893-3 (ebook edition)
ISBN: 978-1-4555-5894-0 (print on demand edition)

To my new grandson, John Solomon.
You are the light of my life.

Acknowledgments

As always, I need to thank my agents—Joanna MacKenzie, Danielle Egan-Miller, and Abby Saul. You ladies are amazing!

Thanks to my editor, Latoya Smith, for always making my books so much stronger. You're such a talented editor!

I'd be lost without the help of my critique partners—Cheryl Brooks, Nan Reinhardt, Leanna Kay, and Sandy Owens. Thanks for all you ladies do for me!

And to my family, friends, and readers for their unending support. Love you!

Sealing the Deal

Chapter 1

One more person.

If one more person told Bethany Rogers how sorry he was that her sister was dead, she might just punch him right in the nose.

She swallowed her irritation. It wasn't her normal response to stress anyway since she much preferred finding the positive in any situation. Of course, she'd never been through *this* kind of stress before. Perhaps this anger was normal for someone who was grieving.

It wasn't often a girl lost her only sister. Nothing remotely positive to be found in that.

I never said good-bye.

That would haunt Beth for a good, long while—if not the rest of her life. Even though she kept reminding herself that not talking to Tiffany wasn't her fault, she couldn't push the guilt aside.

Her sister had been in a war zone. Communicating with someone overseas wasn't easy. The time difference alone made it a daunting chore. While the army allowed Skyping, Tiffany had reached out to her big sister only a few times. Their last video chat had been over a month ago when Tiffany had first arrived in Afghanistan.

And now Tiffany was dead.

Beth went to the chapel early, wanting a moment alone with her sister, only to be denied a private farewell. An army officer stood guard over the flag-draped coffin. While the family had been offered a chance to view the remains, the officer who'd escorted Tiffany to Princeville, Illinois, cautioned them against doing so. The suicide bomber had done his job well, savagely destroying the three people at the guard post that fateful morning.

Sick at heart, she turned to head back up the aisle and nearly collided with Danielle Bradshaw. Her best friend was dressed in a perfect little black dress, wore very little makeup, and had pulled her long, blond hair into a tight bun.

Mourning chic.

"Hey." Beth swallowed hard to keep the threatening tears—the ones she wanted to shed in private—at bay.

"Hey," Dani replied, her tone wary. She studied Beth with her crystal-blue eyes before understanding dawned. Then she opened her arms wide.

Without a moment of hesitation, Beth threw herself into Dani's embrace. Beth was as short as Dani was tall and found her cheek pressed against her friend's shoulder. "Thanks for coming."

"Shit, Beth. Where else did you think I'd be?" came Dani's characteristically acerbic reply.

Having narrowed her vision to focus on her best friend, Beth hadn't realized the rest of the Ladies Who Lunch had arrived as well. Mallory Carpenter and Juliana Wilson came forward to sandwich Beth and Dani between them, a group embrace of four women who needed each other's friendship in a way most people might never understand.

That bond had been formed years ago as the four of them shared their lunch period when they'd all been teaching at Stephen Douglas High School. As time passed, they'd learned to lean on one another through thick and thin. Mallory's breast cancer. Juliana's choice to leave teaching and start a new career.

And now Beth facing the loss of her little sister.

They simply held on to each other for a few precious moments, crying softly. Then one by one, they eased back.

Mallory sniffed and wiped the tears from her cheeks with a tissue she'd wadded in her palm. Her light brown hair had recently been cut into a short, sassy style. After she'd lost her hair to chemotherapy, it had taken her a long time to allow anyone to put a pair of scissors to it. Now that her breast cancer was four years in the past, she'd finally decided to cut it the way she wanted instead of focusing on growing it out. Her dark brown dress matched her eyes. Although those eyes were red-rimmed, they still reflected Mallory's boundless kindness.

Juliana was stoic. Dressed in a navy suit, her long red hair loose around her shoulders, she looked the part of the successful Realtor she'd become. But beneath that rough exterior beat a heart full of compassion.

"Thank you all for coming." Beth gratefully accepted a new tissue from Danielle.

"Where else would we be when you need us?" Mallory asked with a sympathetic smile.

Beth shrugged. "It's about the only thing I can say without getting choked up. I sound like a broken record."

Mallory spared a quick glance over her shoulder. "The guys came, too."

Hanging back a few feet were Ben Carpenter and Connor Wilson. Since Connor wasn't holding two toddlers, Beth assumed the Wilsons had left their twin boys back in Cloverleaf with a babysitter. She tossed each man a grateful smile. They nodded in return.

Dani took her hand and gave it a quick squeeze. "How are you holding up, hon?"

"I'm okay. Still a little catatonic. I just can't believe Tiffany's gone." Beth's gaze drifted to the double doors, and she caught her parents walking in. Carol Rogers held Emma, Tiffany's nine-month-old daughter, against her hip.

"They brought the baby?" Dani whispered.

"They're living in Florida now, remember?" Beth replied.

"Oh, yeah... the retirement community."

Crossing her arms around her middle, Beth tried to ward off the chill that seemed to have settled in her bones. "They don't know anyone here anymore. Neither do I for that matter. We didn't want a stranger to babysit."

"Then why's the service here and not Cloverleaf?" Juliana asked.

"Tiffany's friends are all here. Princeville was home to her."

Dani frowned as she stared at Beth's parents. "Carol looks pissed."

"As usual," Juliana added before looking a bit contrite.

The Ladies weren't overly fond of Beth's mother. They thought she'd always been too critical of Beth, which meant they blamed Carol for Beth's tendency to feel as though she wasn't good enough. Or pretty enough. Or thin enough.

Maybe they had a point.

"She's probably just tired. Emma was really fussy last night," Beth said, making yet another excuse for her mom. "I finally took her from Mom and slept in the recliner with Emma lying on my chest."

"You're a good aunt."

"Mom's good with her, too. You know, they'll have Emma down there until Tiffany's tour of duty ends and—" Beth had to stop and close her eyes. Tiffany's deployment had ended the day she died.

Will I ever stop thinking of her in the present tense?

"Will they keep Emma now?" Dani asked.

That was the same question Beth had been asking herself—especially in the wee hours of the morning as she'd cradled her niece against her. Her parents' condo was smack dab in the middle of a community of fifty-five and overs. It was one thing to keep their granddaughter for a tour of duty. Even then, Beth was going to have the baby as soon as summer break began, because Carol didn't want "to raise another kid." Loving children, especially her niece, Beth had readily volunteered to take Emma for at least June and July, longer if she could arrange good child care when school began.

But forever?

Before Beth could ponder that again, her mother came over. "Can you take Emma for the service? My back's killing me. That's what I get for being nice."

Emma reached for Beth before she could even answer.

Settling Emma on her hip, Beth kissed her cheek.

With an enormous yawn, Emma put her thumb in her mouth and rested her head against Beth's shoulder. As if none of the dozens of people were in the church, Emma fell asleep moments later.

There was no worry about Emma fussing through the service. The child was her mother's opposite. While Tiffany always craved being the center of attention, Emma was calm and oddly quiet for her age. Tiffany had been a reed-thin blonde with blue eyes, while Emma shared Bethany's curly brown hair, brown eyes, and chubby cheeks. Beth wanted children of her own one day, lots of children, and Emma was exactly what she thought a future daughter would look like.

The more Beth thought about it, the more she realized Emma favored her aunt rather than her mother in more than looks. Tiffany and Beth had acted nothing like sisters. Tiffany's wildness came in direct contrast to the tight rein Beth kept on her life. Perhaps their different temperaments were from being the older versus younger sibling.

Beth's pondering was interrupted as the minister stepped into the chapel through the side door. She nodded at her friends as they took their seats in the second row. Then she moved to where her parents waited on the front pew. Before she could sit, her gaze was drawn to the back of the chapel.

A tall, handsome man with short, cropped dark hair came inside and looked around as though he felt completely out of place.

Her heart began to pound. Robert Ashford had arrived. She gave him a small wave, wanting—*needing*—him to come to her. Perhaps that need stemmed from her grief, causing her secret infatuation with the man to intensify. She simply didn't have the time or the energy to add her crush on Robert to her list of things to think about. Emotionally overwrought at losing her baby sister, she couldn't examine her feelings too closely.

About the time she feared he'd given up finding her in the crowd, his brown eyes caught hers. With an insistent flip of her wrist, she begged him to join her. Even though the Ladies and their spouses were only a row behind, she wanted Robert at her side, especially since her parents had seated themselves several feet farther down the pew.

The overwhelming desire to lean on him couldn't be shaken. Robert was her friend, her former colleague—technically her boss as well. But none of those roles explained the keen yearning to have him near.

He strode up the aisle, not even stopping to acknowledge their friends.

"Hi, B. I'm s-sorry about your sister." The way he shifted on his feet spoke of his discomfort. That, and he kept tugging at his tie as though it were too tight.

Come to think of it, she'd never even seen him in a suit.

"Thanks for coming," she said.

"I was, you know, worried about you." His gaze drifted to the full second pew. "Should've known you wouldn't need me."

"But I do!" She didn't realize she'd shouted until Emma stirred and several people gaped at her. Beth lowered her voice. "Can you sit by me? Please?" Why did she suddenly feel as awkward as a girl talking to her first crush?

"Um... sure. If that's what you want."

"It is."

Since the minister was clearing his throat, she took a seat, settling Emma on her lap and letting her rest against her shoulder again. Thankfully, the baby went right back to sleep.

Robert took his place next to her and, as if it were the most natural thing in the world, he draped his arm behind her, resting it on the back of the pew. A few minutes later, after the minister started talking about how Tiffany had given her life in service to her country, Robert's arm moved to rest on Beth's shoulders.

It wasn't until his touch stilled her movements that she realized she'd been trembling.

* * *

Bethany kept a wary eye on Emma throughout the dinner in the church social hall. All of Tiffany's friends were pretty much ignoring Emma, which wasn't a shock. From the time she turned fifteen, Tiffany had been wild—living for the moment and spending her time with people who shunned responsibility. She'd used alcohol, taken drugs, and slept with pretty much anyone. The only reason she had a high school diploma was because Beth had tutored her through her toughest classes.

Although Tiffany had spent time in the local juvenile detention center and the county jail, her first felony arrest sobered her. Up until the judge told her she might be in prison for up to five years, she'd done no more than thirty days in custody. Prison scared the shit out of her. So her lawyer had worked out a deal. If she straightened herself out and joined the army, she'd only be charged with a misdemeanor.

She'd straightened up and enlisted, hoping to go to college one day. Emma was conceived on her mother's first leave after basic training. Emma's father—a man Tiffany refused to identify—wanted nothing to do with being a parent. Since she'd been quite content to be a single mother, Tiffany hadn't even asked for child support.

The problem was that although she'd wanted to be with Emma, she still owed the army time. And that time saw her deployed to Afghanistan.

Beth accepted a drink from Robert. "Thanks. I'm so grateful you're here."

He shrugged. "The Ladies have your back. I just thought..." Another shrug, but his dark eyes didn't leave her.

"It means a lot to me." She saw her three friends drawing near.

"Ah, speak of the devils," he quipped.

"Who are you calling a devil?" Dani asked, jostling Robert with her shoulder. As if she could ever move the man. He was nothing but a mountain of muscle, probably from years of constructing homes.

"If the high heel fits..." His wink and the bantering helped Beth relax.

With a grin, Mallory said, "Actually, I think we're more witches than devils."

"Yeah," Juliana agreed with a nod. "But I left my broom back in Cloverleaf."

"Thank you all for coming." Fighting strong emotions, Beth tried to give her friends a smile. Judging from the unsettling quiet, she didn't succeed. "I mean it. Thank you all for—" A shuddering breath slipped out as a few tears spilled over her lashes.

"Robert," Mallory said, "my husband wants to ask you something."

He frowned, staring at Beth. "In other words, you women folk wanna be alone?"

"Bingo."

His hand settled on Beth's arm. "You okay, B?"

"I'm fine."

He wiped a tear from her cheek with calloused fingertips.

Funny, but his touch helped her regain control of her emotions. "I'm fine. Really. Thanks."

"Then if the beautiful Ladies Who Lunch will excuse me..." With a flourish of his hand and a half bow, he walked away.

"What a flirt," Dani said.

Beth couldn't let that misconception stand. "Far from it. He's really very shy."

"Robert?" Juliana furrowed her brow. "Shy?" She let out a snort. "I've never seen that side of him."

"It's all bravado," Beth insisted. "He stuttered when he was little. Took him a long time to be able to talk to people. His parents were immigrants from somewhere in the Czech Republic, and he used to speak with an accent." *Poor kid.* An accent and a stutter. Growing up must have been rough.

Dani's quizzical stare made Beth uncomfortable. Her best friend knew her far too well, sometimes better than Beth knew herself.

A hot flush spread over Beth's cheeks. "We talked a lot when we were working on one of the houses."

"Beth?" Dani asked. "I was always teasing when I said you had a thing for him, but now? Now I'm not so sure. After all these years, are you falling for our Robert?"

It *had* been years—nine to be exact—since Beth had walked into Douglas High as a new teacher. At the time, all of the Ladies and Robert were teaching there. The women became fast friends while sharing their lives every day at lunch, often pulling strings and calling in favors to be sure they shared the same lunch period. Those precious moments had built a friendship strong enough to weather any changes, even Juliana leaving teaching to become a Realtor.

The name of their group came from one of the women's Chicago excursions to shop and see plays. After watching *Company*, they'd adopted one of the song titles. From that time on, everyone called them the Ladies Who Lunch.

Robert had taught industrial technology. Beth had gotten to know him through spending time on school committees, chaperoning dances, and chatting in the corridor almost every passing period. He had a quick sense of humor and a heart he tried to hide. Then his side business of building custom homes had taken off, and like Juliana, he'd sought greener pastures.

Beth had missed seeing him, even stopping by one of his open houses just to talk to him. The place was nice but poorly staged. After she made a few friendly suggestions, he'd insisted she become his decorator. Since HGTV was her favorite network, she'd loved the new challenge. She'd also quickly discovered they made a good pair. At least when working together.

He'd never once hinted that he wanted anything from her beyond friendship. The women he dated explained his lack of interest. They were all tall. And thin.

Beth would always be a size fourteen—probably a good four sizes above anything he'd ever find attractive.

"He's my boss," she reminded Dani. "Besides"—she quickly found Emma in the dwindling crowd—"I've got other things to worry about now."

"Like your niece," Dani said. "Have you and your parents talked about what's gonna happen to Emma now?"

"Aren't they keeping her?" Juliana asked. "I mean, they had her while Tiffany was in Afghanistan, right?"

Beth nodded. "But having her there was already getting to be a problem. They were going to send her to me for the summer, maybe longer." Something she'd been looking forward to, loving the idea of coming home to a friendly face instead of an empty apartment.

"You said their condo's in a fifty-five-and-over community," Juliana commented. "If they want Emma to live with them permanently, they'll have to move. Not that a retirement community is a good place for a kid, even for a short time."

"Yeah," Mallory added. "Definitely not kid-friendly. No playgrounds. No libraries. No other children."

Dani shot Beth a fierce frown. "And then there's Carol filling her head with the same nonsense she gave you."

"I know, I know. You've all got a point." Beth heaved a sigh. The choice was obvious to her if not to her friends—just as obvious as it had been when she'd made up her mind last night. "I'm taking Emma."

"For how long?" Dani asked.

"Forever."

"Aren't you worried about your job?" Dani immediately asked. Her sympathetic tone grated Beth's already frayed nerves.

"Lots of single moms are teachers," Beth replied, trying to keep the irritation out of her voice. She needed to think good thoughts to help her make this scary leap. "I'll just have to adjust. Emma needs me." *And I need to do this for Tiffany. For myself.*

"I'm sorry, Beth," Dani offered. "I didn't mean to sound so angry. I'm just worried about you. You're right. Emma needs you."

"It's the only solution." Something Beth had decided in those wee hours of the morning as she'd held Emma and fretted about the child's future—and her own. The soldier who brought back Tiffany's body also provided the family with documents she'd filed with the army. Tiffany had requested that Beth raise Emma. How could she not honor that wish?

Sleep had eluded her, and she'd spent most of the night lost in thought. She'd brought back memories of Tiffany. Some good, some not so good. Every now and then, Emma stirred, and Beth soothed her back to sleep by rubbing her back and humming softly the same way she'd soothed away Tiffany's nightmares when they were children.

She'd stroked the baby's soft curls, breathed in her sweet scent, and realized that Emma represented her future. That beautiful little girl was all Beth had left of Tiffany. She'd hold on tight and never let go.

"We'll be here to help," Mallory said with a nod. "My stepdaughter would love to babysit."

"I've got tons of baby stuff to share," Jules added. "Two of everything, in fact." She winked. "Anything Craig and Carter outgrow is yours. What is Emma? Eight months?"

"Nine."

"Perfect. She'll have lots to choose from."

Although she'd known the Ladies would support her, Beth fought tears at the generosity of her friends. "Thank you."

Robert came back, carrying a babbling Emma, who'd been passed to him by her grandmother. She seemed fascinated with his tie, and judging from the stranglehold she had on it, she was close to choking him.

"Here's Aunt Beth," he said, trying to get the baby's chubby fingers to let go of his tie.

"Is that what she'll call you?" Jules asked. "I mean, she's not likely to remember Tiffany. Shouldn't you be Mommy to her now?"

"I…I don't know," Beth replied. "I hadn't even thought about it."

"Mommy?" Robert shifted Emma to his other hip, where she began to contentedly toy with his shirt buttons. "You're taking her permanently?"

"Yeah. My parents can't. Besides, she needs stability right now. Mom and Dad would have to move and—"

"You don't have to explain it to me," he said with a lopsided smile that charmed her. "I know you well enough that I'd already figured you'd be bringing her home with you." After giving Emma's nose a quick tweak, he passed her to Beth. "Need any help getting her stuff home? That car of yours doesn't hold much."

Beth gave him a playful elbow in the ribs. "Hey! I like my Beetle. But no thanks on the help. She doesn't have much anyway. Just what Mom and Dad brought with them from Florida. I suppose there's more in Tiffany's apartment."

Sweet Lord, there was so much she'd have to do in the days to come to wrap up her sister's life. The apartment needed to be cleared out. All of Tiffany's things had to be sorted and a decision made about what to do with them.

How difficult would that be? Beth had spent so much time with Tiffany before her deployment. Every corner of that apartment would hold a memory of time she'd spent with her sister before Emma was born. They'd both been so busy—Tiffany with Emma and Beth with school—that they'd seen less and less of each other. Then came the deployment.

Not only would Beth have to deal with the things her sister left behind, but Tiffany's money would have to be handled carefully to ensure Emma had all she needed, including a college education.

Feeling a bit overwhelmed, Beth bit hard on her lip to keep quiet. If there wasn't something good to say about a situation, better to stay silent. And better to keep from crying in front of everyone. She'd learned that lesson well as a child. Carol always taught her girls to keep their feelings to themselves, that showing emotions simply wasn't acceptable.

Sniff back those tears; swallow that anger.

"If you need help with anything, we're here for you," Mallory said, watching her warily.

Beth nodded and tried to find her voice again. "M-Mom and Dad can help."

"So can we," Jules added.

Robert drew closer and tousled Emma's curls. "Me too. I'll be there for anything you need."

"Thank you all." Beth kissed Emma's cheek, setting the baby to giggling.

The sound filled Beth's heart with joy.

This was the right choice, being a mother to this beautiful little girl. No matter how difficult it became, she would see this through.

"Well, then." He set his hand on Beth's shoulder. "I'll see you at the model home Saturday? Or is that too soon?"

"It's fine," Beth replied. "See you then, Robert."

He'd gone only a few steps before turning back. "You sure you don't need me?"

What she needed Robert couldn't give her—a strong man to lean on. No matter how much she wanted *him* to fulfill that role in her life, a desire that seemed to grow each day, she'd never let him know it. If she so much as hinted that she needed him, he'd bend over backward to be there for her.

But not as anything more than a friend, and she sure as spit didn't want him to feel obligated to be with her just because of Emma. Besides, in all the years they'd been friends, he'd never once even hinted that he wanted something more.

"No, but thanks, Robert. Have a safe drive home."

"You too."

Chapter 2

Beth pulled her blue Beetle into the carport at her apartment complex. She would've breathed a sigh of relief if she hadn't been so exhausted. What she wanted was a glass of merlot, a hot bath, and to sleep for the next twelve hours.

She'd probably get none of those things. In the three days it had taken her and her parents to handle Tiffany's affairs, Beth probably hadn't slept more than six total hours. There had simply been too much to do, and Emma demanded a lot of attention, something Beth provided while her parents acted relieved to let her shoulder the caretaker role.

Emma had cried the whole trip back to Cloverleaf. It was only eighty miles, but after four stops, the journey lasted more than three hours.

What had happened to the quiet, shy baby? Did she miss her mother? Her grandparents? All she did was cry or sleep.

"We're home, sweetie," Beth said in a singsong voice.

Emma's only response was a babble, which was much better than her earlier screaming.

Shouldn't she know a few words by now?

She should've found a way to spend more time with Tiffany after Emma was born. There'd always been something keeping her in Cloverleaf. A school activity. Proctoring the SATs. A weekend excursion with the Ladies Who Lunch.

Beth found herself a stranger to her own niece, a baby who now depended on her aunt to raise her. When she got the chance, she'd have to get her butt online and educate herself quickly on how to be a good parent.

After killing the engine, Beth raked her fingers through her mop of curly hair, which was longer than it had been in years, now brushing her shoulders. Why everyone told her how much they'd love to have her hair, she'd never understand. She considered it unruly and a darn nuisance.

Would Emma feel the same about hers one day?

Coming around to the passenger door, Beth opened it, flipped the front seat forward, and reached into the back to unbuckle the car seat. At least it wasn't nearly as difficult getting Emma out as it had been getting her in. *That* had been pure slapstick.

First, Beth had to fit the contraption in the backseat of her tiny car. Then the seat belt had to be threaded through the base, but it wasn't long enough. So she'd added the extender her mother used in her own car. Then the rest of the seat was supposed to pop in.

It didn't. She hadn't realized she needed an engineering degree simply to operate a child's car seat.

How long would Emma even need one? This one fit her perfectly now, but what happened as she continued to grow? While her teaching job made her somewhat of an expert on handling teenagers, Beth was nothing but a rookie when it came to babies.

After several minutes of fumbling with latches and hooks—and worrying about Emma's increasing agitation—Beth finally got the baby out. She grabbed the overstuffed diaper bag, slung it over her shoulder, and then stared at the rest of Emma's stuff piled next to the car seat base and on the floor of the passenger side.

How was she going to get it all inside? She couldn't leave Emma alone while she hauled it all in. Could she? Wouldn't that make her negligent?

Emma was the first baby she'd ever been around, and although she'd planned to take care of her this summer, she sure wasn't experienced. While she might've held Jules's twins from time to time, she'd never babysat. They employed a nanny, Aubrey Stanton. She was a sophomore in college, and she earned money to pay her tuition by taking care of the twins. Since Juliana and Connor were Realtors, their hours were flexible, and they easily worked around Aubrey's class schedule. *A match made in heaven.*

Beth would have to look into day care just as soon as she could. She'd already missed eight school days, the limit the school offered for bereavement, plus all three of the personal days she received each year. Since she still had things to do for Tiffany's estate and to acclimate Emma to her new home, any time away would come from her accumulated sick leave—if the school corporation allowed it.

When she'd explained the changes in her life to her boss, he'd been sympathetic yet stern. She needed to get back to work as soon as possible.

No wonder. The first round of annual testing to evaluate the students' progress was approaching. Add to that Beth's Service Learning class, a hands-on course where the students earned credit by doing projects for the community. A substitute teacher simply couldn't do what she could.

She dropped her keys twice before she was able to get the apartment door open while simultaneously holding Emma's carrier. Once inside, Beth set the carrier down and finally got Emma out of it.

A look around the apartment revealed a disaster area. After the call had come about Tiffany's death, Beth had gone on autopilot. The arrangements were handled by phone, made easier since Tiffany had filled out a directive about what would happen if she died on her tour of duty. There were instructions on everything from where to have her funeral to which cemetery to bury her in.

Beth sighed, resigned to the fact that she wouldn't be able to do much about the mess or about the two of them living in a studio apartment that was one enormous room with an attached bathroom. She hadn't picked the place out for any reason other than it was inexpensive. The low rent allowed her to save money to buy a house one day. She hadn't expected to be sharing it, especially with a child.

"We'll just have to look on the bright side, Emma. It's cozy. It's cheap. And we've got each other."

Emma chose that moment to arch her back and let out a wail that could wake the dead.

"What do you want, sweetie?" She'd been fed. She'd been changed. She'd been given time to play. "Tell me what you want."

The wail continued, and Beth had her hands full trying not to drop the baby. Figuring the best thing she could do was let Emma stretch after the long trip, she set her on the floor. Then she grabbed an afghan and spread it out before moving Emma onto it. "Here you go. Sit there while I get the rest of your stuff."

All Emma did was roll to her stomach and scream some more.

Dropping to her knees, Beth patted her niece's back. "What? What can I do for you?"

"No, no, no," Emma snapped at Beth. "No!"

So she *did* know a word. "No what, Em?" Good Lord, trying to figure out what a child that age wanted was more frustrating than dealing with a classroom full of the moodiest of teenagers.

Emma flopped over to her back and started kicking, all the while crying as though someone were trying to murder her.

Beth leaned over her and was rewarded with a foot to the face. Her hand shot up, covering her throbbing nose. At least it wasn't bleeding.

"Knock, knock."

She whipped her head around to find Robert standing in the open doorway, holding quite a few of Emma's things. His handsome grin made her stomach flip. "Robert! What are—"

He didn't even let her finish. "Figured you might need some help when you got home."

Although she wanted to ask him how he knew she'd returned, she still had her hands full with Emma. The baby was now on all fours, wailing as she crawled toward the door faster than should've been possible.

Robert came inside and set the folded playpen, the high chair, and the bag of toys by the couch. When Emma reached him, he picked her up, tossed her in the air, and laughed.

Darn if the baby didn't start laughing in return as if she hadn't just spent all that time screaming.

Beth sat there on the carpet, watching Robert handling Emma as though he'd raised a brood of his own. "Where did you learn to do that?"

"Do what?" he asked before he blew a raspberry against Emma's neck, setting her to squealing in happiness.

"*That.* Get her to be happy. She's done nothing but cry from the moment Mom handed her to me."

Settling Emma against his hip, he gave Beth one of his crooked smiles, the kind that always made her smile in return. "Thanks to having four siblings who breed like rabbits, I've been around ten different babies. Boys. Girls. Different ages and very different temperaments. All boils down to one thing—don't ever let them see your fear."

He'd been to her place only once, and she'd cleaned it extensively before he'd arrived, wanting to show him how she could turn even a small apartment into something homey. The wretched condition of her apartment made her cringe. "Sorry."

"Sorry? For what?" He strode to her overstuffed chair and plopped onto it. After a few moments of holding and murmuring to Emma, she fell asleep in his arms.

Instead of answering him, Beth sighed. "You're amazing." And she meant more than just the way he handled the baby. The man was the whole package. Cute. Talented. Witty. Why he wasn't already married was beyond her.

"Nothing to it," he replied, lowering his voice when Emma stirred slightly. "Just takes experience."

"Something I don't have." The urge to start cleaning overwhelmed her, so she snatched up the afghan, folded it, and laid it back on the couch. "I'm sorry this place is such a mess."

"Like you've got anything to apologize for. You've seen my house."

"Yeah, but… you're a guy—and my boss."

"Stop it." He glanced down at the sleeping Emma. "Where are you putting her bed?"

Beth frowned. "She doesn't really have one. I guess she can sleep with me on the foldout. Why are you frowning at me?"

"It's dangerous to sleep with a baby in the bed. God, I'm sorry. That sounded preachy."

"No, no." A frustrated sigh slipped out. "I don't know anything about this. I suppose it's easy for the baby to fall out?"

"That, and you don't want to roll over on top of her while you sleep." His gaze wandered the studio. "You're gonna need a bigger place now. Why are you in such a small apartment anyway?"

"I don't need much. It's cheap, clean"—she looked around—"*usually* clean, and easy to take care of. I'm socking everything away to buy a house. Juliana was going to help me search for one this summer. After all, I'm thirty now. It's…well, it's time."

Robert got to his feet and kept Emma cradled against him. With one hand, he popped open the playpen and snapped the sides into place. He looked as though he'd been a father his whole life. What came so naturally to him was an enigma for her.

"What do you mean *time*?" he asked.

How was she supposed to explain it to him of all people? "I… It's…" She finally just blurted it out. "Since I'm probably not going to have a husband and kids—"

"You've got a kid now," he reminded her with a wink. Then he nodded at the playpen. "Grab that afghan and spread it on the bottom."

Beth jumped to do as he asked. "Yeah. I suppose I do. Instant mom."

"And who says you're not getting married? Thirty isn't old, for shit's sake." His gaze dropped to Emma. "Need to watch my language now."

Beth wasn't one to curse, so at least that was one part of her life that wouldn't change now that Emma was in it. "Don't worry about it. Not like you'll be spending a lot of time with her."

* * *

Robert gently laid Emma down before gaping at Bethany, completely lost as to what the woman was thinking.

She'd always been so open, so easy to read.

Now he didn't have a clue what was flying through her head.

Not spend time with her? With Emma?

Even though he'd been around the baby for such a short time, he already felt attached to her, as though she were another niece. He'd figured Beth would be bringing her along whenever they were at one of the homes she was decorating, which meant he'd be seeing them both. A lot. "Why on earth not?"

"I'm not sure I'll have time to be your decorator anymore," Beth replied.

His stomach knotted at the words he'd hoped he'd never hear from her. He struggled for what to say. It boiled down to one thing.

Robert needed Beth.

He went with humor, hoping to ratchet down the anxiety clearly flowing through her. "You think I'm letting you off that easy?" He added another wink in an attempt to lighten the discussion—even though to him, it was pretty damned important.

Didn't she realize how much she meant to him? It wasn't as if the realization snuck up and clubbed him over the head. He'd been warming to her for quite a while, beginning to see more and more in her that he found utterly appealing.

She was the only true friend he had now, and he depended on her, both personally and professionally. Once teachers left the school, they seldom saw the people they left behind. Building houses meant people came into his life and then went right back out again.

None ever stayed.

He couldn't help but smile when he remembered her first year at school. God, she'd been so young, so very green. Only twenty-one and right out of college, while he'd been thirty and an eight-year veteran. Like most newbies, Beth had thought she could change the world. Perhaps in some ways she had. She'd changed Douglas High for the better.

Beth had created the Peer Board, a group of students who helped deal with problems in the school. If kids were having trouble with anything, from bullying to being habitually tardy, they often went to the Peer Board for advice and assistance. Not only did the group take a lot of pressure off the administrators by solving problems in the early stages, but the climate of the school had improved dramatically.

Her room was right across the hall from what had been Robert's engineering classroom. He'd been an industrial technology teacher before his side business of constructing custom homes took off with a population boom in the community. But for six years, she'd been his neighbor. They'd talked, laughed, and shared every school day. When he'd decided to walk away from teaching, leaving her friendship behind had been one of the hardest obstacles.

His color blindness had been what brought Beth into Ashford Homes. The first house he'd built he decorated himself, using neutral colors and relying on his contacts at the paint store and flooring supplier to help him choose. The house had been constructed beautifully, but it didn't sell. Feedback from potential buyers was unanimous. The inside was dreary and dull. The buyers couldn't look past the colors and emptiness to see the fantastic amenities.

Beth had gone to an open house. Robert had followed her through the rooms, hoping she'd like what she saw. Instead, she'd shifted from her bubbly, positive personality to dead silence. He'd had to nag her to get her to admit what she thought, and it wasn't good.

Yet in her typical style, she'd set about helping him. After she chose new colors for the interior walls, changed up some of the floor treatments, and meticulously staged the place, it had sold in a multiple-bid war.

He'd hired her right after, and they'd worked together ever since.

"I…I need you, B." Robert inwardly kicked himself for sounding as though he was begging, even if he was. "I c-can give you m-more m-money."

Fuck.

He hadn't stuttered in years. After getting counseling when he was in middle school, he'd been able to get a hold of himself and stop his lifelong stutter. The only time it popped up was when he was really upset.

Losing Beth's friendship would leave him devastated.

"I don't want more money, Robert." Beth was still flitting around the place, picking up.

Robert strode over to her and stilled her movements by gently grabbing her wrist. "Stop. Please. I n-need to talk to you."

Her big brown eyes were full of resignation. She looked overwhelmed and defeated.

Beth was facing a war, and she didn't even know it. Raising a child wasn't easy, a lesson he'd learned from watching his siblings struggle, both succeeding and failing, with their families. Worse, she was going to wage that war alone.

At that moment, he vowed she would always have him to lean on.

As Beth usually said—sang, actually—"*That's what friends are for.*"

"I need your help," Robert announced. "Ashford Homes wouldn't be what it is without you."

"But Emma..."

Robert put his hands on her shoulders. "We'll find a way to make it work, B. I p-promise."

Chapter 3

Robert was so agitated he couldn't stop pacing the length of the foyer and back, again and again.

Beth was late.

Beth was *never* late.

Visions assaulted him. Her Beetle smashed by a semi, both Beth and Emma strapped to their seats, bloody and bruised. Beth pacing the floor of the emergency room while doctors tried to retrieve something Emma had swallowed. Never had he felt such an overpowering need to protect another person, let alone two people. But that need had settled deep inside him, and he knew he wouldn't be able to calm down until he saw them both safe and sound.

He'd never been remotely paternal before. A good uncle, yes. But what was it about Emma that roused such a desire to protect and shelter her?

Perhaps it was merely her circumstances, being left alone by her patriotic mother who died serving her country. Perhaps it was because she was Beth's flesh and blood. Or perhaps it was just the right time in his life to develop the need to nurture a child.

Who the hell knew?

A quick check of the time had him fishing his phone out of his pocket again. No texts. No missed calls. He'd wait five more minutes; then he was calling. Again. Or hopping in his car and—

The door opened, and Beth walked in carrying Emma. She looked like she'd just weathered a hurricane. Her hair had been pulled tight away from her face, held by an elastic headband and then restrained in a ponytail that was a mass of messy curls. Her clothes, nothing but a long-sleeved T-shirt and yoga pants, were badly wrinkled. Although he was color-blind, even he could see she wore two different styles of Asics. The shirt had a large stain near her waist. For the first time since he'd met her, she wore no makeup.

She gave him a wan smile. "Sorry I'm late. Emma somehow managed to pull the lid off her sippy cup and spilled orange juice all over herself and her car seat. I had to get her changed and clean her seat before we could leave." She glanced to her wrist and frowned, probably because she wasn't wearing a watch. "You didn't wait too long, did you?"

"Not long," he lied.

Emma started fussing and kicking her chubby little legs.

Robert smoothed a hand over her curls, glad to see she was doing so well. Dressed in a pink shirt and tiny jeans, her looks were a stark contrast to Beth's frazzled appearance. "How you doin', squirt?"

The baby stopped fidgeting and grinned, revealing some tiny white teeth.

Beth's defeated frown took him by surprise. He was used to her being upbeat and positive. At the moment, she looked as though the weight of the world rested solely on her shoulders.

"You doin' okay?" he asked.

Instead of replying, she fished her electronic tablet out of the diaper bag. "We should get to work. I've got to get to the grocery store and then to the Laundromat." Using one hand, she tried to flip open the cover. After three tries, she let out one of the most dejected sighs he'd ever heard.

"Why don't you let me take Emma?" he asked.

"Thank you." Beth passed the baby off to him. It was an easy task since Emma held out her arms the moment he reached for her.

Opening her tablet, Beth took a long look around. "This one's ready to go, isn't it? I didn't realize you'd gotten this far."

"Everything is done. Just needs your miracle touch."

"Tell me about the client. A family?"

Robert shook his head. "This one's a single."

"A house this big?" Beth cocked her head. "Seems odd. This is the perfect place for a family. When you showed me the plans, I drooled."

"Drooled?"

"Yeah. I wanted it *that* bad. But you're out of my price range. So this is a single person... Guy or girl?"

"Guy."

"Age?"

"Middle-aged. Forty."

"Forty's not middle-aged. Heck, Robert, you're close to forty and you look fantastic." Her cheeks flushed red and she fidgeted with her tablet.

Easy for a woman who was only thirty to say, but damn if he didn't enjoy the compliment. "Let's just say it's old enough."

"Tell me about him. Fashionable? Lots of dates?"

Robert shook his head. "Neither. No family, but he wanted

one. Hasn't given up all hope, but he's ready to commit to a house. Maybe if he builds it, they will come."

At least she let out a small chuckle at his movie quip. "Country-western? Hip modern? What's his taste in décor?"

"He has none," he replied with a chuckle. "Told me to have you decorate this place the way you'd want it to look."

"That's downright cruel." Her fingers started to fly over the tablet.

"Cruel?"

"Yeah…I'll make it perfect; then I'll have to hand it over to someone else."

Robert bit his lip. Everything he'd told her about the new owner was true. He was forty and had no prospects for a family. His home decorating taste was nonexistent. But Robert had left out one important detail.

This house was going to be *his* new home.

He'd built this one on spec, a sign that business was booming. Building an unsold home was something he only got to do when there was a lull in activity at Ashford Homes—a rare occasion. Most of the time, Jules or Connor brought him a buyer. That buyer would choose from Robert's catalog of blueprints, and construction would begin.

This home might have started out as a spec, but once the frame started to rise, he knew he was going to keep it.

It was a new model, a blueprint that one of his engineering friends had drawn up based on Robert's idea of what would make the perfect house. Roomy but not overmuch, it was designed for function while still maintaining a welcoming open floor plan. There were four bedrooms in case the owner had company or if he one day found a woman to settle down with and raise a couple of kids.

For some reason, he wasn't ready to tell Beth about being the owner. What would she think? That he wasn't able to land a wife? She knew he dated a lot, so she'd never assume that. But would she understand why he needed this house for himself? Would she think he'd given up on having a family?

What's wrong with me anyway?

Self-doubt had plagued him the last year, probably a result of turning forty. He'd always heard men had a midlife crisis around that time. Some bought sports cars or motorcycles or found themselves a trophy wife.

Robert didn't want a trophy wife. He just wanted a woman he could love. One who shared some of the things he enjoyed and could learn to love him in return.

Angry at himself for getting so maudlin, he tried to focus on the things Beth was muttering as she moved from room to room. It was an endearing habit of hers, almost as though she needed to talk herself into some of the things she wanted.

When she hit the kitchen, the muttering stopped. She set her tablet on the bar and stared.

"What's up?" He came up next to her, shifting Emma to his other hip. She was content playing with the button holding his collar down.

"I really wish I knew more about the buyer. Kitchens are so…personal. I mean, you've got great cabinets, and I love the granite countertop. It's exactly the color mixture I'd pick for myself."

"I know. You've told me how much you love brown and silver mixing. At least the granite guy told me it was brown and silver. Isn't it?"

Her first smile. "It is."

"Thank God. It's too expensive to have screwed it up."

"But the rest?" she asked. "The appliances? The backsplash? A person has to live with those a long time. The wrong choices might make him miserable."

"Pick what you like, B. I'm sure he'll be happy with your work. My buyers always are."

She still didn't look convinced.

He glanced at her pad and saw that she'd pulled up some backsplash samples. Most were tile, but one caught his eye. "That looks like metal. Is that silver?"

"Yeah, it's getting popular to have molded metal. The patterns are interesting, and I like the sleek look it gives a kitchen. Makes it stand out since it's not your typical stuff. But that means no stainless appliances."

"Why not?"

"Too much shiny. Would be silver overload, especially with the silver running through this granite. Black appliances would give a great contrast. Have you asked him if he wants stainless? If he already has them ordered…"

Robert shook his head. "Nope. He was going to order after you chose fixtures."

"And he really doesn't care?"

"He really doesn't care."

Standing to full height, slight though it was, she picked up her tablet. "Then metal it is."

* * *

Beth had been exhausted when she arrived, but now she was positively giddy. This house was her chance to do whatever she wanted, and instead of trying to please a client, she only needed to please herself.

And Robert.

At least this part of her life was under control. Being a mom had turned out to be a lot harder than she'd ever expected. Emma seemed to need her every single moment of the day—and the night. Her perfectly behaved niece had turned into an impossible-to-please child.

Beth's arms and back ached from holding her, but whenever she put the baby down, the crying started all over again. The little sleep she'd gotten had been done sitting up in the chair, letting Emma rest against her chest.

Laundry was piling up, her pantry was empty, and she was just about to collapse from fatigue. Her neighbors were probably having fits over the noise. She'd be amazed if the apartment complex manager didn't ask her to move out by the end of the week.

There would be no help from her parents, but Beth hadn't expected any. They'd hightailed it back to Florida right after they'd wrapped up Tiffany's affairs. Carol had already booked them a cruise now that they were back to being a couple and not burdened—Carol's exact words—with caring for Emma. At least the Ladies were there for her, although Beth was reluctant to lean on them too much. They had lives of their own, and she didn't want to be an imposition.

Besides, she might be a bit frazzled, but things weren't all bad. There were moments she shared with Emma that stole her breath away. A smile. A laugh. That twinkle in Emma's brown eyes. So many times Beth saw parts of Tiffany popping up in her daughter, which made her both happy and a little sad.

As she entered the master bathroom, Beth stopped to stare at her reflection in the mirror.

Sweet heavens. I look like crap!

Robert hadn't said a word about her shameful appearance, nor had he scolded her for being late. She was simply overwhelmed by the sudden changes in her life. Losing Tiffany hadn't truly sunken in because Beth had been so busy trying to learn how to take care of Emma. Clearly she wasn't doing a good job. Emma might be clean and well fed, but she wasn't as happy as Beth thought she should be.

No wonder. She'd spent a short time with her mother, been uprooted when Carol had taken over her care, and now found herself plunked down in the middle of Beth's life in a place she didn't know.

Feeling sorry for Emma, Beth had bent over backward to meet every single whim the baby had. Although she guessed wrong about what Emma wanted most of the time, she was giving it her all.

And it was killing her.

How could she possibly keep this up?

She was supposed to go back to work Monday. The child care was going to cost more than half her teaching salary, and she refused to touch any of the money that was being put aside for Emma from her mother's life insurance and military benefits. She'd have to pick Emma up by four every afternoon or would be charged an extra twenty bucks—even if she was a minute late. When would she have time to grade papers or make lesson plans? Those activities sometimes took hours in the evening. Emma needed someone to play with her and teach her to walk and to read and—

Beth burst into tears, feeling like the biggest failure in the world.

"Bethany?" Robert hurried into the master bathroom. "What

happened?" He skidded to a stop, still holding Emma. "Did you hurt yourself?"

She couldn't stop crying. There wasn't even a towel to grab so she could hide her face.

"B?" His hand settled on her back. "Tell me what's wrong."

"I...I can't...do this..." Everything she touched was going straight to Hades, and the idea that she faced years and years of trying to balance all the responsibilities of taking care of her niece seemed about as likely as her being able to hike up Mount Everest.

Robert wrapped his strong arm around her shoulders and pulled her against his other side. His scent, so masculine and fresh, overwhelmed her, reminding her that he was only her friend no matter how much she might want more. That scent would never be on a pillow resting next to hers. It would never be there whenever she came home and needed a hug after a rough day at work. It would never envelop her as he pulled her into his embrace for passion instead of friendly comfort.

Well, *this* time she'd allow herself to drown in that fantastic scent. She turned to bury her face against his broad chest as sobs racked her body.

Funny, but after several long moments of weeping, Beth felt much better. Reduced to hiccups and shuddering breaths, she tried to ease back.

Robert put his hand behind her head and pushed her cheek back against his chest as if he didn't want to let her go. Her eyes were even with Emma's where she clung to him. Beth hadn't realized the baby had been crying as well until she saw the tears on Emma's cheek and her quivering lower lip.

Beth stared at Emma, and Emma stared back as Robert held them both. Just one happy little non-family. Then Beth ran her fingers down Emma's cheek, thinking they were quite a pair. Two weeping females joined in their grief, both clinging to a man who probably wanted to get them the heck out of the house.

Leaning back slightly, she looked up to find him watching her. The concern she saw reflected in his dark eyes made her heart clench. Here was the kind of man she'd searched for her whole life, one full of compassion and honor and gentleness. Not only that, but he was gorgeous, too. From his thick hair to his perfect body, she'd even loved the light brush of gray on his temples. He'd been right beside her all along.

She knit her brows as he slowly lowered his face to hers, and when it dawned on her that he was going to kiss her, she almost turned away, afraid of allowing her lips to connect with his.

Then she closed her eyes and let it happen.

The touch of his lips wasn't at all what she'd thought it would be. She'd expected a gentle kiss, a friendly are-you-okay-now gesture.

She got… So. Much. More.

Heat raced through her. Her head spun, and when his tongue nudged her lips apart and swept into her mouth, she clutched at the front of his shirt to keep herself anchored. Their tongues rubbed; his insistent, hers hesitant. Her heart pounded hard and fast, echoing in her ears like the beating of a bass drum.

And then he pulled back. His gaze searched hers, his confusion plain. Swiftly on the heels of that confusion came a frown that made her want to throw up.

Robert—the man who had stirred her desire so deeply—hadn't enjoyed the kiss, and she was humiliated, feeling unworthy and defeated.

He let go, stepping back so quickly she almost fell forward. "That won't h-happen again."

He'd barked it loud enough that Emma gaped at him. Then her bottom lip started to tremble. Before Beth could take her back from Robert, the baby let out a squeal that could've broken glass.

Chapter 4

Robert gently laid Emma in the crib. He'd paced miles getting her calmed down, and now, at long last, she was sleeping peacefully. Since Beth was finally getting some well-deserved rest, he didn't want Emma to wake her.

For a moment, he stared down at the baby. She was pretty enough to be on Gerber baby food jars. Chubby pink cheeks. A mop of curly hair. A dimple in her right cheek that popped up whenever she smiled at him.

She was smart, too. Although she only babbled, she could point out every single toy by name, and he suspected she'd be an early reader by the way she could identify the book she wanted read to her. Heaven forbid he pick up *Pat the Bunny* when Emma wanted *Goodnight Moon*.

Her laughter was infectious, and he found himself acting silly just to hear the sound again and again. Whenever Beth joined in the laughter, he felt a contentment settle over him.

Damn if he didn't hand that beautiful little girl his heart at that very moment. The need to protect her swelled up inside him, and if fathers took vows like bridegrooms, Robert was taking his.

Why now? Why Emma?

He wasn't entirely sure. While he was close to his nieces and nephews, he'd never experienced the downright primitive desire to watch over them the way he did Emma. Maybe it was because she needed him, needed a father figure in her life. And from the way she'd wiggled right into his heart, he needed her every bit as much.

To love, honor, and cherish.

'Til death do us part.

God, he was getting sappy in his middle age.

The next task he tackled was making some sense out of the chaos around him. Emma had more toys than she could possibly play with, and every single one of them was strewn around the apartment. Beth had obviously been shopping because there were a lot more things than she'd brought back from Princeville.

A glance at the tiny kitchen revealed a large laundry basket full of clothes sitting on the breakfast bar. Figuring it was as good a place to start as any, Robert dove into the clothes. They were clean, so he folded them into two piles—one for Bethany and one for Emma. Then he used the plastic laundry basket to store all the toys, making a mental note to build her a nice, sturdy toy box.

Dishes, mostly bottles and bowls with tiny bits of cereal clinging to the sides, were next. He mumbled to himself about how Beth didn't seem to eat anything but cold cereal, regardless of the time of day. His final project was straightening the bathroom as best he could manage.

Why did women need so many grooming products? Shampoo. Conditioner. Face wash. Face moisturizer. Makeup. Hell, all he needed was deodorant and toothpaste. Those were in the bathroom as well, and by the time he'd finished, he realized exactly why so many of his female clients demanded so much counter space and storage in their bathrooms.

A yawn slipped out, and he kicked off his shoes. There was no way he'd be able to drive home. He'd fall asleep and smash his car right into a tree. Not that anyone would notice.

He'd left most of his friends behind when he'd turned in his resignation. It wasn't unusual. Even the teachers who retired seldom stayed in touch with those still on the staff. Only the Ladies were actively involved in his life, but the rest of his human contact was with customers and tradesmen.

Not only was he sappy, he was also downright maudlin.

Blaming it all on fatigue, he eyed the spot next to Beth. The poor woman had fallen asleep a good two hours ago. The way she hiccuped softly from time to time told him she might've been crying again when she'd been in the bathroom taking a shower.

No wonder. Her whole world had been turned upside down. As long as he'd known her, he'd picked up on some of her routines. One was that she was the ultimate creature of habit, but her recent life had suddenly become nothing but turmoil. Losing her only sister. Having an infant tossed into her lap. Getting attacked by her boss.

Sappy, maudlin, and full of hyperbole.

He hadn't attacked her. He'd kissed her.

And she'd kissed him back.

That had been a welcome surprise. Even with Emma squeezed between them, he and Bethany had shared a connection, a hot and thoroughly arousing kiss. He'd been so shocked—and so afraid she'd be angry at him—he'd shoved her away, swearing never to kiss her again.

The truth was he wanted to sit next to her on the bed

right now and reenact *Sleeping Beauty*. Except with an erotic conclusion.

His cock hardened at the thought of making love to Beth, just as it had turned as hard as marble the moment his lips had touched hers. She'd tasted like butterscotch, probably because of the hard candies she always sucked on.

Sucked. Even thinking the word and getting a mental picture of Beth doing just that made him groan. He couldn't even close his eyes to escape the image. It had burned into his brain.

Sappy, maudlin, full of hyperbole, and a horny old bastard.

Another yawn. The only place to sleep was on the bed. Next to her.

Liar. The chair's fine.

Robert flipped off the lights, chuckling at the array of night-lights around the tiny apartment. He eased onto the unoccupied side of the mattress and tossed the decorative pillows on the chair. Then he stretched out next to Beth, rolling to face her.

She was lying on her back, but her face was turned toward him. She was so damn innocent. He'd never seen anything but trust in her sparkling eyes, and the way she blushed at the drop of a hat made him wonder what her previous relationships had been like. Her lashes were long, dark, and utterly feminine. Her skin was smooth and pale. And her lips were barely parted and looked terribly kissable.

I'm a cliché. A forty-year-old man wanting a younger woman.

But he wasn't thinking about sex. Well, not *just* about sex. He wanted her. Badly. Each passing minute only made him want her a little bit more. Not only in his bed.

In his life as well.

She was different from any woman he'd ever known, unique

in a way only Beth could manage to be. It wasn't as though he didn't date. He was a regular at the local singles' mixers, and he really didn't have too much trouble getting a woman to go out with him. The problem was that most of the women didn't "do it" for him. He'd sleep with one now and again, but more as a biological function than true passion. Something about the women he'd dated made him shy away from any commitment. They didn't feel... *right.*

Part of that was his own fault. He'd only scoped out a certain type. Blond. Tall. Stacked. Svelte. That was another reason his attraction to Beth was so damned confusing. She was nothing like his "type."

Yet he fantasized about threading his fingers through her curly brown hair. He wanted his palms to cover her breasts, even if they were smaller than what he usually craved. He wanted to pull her close, wrap his arms around her, and indulge in every fantasy he'd ever entertained, including the one about being married to a good woman and having a family.

Her eyes fluttered open, her gaze drifting to the playpen before a relieved sigh slipped out. Then those caramel eyes widened when she saw him. "Robert?"

"Shhh." He touched a finger to her lips. "Go back to sleep." Although he resisted the urge, he wanted to rub his finger over that pouty lower lip of hers.

"But you're in my bed."

"'Cause I'm too tired to drive home."

"Oh..." Instead of taking advantage of Emma sleeping, Bethany slowly rolled to face him completely, her brows gathering as she looked past him. "You straightened up my apartment?"

He nodded.

"Why?"

He shrugged. "You needed some help and some rest. Get some more sleep before Emma wakes up and needs you."

* * *

Beth didn't want to go back to sleep. She wanted to throw her arms around Robert and thank him for being there to rescue her.

She'd been drowning, and he'd been her life preserver. The man was a natural with babies, taking to parenting like a Canadian boy to ice-skating. Emma adored him, obviously more than she liked Beth. But Beth was trying hard to please the baby, probably because she felt so sorry for her.

There was nothing Beth could do to make up for Emma losing her mother. So she'd taken to buying Emma anything that caught her fancy. Most of those toys were now in the nearly overflowing pink laundry basket. A brilliant thought on Robert's part, turning it into a makeshift toy box, although Beth hadn't thought past the next few hours to worry about stuff like storing Emma's toys or clothes.

The time had come to buy a house. She'd managed a decent savings for a down payment. Maybe not enough to afford the type of home Robert could build, but something cozy was within reach. Emma deserved a real home, not an efficiency apartment. She should have a room of her own, a place to keep her clothes and toys, and maybe even a bathroom to herself as she got older.

Beth had shared a bathroom with Tiffany, and they'd fought about it all the time. One sink plus two girls equaled frustration—and sometimes fistfights.

Emma had lost her mother; she should at least have her own bathroom.

"You're thinking awfully hard for someone who should be sleeping." Robert's voice was a whisper, as though they were a couple sharing a few intimate words of pillow talk before they went to sleep.

Bethany answered in kind. "I was thinking this place is too small now. I'm gonna have to buy a house."

"I can build you one." He sounded so darned sincere she could almost believe him.

"That's sweet." She smiled despite her embarrassment at her lack of finances. Teachers simply didn't make a lot of money, and he knew that well. "I don't have that much saved yet. And Emma needs something now."

"I have one that's almost ready."

Her mind flew through the houses she'd decorated for him. All of them had already sold. It was rare when one of Robert's even made it to market. Most were built to a buyer's specifications, although he'd do a house on spec from time to time.

Only one possibility came to mind. "You can't mean the one I saw today."

"Yesterday," he teased. "It's after midnight. And, yes, that one."

"I can't afford that house, Robert. Besides, I thought you had a buyer."

"A maybe buyer, but you need it more." He let out a yawn that shook his whole body, and once she stopped to consider him, she realized his eyes were barely open.

"Get some sleep," she said, feeling selfish. After all, he'd exhausted himself taking care of her and Emma.

"Hmmm..." His hum was followed by him closing his eyes the rest of the way.

Beth lay there in the dark and continued to stare at him, glad he didn't know exactly how much she wanted him. At least when he was asleep, she could look her fill and not worry about him thinking she was being ridiculous.

Robert was her boss. Her *friend*. Not once had he even implied he wanted more from their connection. He was a player, as Jules always said. It was ludicrous to think of him taking a romantic role in her life.

But she thought about it. A lot. She remembered how natural he looked holding Emma, how wonderful he'd be with more children. Their children. What a great husband he'd be.

How could he not be married already?

The women at school claimed he'd never settled down because he was such a tomcat, a new woman on his arm every time they saw him. They were right. He went out with a lot of women, and he never seemed to have trouble scaring up a date. No guy that good-looking would ever be alone.

Maybe he didn't want to settle down. Some people didn't, although Beth had a hard time understanding them. She was truly of another generation in her values. A woman got married and had a family. That was the goal, which was why she sometimes felt like such a colossal failure. Guys just weren't attracted to her.

No wonder. She was twenty pounds too heavy. She lacked the big boobs guys liked. She had mousy brown, far-too-curly hair. In her mind, she was everything they wouldn't want, probably because she'd heard that sentiment from her mother far too many times.

But that hadn't stopped Robert from kissing her.

Comforted by that, Beth rolled over so she could stop staring at him and get some sleep before Emma woke up.

Sleep was a long time in coming.

* * *

So warm and sweet.

Shivers ran the length of her body as Beth smiled, loving the way Robert was nuzzling her neck and rubbing her hip. Heat bloomed low in her belly, fanning through her as she wiggled her backside against the groin pressed hard against her.

"Hard" being the key word. The erection was easy to feel, even through their clothing. She wriggled again, loving how he growled against her skin and then ran his tongue around the shell of her ear.

His hand covered her breast, squeezing lightly before returning to her hip. Even more heat shimmered through her. She arched into his touch with the fleeting thought that it had been so long since she'd been with a man.

Years, actually.

But *this* man? This was the one she'd wanted for a long time, longer than she was willing to admit to herself. She'd always kept her distance, drawing clear lines between her and her colleague, who then became her boss. Besides, he'd never shown an interest in her before. Ever.

She'd only seen him with Barbie dolls. There had been more than a few. Come to think of it, she'd never seen him with the same one twice. Robert was a player, and Beth hated players.

So why this strange fascination?

Robert's warm lips were on her neck again, and he hoarsely whispered, "Bethany..."

Until he'd said her name, she'd wondered if he was just in the throes of some erotic dream and had reached out to conveniently find a warm woman lying next to him. But he wanted her. *Bethany.*

The fire inside her flared to an inferno. She needed to show him how she felt, hoping he'd bare some of his own feelings in response. "Robert..."

His insistent hand on her hip turned her to her back. Then his body blanketed her, and his lips settled on hers. With little prelude, his tongue thrust deep into her mouth.

Beth couldn't have stopped herself if she'd wanted to. And she sure didn't want to. Returning the ferocity of his kiss, gliding her tongue over his, she looped her arms around his neck and arched into him.

His scent—masculine with a touch of pleasant, spicy cologne—intoxicated her. His taste was quickly becoming familiar, and when his knee nudged her legs apart, she welcomed him and the way his pelvis settled between her thighs.

The kiss continued, a chase of tongues that went on and on. Robert slid his hand over her breast again, squeezing with the perfect amount of pressure as he pressed his hips into her core.

This was going to happen. It was really going to happen.

Until Emma started crying.

They broke apart like a couple of teenagers caught necking by their parents.

Beth scrambled off the sofa bed while Robert retreated to the bathroom.

Confused and reining in her passion, Beth went to Emma. She felt ashamed, but she wasn't sure exactly why.

Was he upset by her weight? Her small breasts? What scared him away? He'd rushed off so swiftly, like he desperately needed to put some distance between them. Although he was clearly aroused, Emma's cries had evidently made him sober, as though he really *had* been lost in a dream, probably thinking about his usual type of woman.

Beth tried to shrug off the rejection, telling herself it was for the best anyway. He was her boss, and God knew she needed the money now.

For the first time, Emma stopped crying the moment Beth picked her up. Not sure how to respond to that blessing, Beth grabbed a fresh diaper and laid her niece on the mattress. She had just finished changing the diaper and redressing the baby when Robert came out of the bathroom.

He plopped on the far side of the mattress and jerked on his shoes. "I need to go."

"I can make us some breakfast," she offered.

Robert snorted. "With what? Your fridge is almost empty."

Her face flushed hot. "You're right. I'm going to the grocery store later today." As if that would matter now…

He swiped his hand over his face. "I'm sorry, B-B."

All she did was shrug, mostly because she had no idea exactly what he was sorry for. For the rather sharp quip about her empty fridge? For the fact he'd almost made love with her?

She needed some coffee. Now. Despite finally getting some sleep, her brain couldn't seem to function, and she swallowed hard as she tried to force back her emotions. There was no way she'd let him know exactly how much he'd hurt her.

"I need to go," Robert said again. "Got a lot of stuff to do today anyway." He came to stand at her side. "C-can I tell Emma good-bye?"

"Sure. I'm gonna throw this away." Beth snatched up the dirty diaper while he picked up the baby.

Emma smiled and babbled at him. She put her hands on his cheeks, and he rubbed his beard stubble against her palms, setting her to giggling. When Beth came back to them, Robert kissed Emma on her chubby cheek.

"Love you, squirt," he said before handing the baby back to Beth. "See you later. O-k-kay?"

"Sure, Robert. Whatever."

The tears didn't fall, even after he'd shut the door behind him.

Love you, squirt.

He'd said it so easily, so naturally. Emma had charmed her way right into Robert's heart.

Was it stupid to be jealous of an orphaned baby?

Only a few moments ago, Beth had been close to casting aside all her self-imposed rules about sleeping with guys. She might know Robert well, but they had no relationship save being friends and colleagues. Yet she would have stripped out of her clothes faster than a burlesque dancer and let him make love to her without even considering things like safe sex or possible pregnancy.

But he didn't want her. All the kisses they'd shared might have seemed passionate—at least to her—but he obviously regretted each and every one. She'd cried more over him the last two days than she had over losing Tiffany.

Or was her sister's death one of the reasons Beth was being overly emotional now?

"You know what, Em?" Beth sniffed hard. "Your aunt needs to stop being silly. Robert just felt sorry for me. That's all."

Emma happily babbled something, but Beth still didn't understand her niece's infantile vocabulary. She kissed the baby's cheek and was rewarded with a sweet, innocent smile.

Despite her churning thoughts, Beth couldn't help but smile back. "You know what, *squirt*? I love you, too."

Chapter 5

I'm sorry to force the issue, Beth." The voice of Jim Reinhardt, her principal, buzzed in Beth's ear. "I know everything you've been through, and you know you've got my sympathies. I just need to have a date for your return so we can plan for your subs."

"I understand." And she did. The kids were in school every weekday. Only she wasn't, making her feel guilty for not being there for her students. That, and she was almost out of paid time off.

"Unless you need a formal leave of absence," Jim said. "That would be a different story altogether. You know you can take more time off, right? You've burned through the paid days, but I can help you do the paperwork for an unpaid personal leave."

"No. I can't afford that." There was money from Tiffany's life insurance, but Beth didn't want to use that for Emma's day-to-day expenses. Emma was going to college one day, and who the heck knew what tuition would be in eighteen years? Plus, she deserved a nest egg, and that money would provide it. If Beth handled everything well, those funds would pay for Emma's education and perhaps be a good down payment on a home.

No, Beth wasn't going to touch Emma's money unless she had no choice. "I need to get day care arranged. If I can do that, I'll be back next Monday."

"Talk to some of the other teachers," Jim suggested. "Best way to find a good babysitter is to talk to someone else who uses one. That's what Rose and I did when our kids were younger." He snorted a laugh. "About a million years ago."

"I will. Thanks for the advice." She already knew who she wanted to be responsible for Emma during school days—Jules's nanny, Aubrey. But could Beth afford her? And would Jules even allow Emma to have the same nanny as her twins? It would mean Beth dropping her niece off every weekday at an ungodly hour. Since Jules was her own boss, she might not appreciate the intrusion. It was widely known that Jules was horrible to be around in the morning. Shoot, she even joked that she was a "psycho hose beast" before nine.

"I'll call by tomorrow with a definitive date for you," Beth said.

"Take care of yourself, Bethany. We miss you." On that, he hung up.

Beth immediately called Jules, who thankfully answered on the second ring. More often than not, calls to the über-busy Realtor went directly to a chipper voice mail message. "Hey, Beth. What's up, buttercup?"

Just cut to the chase. "Do you have a few minutes to come by my apartment?" It would be so much easier to ask Jules about the nanny in person. There was also another topic she wanted to discuss. "I know you're really busy... but I need your help."

"Ask and you shall receive," Jules replied with a chuckle. "That is, if I can provide it. You caught me at the perfect time. Just finished a closing, and I've got a solid half hour with nothing on my schedule." In her typical irreverent manner, she gave the last word a British pronunciation. "See you in ten?"

"Thanks, Jules."

* * *

Balancing Emma on her hip, Beth opened the door to Jules's knock. "Thanks for coming over."

Jules smiled, kissed Emma's cheek, and marched into the apartment. "Damn, Beth. I forget how small this place is. Don't you get claustrophobic?" She winked to take the sting out of her comment.

"You know I'm saving for a house, which is actually why I asked you here."

Jules took a seat on the chair while Beth plopped onto the mattress, letting Emma stretch out on the quilt. The baby had been fed and changed, and sleep was rapidly overtaking her. Refusing to lie down, Emma reached for Beth. With a small sigh, Beth picked her back up and cradled her against her shoulder.

"So you're ready to take the plunge?" Jules asked.

Beth rubbed Emma's back while she discussed business with her friend. "I am. Emma needs to grow up someplace with a yard and a bedroom of her own."

"Price range?" As always, Jules got right down to business.

"Not really sure. I'd like to see what my money can get. I've got about twenty thousand for a down payment. Is that enough?"

"Depends on what you want." Jules pulled her e-tablet out of her enormous purse, and her fingers started flying over it. "You're a property virgin, so best thing to do is start with what I call the 'Goldilocks Plan.' "

Beth quirked a brow. "Goldilocks?"

"Yeah," Jules replied with a lopsided smile. "I show you one that's really pricey, one on the low end, then one that's in the middle. You get to decide what's just right. Helps narrow down exactly what you're looking for."

A good plan, considering Beth really had no idea what she needed, let alone what she wanted. All her Pinterest posts about houses had been one of two extremes. A house for her to share with her husband and children or a house for a lady who would be single for her whole life. What kind of house did a single mom get?

"That sounds like a good plan, Jules. I honestly have no idea what would work for Emma and me."

"Don't sound so forlorn." Jules raised her gaze from the tablet. "We'll find something perfect. I promise. I'm pretty good at my job."

"That's why I called you." Beth drew her lips into a thin line. Even forming the question about child care was difficult. She finally decided to just spit out the request. "I need another favor. You're always telling me how much you like your nanny."

"God, yes. I'd never survive without Aubrey." She let out a throaty laugh. "Twin boys. I still wonder what I did that karma came back at me by making me the mom of twin boys."

"Would Aubrey be able to watch Emma, too?" Hurrying to explain, Beth added, "I'd pay her. I just…I don't want Emma spending her whole day with some stranger."

Instead of immediately responding with a hearty, *Sure, bring her over,* Jules stayed silent. The answer, however, was there in her eyes.

Any other time, Beth would have immediately withdrawn the request. Getting on Jules's bad side was never a good thing, and asking if Emma could stay with the twins had obviously annoyed her. Asking Jules why would only compound the problem.

Time ticked by in long seconds until Jules finally sighed. "I guess it's okay." She might as well have been telling a dentist to go ahead and drill without Novocain.

"Never mind," Beth said, trying not to make eye contact. There was no way she'd impose on Jules when the woman was so obviously put out by the request.

In all the years she'd been part of the Ladies Who Lunch, Beth had felt nothing but affection and support from Jules, Mallory, and especially Danielle. Now she could almost see a wall being built between herself and Jules, like some silly cartoon where the bricks stacked up row after row after row.

"Beth..." Jules heaved a sigh.

Beth held up a hand, palm out. "Stop. You don't owe me any explanation. It's fine." She wanted nothing more at that moment than for Jules to go home to her handsome husband, her robust twin boys, and the huge historical building in downtown Cloverleaf she and Connor called home.

Go back to your perfect life, Jules. I'll handle my own disasters.

"Beth...it's just—"

"I've got to get Emma ready for her doctor's appointment." Although the statement was far from subtle and a blatant lie, Beth went to the door and put her hand on the knob. "Thanks so much for coming over. I'm looking forward to seeing what kind of place you can show me."

Jules hefted her purse onto her shoulder. She stopped at the door, her face full of an emotion Beth couldn't read. "I'll send some e-mail links after I get back to the office, and I'll start the paperwork to get your mortgage preapproved." On that, she thankfully left.

After Beth shut the door, she leaned back against it, holding Emma against her chest since the baby had fallen asleep. Beth pressed a kiss to her temple before sighing.

The world had gone from orderly to confusing so quickly, she couldn't quite make sense of it yet. Her adult life had been consumed with being a teacher. In the back of her mind, there had been vague plans of a husband, a family. But Bethany Rogers was a teacher, one with a plan to buy a nice little house. Someday.

For now, she was a single mother with no reliable child care, an efficiency apartment, and a tiny car.

"Oh, Em. For such a small girl, you sure knocked me for a loop."

After she laid the peaceful Emma in the playpen that served as her crib, Beth fired up her laptop for the first time in days. Sixty-three e-mails, most of which were easy to delete before she even read them. The only one that interested her was from Robert.

Since when did Robert e-mail her? Why hadn't he texted? Or called?

Beth opened the message.

Sorry, B. Left you on a bad note. Want to come to the new house tomorrow? Some of the fixtures arrived. Thought you'd like to see them. Will bring dinner. See you at six?

Which meant he'd be there with a bucket of KFC and a couple of sodas. At that moment, it sounded like heaven.

Robert. She had so much to think about where he was concerned.

Or did she? Sure, they'd shared a couple of kisses. Hot, soul-stealing kisses from her point of view, but he'd literally run away. Was he running from her or from the idea of commitment? He knew her well enough to know she'd never be one of his arm-candy girls. If he got involved with her, it would be for something more solid.

But it looked like Robert was ready to have things return to status quo. Otherwise he would never have left so darn fast after they'd kissed. It was probably for the best.

She typed her reply.

The munchkin and I will see you then.

* * *

Robert looked out the window again, thinking for the third time he'd heard Beth's car in the driveway.

Wrong again.

She wasn't late. Not yet. He worried anyway.

Ever since he'd left two days ago, he'd been at loose ends, worrying about whether she hated him for taking advantage of her. His own thoughts about what had happened between them were in tangles.

He'd practically tried to seduce her while she was asleep. It was a damn good thing she hadn't hauled off and punched him in the nose. When he'd awakened to her scent, feeling her curves molded to his body, instinct had taken control. He'd needed to touch her, to possess her. Thank goodness he'd gotten a hold of himself before things had gone too far. Yet that interlude haunted his every minute.

It had been a long, long time since he'd felt that kind of

connection with a woman. Hell, he'd never wanted a woman that badly before.

Was it because she was forbidden fruit? A colleague rather than a conquest?

Did he like the idea of winning the "good girl" for once?

Or did this have nothing at all to do with *her*? Was this what every man went through when he turned forty? Flirting with younger women?

There was a third possibility. The way he'd been acting might not be due to either Beth or himself. Did holding Emma trigger some fatherhood gene that had thus far been dormant? Had he spontaneously developed some evolutionary need to be a dad?

His brain couldn't seem to do anything except offer up question after question. The answers were far out of his grasp.

A sound drew him back to the window. At least this time his ears hadn't tricked him. Beth was here. He hurried out the front door to help her with the baby. "Hello there, ladies."

"Hi, Robert." Beth spoke over her shoulder as she worked on wrestling the complicated car seat out of its base.

"Need some help?"

With a grunt, she tugged the carrier loose. Maneuvering it around the front seat and seat belt wasn't easy, but soon Beth had Emma out of the Beetle. "We're good. Want to take Em or grab her diaper bag?"

"I'll take the baby." His hand shot out to grasp the handle Beth had pulled up so the seat now became a baby carrier. "Hiya, squirt."

Emma stopped sucking on her thumb and grinned at him as spittle ran down her chin.

"You're a mess," Robert joked.

After slinging the bag over her shoulder, Beth slammed the car door. "I think she's teething. Started drooling like crazy after her nap. She keeps putting her thumb or her fingers in her mouth."

"Have you tried an ice ring?" Funny how much he remembered from when his nieces and nephews had been Emma's age.

"A what?" Beth followed him to the front door.

"My sister had this toy that had water in a plastic ring. She'd toss it in the freezer, then give it to her kids when they were teething. It's supposed to soothe their gums or something."

"I'll have to stop by Toy Junction on the way home and get her one. It's a better suggestion than my mom made."

"What did she say?"

"Told me to rub whisky on Emma's gums. It's a wonder Tiffany and I survived childhood," she teased. As she walked through the door he held open, she murmured her appreciation. Then she stopped only a few steps inside. "Wow. You've been busy."

He shrugged. Getting the flooring, bathroom tiling, kitchen cabinets, and granite in quickly hadn't been easy, but he needed her to see the house taking shape. By the beginning of next week, everything would be in place, and the furnishings would arrive in ten days.

As Jules always told him, it was easier to sell a staged home. But this time, the deliveries weren't going to be rentals and they sure as hell weren't to stage the place. They were going to be his own furniture in his own house.

They both kicked off their shoes by the door.

"The hardwoods look great." Beth gave him a little laugh that made his throat clog with emotion. "Even if that does sound egotistical."

He might not be sure exactly what it was that he felt for Beth, but one thing was damn sure. It was something strong, and he was getting too old to be patient. After dinner, he'd spring his surprise.

"You have a right to crow," Robert replied. "You did a great job on this. As usual." He cuffed her on the shoulder as he led the way to the kitchen. "Ready to eat?"

She set the diaper bag on the kitchen island. He loved that her fingers roamed over the granite surface for a few moments.

"Depends," she replied.

He quirked a brow. "On what?"

"On if you only got the downstairs floors and fixtures."

"N-no. Ups-stairs is done, too." His nerves were showing.

"I'm heading there first. Then I'll eat." She strode to the staircase before glancing over her shoulder. "You coming?"

Robert finished disengaging all the straps holding Emma in her seat. "Nah. You go on. The munchkin and I will get the drinks ready."

As soon as Beth disappeared up the staircase, he kissed Emma's cheek. "Counting on you to help me pull this off, squirt."

She babbled something before sticking her thumb back in her mouth.

"I'll take that as a yes." He chuckled at her. "You keep that up, and I'm gonna have to pay for braces one day." At least that's what his sister always said about thumb-sucking.

But would he still be in Emma's life by then?

* * *

Beth climbed the stairs, loving the feel of the frieze carpet beneath her feet and wondering why Robert had hustled to get the house floors in. He'd talked about a buyer as though it wasn't anywhere near a done deal, and yet he'd put aside two of his other projects that were contracted earlier to focus on this house. What was the rush?

While everything she'd told him to buy wasn't there, he'd made a good start. The rest would come in time.

She loved the play of colors in the master bedroom. The pleasant gray paint blended with the blue and white tiles she'd selected for the en suite bath. The carpet was a darker shade of gray, and she could feel the bounce of the new padding as she paced across the room. A peek inside the guest rooms, laundry room—something she'd insisted on when Robert showed her the plans—and spare bathrooms revealed a house nearly ready for a growing family.

Still, she wondered if a family would ever live in this beautiful house. The more she thought about it, the more she suspected that this house would be Robert's. He'd hinted as much by coyly answering her questions about the buyer. Deep down, she had to admit she'd chosen the tile, carpet, and hardwoods with him in mind.

Intuition?

Or wishful thinking?

Get off it, Beth. He kissed you. So what?

Padding back down the stairs, she smiled when she found Robert dancing around the kitchen with Emma, humming some silly tune she didn't recognize. The poor guy wasn't only color blind, but he was also tone-deaf. But the picture they presented of happy father and daughter made her heart sing.

So why were tears blurring her vision?

"Look, squirt! There's Mommy!" Robert grinned at her before his lips dropped. "What's wrong?"

Beth shook her head and forced another smile. "Nothing. Nothing at all."

He didn't pass her the baby, seeming content to hold her. Emma was clearly enraptured with Robert. Her gaze never left his face as she contentedly sucked her thumb. "Don't you like the place?"

"Are you kidding? I *love* it."

"So do I, which is why I'm keeping it."

Her heart skipped a beat before slamming against her rib cage. Her intuition had been spot-on—except for one very important thing. Why did Robert suddenly want a house? Had he finally found a woman he was serious about?

Beth had come to terms with his dating, but if he'd finally decided to settle down with a woman to make her a permanent part of his life, she'd be devastated. He hadn't mentioned anyone. Not once.

With trembling fingers, she started unpacking the groceries Robert had brought. Paper plates. Plastic cups. Anything to keep her hands busy so she could pretend her world wasn't falling apart. "I had a feeling…" She shrugged to feign indifference when her emotions were caught in a hurricane. "I mean, it's an awfully big house for just one person." *Oh yeah, Beth. That was nonchalant.*

"I'm not planning to be alone. There's a w-woman I'd like to share it with me."

There was no way she'd cry in front of him. She'd been the one to take a few kisses too seriously. But she ached to punch him in the nose for leading her on when he was in a relationship with another woman.

He kissed me! How could he kiss me when he's in love with someone else?

"Does your girlfriend like the stuff I chose? I mean, are the colors all right with you?"

"Like colors would m-matter for me. And about that girlfriend... We need to talk."

All Beth did was shrug again. There was no way she'd be able to choke down food, so she planned to do everything she could to make a quick escape. Even looking at Robert made her heart hurt.

Balancing Emma on his hip, he put his free hand over one of Beth's. "Stop for a minute. I... I need to ask you something."

Beth set down the napkins, picked up the plastic forks, and stared up at him. She'd never considered how tall he was, and it dawned on her she always had to tilt her head back pretty far to look into his eyes. She loved tall men, especially tall men with a face so handsome it took her breath away.

But now he belonged to someone else.

She put on a mask of indifference, figuring he was going to ask for some décor changes to please his new woman. "Ask away."

"D-do you like this house?"

She let out an inelegant snort and answered with uncharacteristic sarcasm. "Duh. Of course I like it. I decorated it, remember? Besides, my opinion doesn't matter." Her voice was strained as she fought the desire to weep.

"D-do you like it enough to live in it?"

Rendered momentarily speechless, Beth dropped the plastic forks, wincing as most of them bounced on the granite and fell to the floor. "But... but... I thought you were moving in with a girlfriend."

"Girlfriend? What on earth made you think I had a girlfriend?"

"You said you were going to live with a woman."

"W-what if you were my r-roommate?"

His stutter betrayed his nervousness, but all she could do was blink in confusion. With one question, Robert had thrown her mind into bedlam.

A question spilled out. “You don’t have a girlfriend?”

“N-no.” He gave her a shy smile. “At least not yet.”

Gathering her brows, Beth tried to read his eyes. All she found was worry. “What are you saying, Robert?”

He took a deep breath and then blew it out through his mouth, as though gathering his courage. Or perhaps he was just concentrating so he could stop stuttering. Then he spit out whatever he’d been struggling to tell her. “I want you to move in with me. Here. Just as soon as the house is done.”

Chapter 6

I beg your pardon?"

Robert had expected Beth to resist, but the incredulous frown that spread over her face was almost his undoing. Sure, things were moving pretty fast. With a few kisses, they'd gone from friends to something more. But what?

He wasn't sure, and Beth's reaction told him she was every bit as confused.

That confusion had helped him form a plan. They needed time together to figure out exactly where they were going. With all the changes in her life, she had to feel as though she were standing on quicksand. He'd offered her a home, a place that would work much better for her and Emma to help her find some solid ground.

He wasn't asking her to his bed. Not yet, at least. Just asking if she'd be his roommate had taken every ounce of his courage. He wasn't about to lose the chance to have both Beth and Emma in his life.

He'd never been able to commit to one woman for too long. Deep down, he was afraid his infatuation with Beth would abruptly end. That was the normal course for his affections. If it did, it would be damned awkward having her and Emma living in his home. But that was a chance he was willing to take.

All Robert knew was that Emma represented something he'd always wanted desperately. Fatherhood. A family. Emma was such a unique child, and his bond with her was irrevocable.

As far as what he felt for Beth, he figured once she and Emma moved in, he would have more time to ponder the whys of their attraction. Then he could sort out his feelings.

"I want you to move in with me. Here." He buckled Emma back in her seat and then set the seat on the enormous kitchen island. "Emma needs something bigger than that studio apartment you live in."

Beth's cheeks reddened. "I've already got Jules looking for a house. We've got three showings set for tomorrow."

That news was exactly what he didn't want to hear. "What's wrong with this p-place?" Robert stopped, concentrating so he'd stop stuttering. Beth had him more flustered than any other woman he'd ever known. It had been years since he'd had this much trouble speaking. "What do those houses have that this doesn't?"

"They're nothing like this. I can't afford something this big."

"Think about it, B. You love this house. You told me so. It's got plenty of room for all three of us, and I'll build the best play yard in Cloverleaf in the backyard for Emma. A small climbing wall. A slide. Swings. Only the best for the squirt."

"Robert…I…You…" She shook her head. "You're generous to offer, but I would never put you out like that."

"Put me out?"

"You don't need to take us in as though we're street urchins."

Ah, so her pride was hurting. "That's not what I'm thinking at all. I just…" He ran his hand over his face and spit out the truth. "I want Emma to have someplace nice to live."

Her chin rose defiantly. "You think I can't provide a decent house for her?"

"I never said that. But look around you. Emma would be happy here. She'd have that big bedroom upstairs with her own bathroom. I'll finish the basement so she can have a place to play with her friends and not get under your feet."

"She is *not* under my feet. I love Emma."

"So do I!"

Everything was coming out all wrong. His words only seemed to strike nerve after nerve. He'd wanted to offer her a sanctuary. Instead, she acted as if he'd denigrated her.

Robert put himself in front of her and placed his hands on her shoulders. Beth looked everywhere except at him. "Look at me, B."

"I should go…"

He gripped her chin. "Look at me. Please."

There were unshed tears in her eyes.

"What's wrong?"

"Why does everyone think I can't raise Emma?"

"Everyone?"

She looked so damned forlorn. "Jules. My parents. You."

With a shake of his head, he tried to set her straight. "First off, I have never—I repeat *never*—said you can't raise Emma. In fact, I think you're doing a fantastic job with her." He glanced at the munchkin. "Look at her." Emma smiled on cue, all tiny teeth and drool. "She's doing really well with you. What did your parents say?"

Beth's pouty lips strongly tempted him to kiss her again. "They told me it might be better to put her up for adoption."

"Are you serious?" What kind of grandparents would say something so cruel? How could they even consider giving up their only grandchild?

"Dead serious. They made such a fuss over how much taking care of her while Tiffany was gone inconvenienced them. I was going to take her this summer, maybe even longer."

What did a person say to something like that? "That's cold."

"I know, right? Besides that, my folks are really old-fashioned. They think a child should have both a mom and a dad." A smile threatened. "I think Tiffany had Emma as a way to piss Mom off. Kind of her way of saying, 'I'm a single mom. Take that, Carol.' "

"They're wrong. You know they are."

Although she glanced away, he saw the hurt in her eyes. "They've never really had a lot of confidence in me."

Since his parents always encouraged their gaggle of children to reach for the stars and told them they all had the ability to do just that, he had a hard time picturing what it must have been like to grow up with parents like Beth's. "Then they're not too smart, 'cause you're somebody who deserves their confidence. You're amazing."

Her gaze came back to his, but there was disbelief in her eyes.

"I mean it, B. Look at all you've done at school. Everyone admires you."

She gave him a small snort.

One thing he'd have to do when they lived together was help give her more self-esteem. But he had to convince her to move into this house with him first. "What did our ever-tactful Jules have to say?"

"It was wrong to tell you she said I wasn't good with Emma."

"She didn't say that?" Robert asked. He still stood in front of

Beth, and now he held both her hands in his. It felt so natural. So right. Like two people in love sharing a conversation.

But Beth didn't love him, and he was still pretty mixed up about how he felt about her. That was why he thought she and Emma moving in would be so great. He would have Emma in his life, and he and Beth would have time to share their lives, to see if the kisses and caresses led to—or away from—something special.

Beth shook her head. "She got weird when I asked if her nanny could watch Emma when I go back to work next week."

"You're going back so soon?"

This time, she nodded. "I'm out of paid time off."

"Why not take a leave of absence?"

Her laugh was always so sweet to his ears. "'Cause I like to eat, and I imagine Emma does, too."

"Didn't Tiffany have life insurance? I thought all soldiers did."

"I won't touch that money. Not unless I absolutely have to. It's a nest egg for Emma. She can pay for college and maybe even buy her first home with it."

The response was pure Beth. Always putting others before herself. She was going to raise that baby on a teacher's salary, a salary that seldom saw increases. She'd have her work cut out for her being a single mom who got paid diddly-squat.

"Well, then," Robert said. "That seals the deal. You move in here. There's one less expense." She had to agree. She just had to.

"I'd pay you rent," she insisted.

"The hell you will!"

She jerked her hands free. "I'm not a charity case, Robert. Emma and I aren't living in a homeless shelter or anything. I already told you Jules is looking for a house for us."

Why had everything he said in this conversation come out wrong? After raking his fingers through his hair, he tried again. "B, p-please. Please move in with me. I want Emma here. I want you here."

"Why?"

A man could only take so much provocation. Her belligerent frown that wouldn't scare a fly. Her brown eyes that flashed with fire. The way she crossed her arms under her full breasts. Everything about her made him want to kiss her.

So he did.

Robert grabbed her hand and tugged Beth into his arms. He stopped when his lips were almost touching hers. "Because of… *this*."

* * *

When Robert kissed her, every ounce of Beth's anger evaporated. All there was in her world was the feel of his warmth surrounding her, invading her. His lips were firm and insistent, and she opened her lips before he even tried to nudge them open. A throaty groan followed as his tongue thrust into her mouth, rubbing across her tongue in a caress that reached down to her soul.

Instead of looping her arms around his neck, she grew bolder, pressing her palms against his butt. She'd admired it for so long as she'd watched him work. He had such a sexy backside.

The kiss went on and on, drowning her thoughts of buying a place of her own. She wanted to move into this gorgeous house with this handsome man she cared for, but she wasn't sure why he'd extended the invitation. Every time she asked him, he evaded a true answer.

As though he realized her mind was wandering, Robert eased back, still keeping her in his embrace. "Don't you want to see where this is going?"

"This?"

He nodded. "Us. If we're here, spending time together, maybe I can figure out why I can't keep my hands off you."

"That was blunt."

With a little laugh, he shrugged. "I can't stop touching you. It's the honest truth."

She had to ask, but finding the words wasn't easy. "Would you…I mean, would we…Do you expect…" She sounded like an idiot.

A smile bloomed on his face that told her he understood. "You'll have your own room, if that's what you're asking."

"It was. I just wasn't sure."

"Neither of us is ready for more. Right now, we need to focus on Emma." Robert grasped her shoulders again. "Look, B…it's a good idea. Besides. I w-want you two here. With me. I'm kinda lonely."

"Lonely?"

He nodded. "Admit it. This is the r-right thing for all of us. Don't let your stubborn pride convince you otherwise."

He was right. Of course he was right. Beth only wished she could have a few moments of being able to read his mind to know what was truly driving his invitation. Was it how he felt about her? Or how he felt about Emma?

When Robert talked about them moving in, he spoke of how much he loved Emma. *Would he even be interested in me if Emma hadn't come into my life?*

Not once in all the years Beth had known him had he ever shown the smallest amount of attraction to her. Now he claimed he couldn't leave her alone. It seemed so convenient that the fascination appeared when Emma did.

He'd hit the nail squarely on the head when he'd called her stubborn. It was Beth's worst fault. Would she let that pride and a touch of unreasonable jealousy be the reasons she denied Emma the privilege of living in this veritable mansion?

"I should pay rent at least," she insisted.

"Nope. You can earn your keep by helping me finish this place. We need to choose furnishings; then there's the basement to work on. You'll do plenty to work the rent off."

"You're being ridiculous, Robert. I can't live here rent-free."

"Pay for your groceries, then."

"I was going to do that anyway." If this was going to happen, she didn't want to feel like a charity case. "I won't take a dime for decorating this house—or any others for as long as I live here. All right?"

"We've got a deal!" With a quick kiss, he whirled around to fish Emma out of her seat. "Hear that, squirt? We're gonna be roomies!"

Chapter 7

You're *what*?"

Beth winced at the way Danielle screeched the question. "I'm moving in with Robert."

"But...but..." Danielle stared at her wide-eyed from across the table at the coffee shop. "You didn't even tell us you were going out with him." Her voice held a note of censure, as well as a touch of hurt and a lot of anger.

Mallory and Jules were glaring every bit as hard, and Beth was sure to hear their displeasure soon as well.

Why were they all against her when they didn't even know the particulars of the situation?

"That's 'cause we're *not* going out," Beth said. Knowing that answer was going to trigger a slew of questions from the three Ladies Who Lunch, she hastened to explain. "Robert and I are friends. That's all. He knows how hard it is for me to raise Em all by myself. He built that big house over in Stone Haven for himself, and he decided he wants us to move in with him."

"I don't get it." Dani pushed her empty coffee cup farther away. "Why build a house like that for himself?"

Beth shrugged since she'd been asking herself the same question. "Maybe he wanted to hold it while the value appreciates? Maybe he decided he liked it while he was building it? All I know is Emma will have a great place to live, and I'll have a friend to help with watching her."

The scowl Jules tossed her way told her she'd hit a nerve.

Good. If Jules hadn't been so selfish about letting Aubrey watch Emma with the twins, Beth might not need Robert's help.

Who was she kidding? Her feelings for Robert grew each day, and Jules's rejection would never change that. Even if Aubrey had Emma every school day, Beth would still be taking Robert up on his generous offer. They needed time to see if they could become more than friends. Much more, she hoped.

Dani's brows knit. "So you aren't a couple?"

"No. No way," Beth replied. *Not yet.* Although she feared her heart had already settled on Robert. She had no plans for a relationship beyond sharing the home and seeing if a true relationship grew from the time they spent together. For all she knew, he might decide she wasn't at all what he'd expected, especially because living together he was sure to see her at her worst.

Since when did she feel the need to lie to her friends, especially Dani? The Ladies shared everything. The four of them had always been close and entirely open with one another. Now there was a wall between Beth and Jules over the nanny request, and more walls were going up between Beth and the group with each half-truth she told.

She just wasn't ready to share what was budding between her and Robert—if there was anything even budding between them. She had no confidence it would last, and if the Ladies knew, things could get awkward if Robert changed his mind and just wanted to be platonic roommates.

Once she was sharing a home with him, he might realize exactly how high maintenance she could be and give up on even thinking about being intimate. Isn't that what her last two boyfriends had told her? She was too fussy, too particular? Why should Robert be any different?

Beth liked what she liked. That was that. She tried to never be insistent or contrary, but when it came to food or beauty products or even clothing, she had certain preferences. She also hated things to be disorganized.

Emma had thrown a kink in Beth's orderly life from the first moment she chose to take over her care. Having a baby and keeping things neat and clean weren't compatible. After seeing how much Robert had straightened up her apartment while she slept the other night, he might have assumed she was as messy as he was. Far from it.

She'd been to his home and his office. God love him, the man was a slob. Surely once he realized how fussy she was, he'd ask her to move right back out. If she hoped to keep her sanity, perhaps she needed to learn to relax some of her standards, which might make things easier for Robert and Emma.

"Are you doing this because of Aubrey?" Jules asked, drawing Beth out of her thoughts.

Although her anger at the rejection had faded, Beth wasn't ready to let Jules entirely off the hook. She still thought it was odd that Jules wouldn't let her nanny take care of Emma. "Not completely. It will be great to have Robert watching Emma."

"We can talk about it more…maybe?" Jules's voice held little promise that she'd change her mind.

So why even offer? Beth cut her off before she could say

anything else to stir the anger back up. "No need. Robert's oldest niece runs a day care out of her house. She's going to take Emma when Robert and I can't be with her. Since he works from home a lot, it won't be too many hours."

"That's asking an awful lot of commitment from him," Dani said. "Especially if you two aren't even dating."

"She's right," Mallory chimed in. "Why's Robert willing to take on all this new responsibility?"

The same question Beth had asked herself a million times. She kept coming back to the same entirely inadequate answer. "We're friends, and friends help each other out."

Mallory didn't look convinced. "Robert must be in a hurry to get you and Emma under his roof. Ben's been pulled off the house in Windsong to work on Robert's... um... your... er... the house you two are going to share."

Mallory's husband was one of the best contractors in the county. Ben liked being his own boss and wasn't ready to commit entirely to Ashford Homes, but Robert used his services whenever he had a client who was overly particular or one he wanted to impress. Ben had done a lot of the work on the house Robert was moving into. Seemed like Ben would be putting on the finishing touches as well according to Mallory.

"I'm glad," Beth said, shifting her coffee between her hands. "Then it'll be perfect."

"What about gossip?" Dani asked. "You're telling us that there's nothing going on between you and Robert, but do you think everyone in Cloverleaf will believe that?"

"I'm not that naïve." With a sigh, Beth said, "We'll just make it clear that we're friends sharing a fantastic house for the good of a poor orphaned baby."

Jules let out an inelegant snort, the first sign of her normally vocal sense of humor. "You make Emma sound like Oliver Twist."

"I was being facetious," Beth retorted, but she smiled as well. She'd laid it on a little thick. "The people who know me will understand."

"But will the parents or Jim Reinhardt or the school board?" Mallory drew her lips into a grim line. "Cloverleaf is stuck in the 1950s, Beth. There could be repercussions for your job."

"Not if they don't want me to sue their butts from here to Timbuktu." And Beth meant it. There were no laws against adults cohabitating, married or not. "It's time for Cloverleaf to take a leap forward in time. There's nothing wrong with Robert sharing a house with me and Emma. Even if we were a couple, that's no one's business but ours."

She might be cavalier with her friends, but Beth's gut tightened. Being the center of attention anywhere except her classroom made her uncomfortable. She wasn't like Jules, craving the spotlight. The idea that living with Robert would make her the target of gossip, something that plagued Cloverleaf, almost made her change her mind.

Jules had been fiddling with her cell phone more than paying attention to the conversation. She got to her feet and hefted her purse off the floor. "I've got a house showing in fifteen minutes." She directed her gaze at Beth. "I take it you don't want to see those houses tomorrow." Sarcasm dripped from her words.

"No, but thanks for arranging them," Beth replied. Things between her and Jules were tense enough that the other Ladies had to be picking up on it. Hopefully, time would soothe the rift.

"See you all later." On that, Jules strode out of the coffee shop. The bronze bell hanging at the entrance rang as she opened and closed the door.

"I should head out, too," Dani said. "I've got a crapload of papers to grade." She frowned at Beth. "Call me if you want to talk."

Beth nodded, but the only person she had any intention of talking to was Robert. *He* understood. *He* cared. After Jules let her down, she began to fear her friendships with the Ladies meant more to her than they did to the three of them.

"Mallory?" Dani asked. "You coming?"

"Go on, Dani," Mallory replied. "I wanna talk to Bethany for a second."

Bethany. What Mallory always called her whenever she was frustrated with her. Just like a mother getting ready to scold a child.

Dani left on a snarky, "All righty, then." The bell marked her departure as it had Jules's.

"Why do I get the feeling you're going to start in on me, too?" Beth asked. Her coffee was empty, and the smell of the freshly baked muffins called to her. Baked goods were always her favorite comfort food, but she wouldn't wolf one down with model-thin Mallory staring at her.

"You're really moving in with Robert?" Mallory asked.

Beth nodded, not feeling the need to keep justifying her choice by explaining it yet again.

"But there's nothing romantic? Nothing at all?"

Shouldn't lying to friends get easier with each new telling? "Nope. Nothing at all."

"I don't believe you." Where Jules was brutally honest, Mallory used tact. Those four words were a polite way of her calling Beth a liar.

Which she was. She simply shrugged. "Believe what you want."

"Bethany… We all care about you. You know that. But I also know you've had a crush on Robert for a long time."

"A crush? You make me sound like one of my students."

"Then call it something else," Mallory countered. "An attraction. An infatuation. Desire."

"What makes you think I'm attracted to Robert?" If Mallory saw how Beth felt, surely others would as well. Just more fodder for the gossips…

"It's the way you look at him when you're together, and you can stop looking like you're about to have a panic attack." Mallory let out a little chuckle. "I doubt anyone else sees it as clearly as I do. Or am I wrong?"

Beth stood at a crossroads. Here was her chance to confide in someone about her feelings for Robert and what her fears were about why he was inviting her and Emma to move in. Mallory was someone she could trust to not repeat anything Beth told her, not even to Jules or Dani. Probably not even to Ben.

But if Beth confided in Mallory and Dani found out, she'd be hurt. Dani had always been Beth's closest friend. Her confidante. If Beth was going to spill her guts to anyone, it should be Dani.

If Ben found out, he'd probably go right to Robert. The last thing Beth wanted was Robert knowing she was jealous that he seemed to want Emma in his life more than her.

Mallory's hand covered Beth's where it rested on the table. "It's okay. I understand. I just…I've always felt like I owe you, and helping you with this would be my way of paying you back."

"Why would you owe me anything?" Beth asked.

"You were the one who helped Ben and I reconcile."

When Ben had come to Beth to ask for help when he and Mallory had temporarily split up, she'd arranged a big event at Douglas High's volleyball team's senior night. Ben showed

Mallory how much he supported her in her breast cancer battle by letting Beth shave him bald right in front of everyone. Then he'd gotten down on one knee to propose. How could Beth resist helping true love find a way?

Beth waved Mallory's comment away. "If I hadn't helped him, you'd still have worked it out. You two are meant for each other."

"Just like I think you and Robert are supposed to be together. And for heaven's sake, learn to take a compliment! Ben said all he did was ask for your help, and voilà, there's Ben in the center of the gym. Not only did you give him the perfect way to apologize and make amends, but you also raised a couple thousand dollars for breast cancer research."

"It was nothing."

"To me, it was a helluva lot more than *nothing*." Mallory leaned back. "I—*we*—want to help you. Raising Emma won't be easy, and you'll need your friends' help. Don't shut us out."

Which was exactly what Beth had been doing. Beth needed to hear the warning, but she'd already made up her stubborn mind, probably because of Jules's rejection at the first favor Beth had asked of one of her friends.

Instead of tossing out yet another lie, Beth said, "Robert will be there for Emma. You should see him with her. If I didn't know better, I'd think she was his biological daughter."

"Why do you think he's so attached to her this quickly?" Mallory asked.

Since Beth had asked herself the same question over and over, she gave the answer she'd finally arrived at. "I think he's finally ready to settle down."

"Turning forty will do that to a guy," Mallory said with a smirk. "So you think this is a midlife crisis?"

"Not at all. He loves Emma. I have no doubt of that. He talks about how smart she is, even claims she's brighter than any of his nieces and nephews."

"But how does he feel about you?"

Beth hesitated, not sure she was ready to confront her fears let alone share them with Mallory.

"Beth?"

"We're just friends, Mallory. That's all." How could she tell any of the Ladies how afraid she was that Robert wanted Emma and was willing to settle for Beth since they were a package deal? He was so open about how he felt about Emma, and although he was physically attracted to Beth, that didn't mean he held any true affection for her.

With a frown and a shake of her head, Mallory pushed her chair back and stood up. "Be careful."

"With Robert?"

"That, and with the Ladies Who Lunch."

"What's that supposed to mean?" Beth asked. The statement held a note of threat that made her bristle.

"That means don't push us all so far away that you can never find your way back."

Chapter 8

Beth looked around her classroom, tears blurring her vision. There were balloons, streamers, and hand-painted signs welcoming her back. Since the principal normally frowned on parties during school hours, she was shocked to see an enormous sheet cake on her worktable. Next to it rested a pile of paper plates, napkins, and plastic forks.

"Oh my…" She sniffed hard, willing herself not to cry in front of the kids. Her gaze swept the faces of the students in her Service Learning class, the clear organizers of this little gathering. Most were grinning, but a few girls had tears in their eyes as well. "Thank you all."

For some odd reason, a teacher showing too much emotion freaked out students, as though teachers were supposed to constantly be in total control of themselves. Laughter was allowed. But tears? Never.

"This is so sweet." Beth turned to see Mallory and Dani standing in the doorway, smiling.

No surprise the Ladies Who Lunch helped make this happen.

While Beth's students started bustling about, cutting the cake and handing it out, she went to her friends.

Brushing aside the guilty feelings that had dragged her down after the tempestuous lunch a few days ago, Beth hugged each of her friends and murmured her thanks.

"We're glad to have you back," Dani said before embracing Beth. Then she brushed away a stray tear. "Douglas High wasn't the same without you."

"We've missed you," Mallory added with a quick hug. "Oh, and Jules is coming by soon. We'll be the Ladies Who Lunch again today, if only for the half hour we have to eat."

"That'll be heaven."

* * *

By the time lunch period rolled around, Beth was already exhausted. She'd have to dig deep to face the three classes she still had to teach. After being gone for almost three weeks, there was a pile of paperwork to do, grading would probably never end, and just catching up on absences and tardies took a good portion of her prep period. Her mother used to scold her for going to school and trying to teach when she was ill. Beth had always explained it was easier to be there and be sick than to try to get things ready for a substitute and get back up to speed when she returned.

As she pulled her classroom door shut, heading to meet with the Ladies, another pang ran through her. How was Emma? Was she getting along with the other kids? Did she miss her *matka*? Robert had started calling Beth that when speaking to Emma, claiming it was what he'd called his Czech mother. Beth loved him for finding the exact right thing. Tiffany would always be Emma's "mommy," but Beth was now her "*matka*."

Matka sure misses you, Em.

Mallory and Dani smiled when Beth swept into the break room at five minutes past noon—the same time she'd eaten with her friends year after year. After grabbing her food from the fridge, she plopped down in an empty seat. "Geesh. Feels like I've been gone forever."

"Three weeks *is* forever in teacher years," Dani replied.

"Where's Jules?"

Mallory shoved the phone she'd been fussing with back in her sweater pocket. "On her way. Clearing security as we speak."

Bethany owed all of them an apology, but she wanted to wait until Jules arrived so she could say the words just once. While they waited, she set out the leftovers from the supper Robert had bought her last night.

"Is that from China Teahouse?" Dani peered at the container.

"Yeah," Beth replied. "Got carryout last night. Robert and I were exhausted after spending the whole day shopping for furniture."

"Speaking of furniture, when are you moving in with him?" Mallory popped open her Diet Cherry Coke. "Ben's working his cute little butt off to get it done quickly."

"Robert's packing his place up now." Beth smirked. "Although he's in the same predicament I'm in. Most of his furniture is falling apart. We're donating a lot of it to Goodwill. I'm really excited, though. I get to pull my grandmother's armoire out of storage for my bedroom."

Dani arched a blond eyebrow. "You'll, um, have your own bedroom? You're not sharing the master?"

Just as Jules marched into the break room, Beth said, "I'll have my own room. Besides, if Robert and I had slept together, don't you think I'd have told you?"

"I'd hope so," Jules said, lightly touching Beth's shoulder as she passed behind her. After she took her seat and set down her McDonald's sack and drink, she grinned. "I always pick the perfect time to jump into a conversation, don't I?"

"Always," Mallory drawled before shifting her gaze back to Beth. "I guess we all assumed…I mean, you're moving in with him."

"Yeah, well, you know what happens when you assume," Beth snapped. Then her shoulders sagged. She was supposed to be apologizing, not getting angry all over again. "It's… complicated."

"All relationships are complicated," Dani countered.

Beth gave her a brusque nod. "Look, I'm sorry. I've just been so overwhelmed. And when Jules, well…" She picked up her fork and stared at her lunch. "I'm sorry. Okay?"

"When Jules what?" Mallory asked.

Jules was the one to answer. "When I blew her off about Aubrey watching Emma."

Mallory knit her brows. "Why would you do that?"

"Because I'm a selfish bitch," Jules replied, yanking her wrapped sandwich out of the bag.

"You are not." Beth was surprised by Jules's response. The woman was never one to so quickly and emphatically admit her mistakes, but calling herself a "selfish bitch" was going overboard.

"I was," Jules insisted, fishing the box of fries out and dropping them next to the sandwich.

"Then why'd you make her take Emma to day care?" Dani asked.

Jules let out a sigh. "The twins are getting to be a handful. Two toddlers aren't easy, and with Carter's allergies and Craig's apnea, Aubrey's working her skinny little ass off. I just thought adding Emma to the mix would be too much for her. That, and I selfishly didn't want her taking Aubrey's attention away from the boys." Her eyes were full of regret. "I'm sorry, Beth. If you still wanna give it a try..."

With a shake of her head, Beth let Jules off the hook. "Robert's niece is wonderful. She's got the entire basement of the house to use since Robert's turned it into Emma's play area. He cleaned Toys 'R' Us out of educational toys the other day. Emma didn't even cry when I left her this morning."

Which had actually hurt a little. When Robert left the apartment after supper, Emma had clung to him and wailed as though her heart were breaking. But when Beth had made a quick run to the store and left her with Robert, Emma hadn't even waved farewell.

"What's wrong?" Dani's hand covered hers.

"I'm just..." Beth wasn't sure how to put her concerns into words. With the exception of Dani and the Ladies, Beth had always lacked support. Yes, she had two parents and a sister. But they'd always made her feel...wrong. Like she didn't belong. Like nothing she ever did would be good enough.

Emma should love Beth as unconditionally as Beth loved Emma. Period. Instead, Emma and Robert would probably do fine if all they had was each other. "This mom stuff isn't easy."

Jules let out a boisterous laugh. "Understatement of the year!"

"It's more than that," Dani insisted. "I can tell."

Beth nodded. "Emma doesn't seem to need me. Not like she does Robert." This time, she was the one to let out the weighty sigh. "Maybe I'm not cut out to be a good mom."

"For pity's sake." Mallory laid down the sandwich she was just about to bite into. "It's been three weeks since you both lost

Tiffany. Give it time. Emma needs to adjust to you, exactly like you need to adjust to her. That's all."

If only it were that easy.

More and more Beth worried about whether she would be enough for Emma. In her mind, Beth had images from Hallmark commercials spinning and twirling and making her crazy. The perfect mother. The perfect daughter. What they'd shared so far was anything but perfect. Emma fussed most of the night. She seemed to lean away whenever Beth kissed her cheek. She squirmed when Beth tried to hold her too long.

Everything was the opposite with Robert. Emma clung to him, laughed with him, and gave him sloppy kisses without prompting. While Beth was thrilled they'd bonded, there was jealousy there, too. Immature and very selfish jealousy. She was Emma's mother now. Shouldn't Emma love her? Or was love like trust and had to be earned?

Then why did Emma love Robert so darn much?

"What can I do to help?" Dani asked, her gaze sincere.

"I was hoping I could count on you to watch Emma while Robert and I move my stuff on Saturday. I wasn't sure if you had plans."

"I do." The smile was pure Dani—full of mischief. "I plan on playing with Emma in that basement full of new toys."

"I've got a better idea," Jules said. "Let Emma spend the night with the twins. That way you'll have plenty of time to get everything done before you take her to your new home."

* * *

The box split when Beth dropped it on the floor, the corner gaping open.

No wonder. She'd packed it pretty full of her winter clothes, and it had been a well-used box to begin with. Packing had been a chore. Unpacking would be even more so.

How could she have had this much stuff in a studio apartment?

She chuckled as she glanced around her new bedroom. The dresser, mirror, nightstand, and bed frame had been delivered. So had the beautiful head and footboards of the large four-poster bed. Her grandmother's armoire stood against the wall next to the window. No mattress yet, but there were more than enough clothes strewn about the room to fill her new walk-in closet.

Why could she never find anything to wear in the morning? Surely a woman with four full boxes of clothes and shoes should have plenty of outfits to choose from.

Alas...Women with big butts never liked anything they put on.

Robert strode into the room, dropped the box Beth had packed with her toiletries in front of her en suite bath, and then leaned against one of the bedposts. "I am *never* moving again."

Her first thought was to say, "Me neither." But then she considered how that might sound. She didn't want him to think he was stuck with her. "I hate moving, too." She grabbed another pair of pants out of the box and a hanger from the pile next to her. "But this place is going to be good for Emma."

"And for us, too." His voice was slightly husky, and his gaze captured hers. "This could be great, B. A new start for all of us."

She nodded, not trusting herself to speak. Every time she thought about what Robert was doing, everything he was sacrificing for her and Emma, a lump clogged her throat. Her feelings for him were getting entirely out of control, and if his affections were only for Emma, Beth could make herself out to be the greatest of fools if she revealed too much.

He pushed himself away from the post and hurried to her. "What's wrong?"

If he could read her face that easily, she was in a world of trouble. "Nothing. Just tired."

His lopsided smile set her heart to pounding, and a warm flush spread over her face. "No wonder," he said. "It's been a long day." He directed a glance at the window. "Probably close to suppertime."

Beth nodded. "I'm getting hungry."

"Then we should get a bite to eat."

"I should pick up Emma first."

"Isn't she staying at Jules's house tonight?"

"She's supposed to. It was the only way we could get any work done today. I just…" She shrugged. "I feel bad putting Jules out."

Robert chuckled. "Aubrey's probably watching her and the twins. I'll give her some money if it'll keep you from feeling guilty. Besides"—he grasped her hand—"I figured we could make this a date night or something."

"Date night?" Darn if her voice didn't squeak.

"Yeah." He took her other hand. "We've been so fixed on Emma, I think we need a little 'us' time. Thought I'd buy you a nice dinner; then we can come back here and watch a movie or something."

"The satellite guy came?"

"Yep. We've got all the movie channels. I know how much you enjoy watching movies."

"Oh, Robert. I didn't expect—" Before she could finish the thought, he tugged her into his arms and kissed her. One quick kiss before he eased back and stared down at her.

"That's what I love about you, B. You never expect. You're grateful for anything people do for you, but not once have you expected someone to help you. And yet, you've made great strides in caring for Emma and yourself despite the loss of your sister."

The praise and the kiss made her face flush warmer. Her childhood had been sadly lacking in approval, not that she blamed her parents. She'd been a handful as a child. Curious and unafraid. A dangerous combination. More often than not, Beth would get herself into situations that made her parents shake their heads and wonder aloud if she was truly their daughter. Surely their daughter would have been more demure.

By the time she'd hit adolescence, she'd settled down. Probably because Tiffany had more than picked up the slack in the creating trouble department.

Hearing praise now only made Beth downright uncomfortable, so much so she'd shake her head and look away.

Robert used a gentle touch to draw her face back to his. He brushed another kiss over her lips. "You will learn how to take a compliment. Even if it kills me."

Although she didn't agree with him, she nodded.

"So will you let me spoil you and take you to dinner? How often do you think we'll get a chance for a night to ourselves once this move is done?"

"You're right. I just…I haven't been away from Emma since the…the…"

"I know." He cupped her face in his hands and stroked her cheeks with his thumbs. "You need a break. Maybe Emma does, too. Let's get some good food, pick a good movie, and have a good time. Just the two of us."

"Our first date," she couldn't help but point out.

"So it is. Well, then." He dropped his hands and started

marching across her bedroom. "I'm going to need a shower and some clean clothes." Robert was gone before she could say another word.

Beth fumbled through the boxes of clothes for something suitable for a date. Her stomach fluttered in nervousness. The way he couldn't seem to stop touching her, and the fact that she wanted him to keep on doing so, boded ill.

Or did it bode well?

Was she ready to take that last step toward intimacy? Her body was screaming *yes!*

She finally grabbed some clothes, snatched her jasmine shampoo and soap from the toiletries box, and took her first shower in her new home.

Chapter 9

As soon as they got home, Robert kicked his shoes onto the rug by the foyer closet. He wasn't at all surprised when Beth toed her flats off, picked them up, and set them in the shoe cubby she'd picked out for the closet. Feeling properly scolded, he grabbed his own and put them in the cubby alongside hers.

Funny. That image, his sloppy shoes next to her blue flats, seemed like a metaphor for his ultimate goal. Being side by side with this woman.

Their shoes in the cubby. Their clothes in the closet. Her head on the pillow beside his.

When had he turned into a hopeless romantic?

The moment he'd realized exactly how wonderful Beth really was.

He was going to have to work harder at picking up after himself. A horrible slob by nature, he worried that he would offend Beth if he acted like himself. Forty was kind of old to be changing habits. For her, though, he'd give it his best try.

The house had really come together nicely. Another great job by his favorite decorator. He could see the special attention she'd given the place even before she'd known it was going to be their house. His clients constantly raved about Beth's good taste and how she always thought of a house's functionality. Since he didn't know what colors went well with others, he'd been grateful for her help. He also despised change. Once a room was done, it wasn't going to get painted again until the last coat peeled.

Now he knew why his clients loved her so much. She embraced change, always knowing about the latest and most versatile gadgets, all the things that turned a house into a home. This place practically screamed "home" to him—and hopefully to her.

Robert would definitely have to try harder to remember to hang up his jacket instead of just draping it over a chair. He'd have to use coasters so he didn't ruin the stunning new furniture. He'd have to put dirty dishes in the dishwasher rather than simply pile them in the sink until they leaned like the tower in Pisa.

There was another good reason to stop being a pig. He needed to be a good role model for Emma. There would most likely be home visits since Beth was planning to officially adopt Emma, and he wanted to help in any way he could. That road should be as smooth for his girls as possible.

My girls.

That's exactly what Beth and Emma were now. Fate had been kind in sending him a family that was ready-made. One that needed him. But he'd still have to win Beth's affections to seal the deal.

An easy smile crossed his face. Judging from the way she'd kissed him, he might already be well on the way to that goal. Once he convinced her to stay with him, maybe even marry him, then he'd stop worrying that he could lose her. Even thinking about her not being a part of his life, a part of each day, made his blood run cold.

Not only did he want Beth in his life, but Emma was something special, and watching her grow up would be a joy. There was no way he was going to miss out. His heart had already accepted her as his daughter. No one was going to take her away from him.

"What movie do you want to watch?" Beth asked, drawing him away from his musings. After picking up the remote, she held it out and wiggled it. "DVD or take our chances on finding something on TV?"

Striding over to her, Robert draped his arm around her shoulders and playfully pulled her down onto the sectional with him. Then he nudged over the ottoman and propped up his feet. "Let's see what we can find."

She put her feet up as well, and then she turned on the TV and started scrolling through channels until she found some romantic comedy. "Is this okay?"

Since his interest was fixated on the woman sitting next to him rather than any movie, he shrugged. "Doesn't really matter."

He couldn't stop staring at her. God, she was beautiful tonight. She'd pulled her dark curls away from her face with a headband, and she wore only a light layer of makeup, just a hint of blue around her eyes. Her light, gauzy shirt hid the curve of her breasts, which he found teasingly frustrating. He loved those breasts. He loved her round shape, too. Thankfully, Beth didn't feel the need to starve herself to try and look like a skeleton. She was the most feminine creature he'd ever seen, and he ached to run his hands over every inch of her soft skin.

Her teeth worried her lower lip. "I thought you wanted to

watch a movie." She offered up a hesitant smile. "If I had my choice, we'd be glued to HGTV."

"Wouldn't matter to me. All I wanted was to spend time alone with you." Robert tugged her closer until she was pressed hard against his side.

"Oh..." If she bit her lip any harder, she'd draw blood.

He'd waited the whole damn night to have her in his arms. Dinner had barely had any taste, because the only thing he could think of was that they'd be all alone in their new home—the perfect time to take their budding relationship to a higher level.

Robert wanted to make love to her. *Tonight.*

His cock was hard as a rock, not a very comfortable situation. It wasn't as though he could pop open his fly and let the poor thing out of the tight confines of his jeans. Wondering how Beth would react if he did made him chuckle.

"What's so funny?" Her eyes searched his.

He almost blurted out exactly what was amusing him but refrained before the words slipped out. He was trying to seduce her, not send her running away because she thought he was some pervert. "Nothin'."

In all his years of dating, he'd never been this unsure with a woman. If she showed interest, he'd take her up on whatever she offered. With Beth, he worried about each touch, each kiss, afraid he'd take a misstep. He cared about what she thought, wanting to guard her obvious innocence and not come on too strong. The last time he'd weighed his every word and every action this way was when he'd been a teenager.

He was going to drive himself insane. It was time to stop over-thinking and just let their attraction unfold.

"Oh. Okay," she murmured.

When she glanced away, Robert nudged her face back to his. Then he pressed a kiss against her lips. Then another. God, he wanted her.

Gentle kisses weren't enough. He tugged her closer and gave her the kind of kiss he'd been thinking of all evening, one of total possession. He ground his lips against hers and thrust his tongue into her mouth, demanding she respond, that she feel the same gnawing sexual need consuming him.

Beth looped her arms around his neck, wriggling around until she could press her breasts against his chest. He let out a rumbling growl and moved his hands to her hips so he could guide her to straddle his lap. She rubbed against his erection, drawing a groan from deep inside him.

Once she'd threaded her fingers through his hair, she held him right where he wanted to be as she rocked her hips, simulating the act he so desperately wanted. No woman had ever responded this honestly, revealing her desire so clearly. In his experience, most women needed more coaxing and cajoling. A few even made it seem as though they were doing him the greatest of favors by allowing him to be intimate with them.

Not his Bethany. Her tongue was every bit as wild as his. Despite her suffering from a lack of self-esteem, she was nothing but open and direct with her passion—and perhaps not so innocent after all. When he got her clothes off, Robert hoped she didn't draw back into her shell. He couldn't bear losing this kind of connection.

Easing back, she stared into his eyes, searching for something. Desire? Commitment?

He'd give her both those things and more. "Say yes," he whispered. "Say you want me as much as I want you."

Her eyes widened and her fingers tightened in his hair.

"Say yes, B." He pulled her down for another kiss, stroking his tongue over hers and loving the responding mewl from the back of her throat.

Robert slid one hand up her side, under her loose shirt until the lace of her bra tickled his fingertips. Boldly cupping her breast, he shifted his lips to her neck, nuzzling the soft skin as he breathed in her scent. "Please, B." He tugged on her earlobe with his teeth and squeezed her breast. "Say yes."

She tilted her head and breathed out a contented sigh. "Yes."

He wasn't about to give her time to change her mind. Wrapping his arms around her, he stood, intending to carry her straight to the bedroom, hoping once she was there she'd quit worrying about the missing mattress in what was to be her room. The master could belong to both of them from now on.

Beth untangled her legs and put her feet on the ground.

"I was going to carry you," Robert insisted.

"I'm too heavy," she scoffed.

Had he not worried at dampening her desire, he would have taken a moment to scold her for the denigrating remark. Instead, he took her hand and gently tugged her to follow him to the stairs.

On the first step, she planted her feet, almost jerking him off his.

"What?" he asked, angry at himself that he couldn't hide the desperation in his voice. If she stopped this interlude, he'd be tied up in knots for days.

"I don't know. I mean…"

Robert had been one step above her, so he went back to where she was and turned her to face him. Then he kissed her again. A long, slow, sensuous kiss. He was panting for air when he finally ended it, as was she. If she could turn him away now, she had a hell of a lot more self-control than he'd ever be able to muster. "I want you."

"I want you, too, Robert. I just..." She was back to nibbling on that bottom lip. "Do you have, um, protection?"

"Condoms?"

She gave him a brusque nod.

He returned the gesture, hoping she wouldn't think he was a cocky bastard for having bought them this afternoon.

Without dropping his hand, she hurried past him, climbing the stairs. "Well, then, what are we waiting for?"

Would she ever stop surprising him?

Robert shut the door behind them out of habit. There was no one to shut out tonight. They had all the privacy they needed. Instead of snatching off his clothes, he leaned back against the door and watched her. Contentment settled over him simply seeing her in his bedroom. This was where she belonged. With him.

She'd jerked her shirt over her head before stopping to stare at him. Clutching the shirt to her chest, she watched him warily. "D-did you change your mind?"

"Are you kidding me?" After pushing away from the door, he strode purposefully across the room, grabbed her around the waist, and tackled her to the bed. "I've waited *forever* for this."

And he damn well wasn't going to let her change her mind without showing her just how much he desired her. With his kiss. With his body. With his heart. So he kissed her, his tongue tracing the line of her teeth, stroking the roof of her mouth.

Beth tugged at his shirt, pulling it out of his waistband and getting in his way as he tried to touch her body. He leaned back, yanked the shirt over his head, and let out a sigh when he blanketed her body again, putting a knee between her thighs to open them wider. His cock was nestled against her, and he sighed again. "I've waited for this forever."

"You already said that." Her fingers skittered across his back, sweet and light as air before her palms covered his ass. She raised her knees and held him to her core. "Besides, it's not as long as I've waited. I've wanted you for *years*."

"Seriously?"

"Oh, heck yeah. Your butt?" She squeezed his cheeks. "It's been driving me crazy since the first day we met." Beth rocked her hips up. "Make love to me."

As though she'd have to ask twice.

Pushing back, Robert took her hand and pulled her to her feet. His gaze locked with hers as he reached for her waistband, lovingly popping the button and dragging down the zipper. He pushed them past her hips by letting his hands slide down her sides. She kicked the khakis aside after they'd puddled around her ankles.

She stood there in a white lace bra and pale pink panties, and he hoped to hell he wasn't drooling all over himself.

He leaned in to kiss the small tattoo of a pink ribbon on her left breast, right over her heart. The name "Mallory" was etched inside the border of the ribbon. "Do all the Ladies have one of those?" He traced the shape with his fingertip.

"Me, Dani, and Jules. It was to celebrate Mallory being well again."

"Bet theirs aren't as beautiful as yours."

"They're exactly alike."

"But this one's on *your* breast. That's what makes it so special."

With speed rather than finesse, he took off his jeans and boxers, not even thinking to take his time and almost tripping in the process. He wasn't patient enough to try to entice her by stripping slowly. Besides, she didn't act like she needed to be coaxed.

His cock had bobbed forward, like it was trying to stare at her. She stared back, her mouth forming an O.

Damn if he didn't glance down at himself. He was kind of big, but certainly not big enough to scare a lady away. "B?"

With a seductive smile, she moved her hand behind her back and popped the hook on her bra before shrugging out of it. Then she discarded her panties. Standing before him, she gave him a sheepish glance, her lips pulled into a tight line. Moonlight shone through the skylight over the bed, giving him the ability to see all of her quite well.

"Gorgeous." It was the only word he was able to utter. She was perfect. Soft and round with pale skin. Her breasts were fuller than he'd imagined, and just looking at the V of dark curls between her thighs made his erection twitch.

* * *

Beth clenched her hands into fists, trying with every ounce of her being not to act like some shy virgin and hide herself from Robert. Sure, her body might not be slim and sleek, but judging from the swollen cock pointing in her direction, the man liked what he saw. So why hide?

The way he'd growled out his compliment had sent shivers racing over her skin. She was past playing coy. Stepping closer, she wrapped her fingers around his erection, loving the incredible heat that greeted her touch. He was so full and thick, and she wanted to play with him a little before they covered up all that masculine beauty with a condom.

He growled as she stroked him. With a smile, she moved up

and down, stopping at the cap to rub it with her thumb and then squeezing his sac each time she reached the base. But he didn't kiss her, just kept his gaze fixed on hers.

Too soon, he brushed her hand away and snaked his arms around her waist. Picking her up, he took her to the bed, letting her fall back against the mattress as he dropped to his knees and spread her thighs. Before she could utter a single word, his mouth was on her, his fingers separating her folds while his tongue probed and licked her until she was squirming. She threaded her fingers through his hair and tugged, probably a bit too hard. But the man was making her body scream for release, and she wanted him to share the experience. Since she couldn't utter a coherent word, she kept pulling on his hair, trying to get him to understand. She wanted him inside her. Now.

This was all so new. The times she'd been with other men, she'd had to perform as though she were striving for an Academy Award. Her fault, because she'd never let her guard down, never faced another man with the same bravado she'd shown Robert. And she'd always faked the orgasm at the end.

With this new bravado came true confidence. She'd stood bravely before him, naked and uncaring if she had a big butt or far too much padding on her hips or a bit of a belly. Seeing that huge cock, arrogant and ready for her and her alone was a potent aphrodisiac.

"Robert, please." She tugged on his hair again.

With a groan, he got to his feet. "Scoot back, B." He jerked the nightstand drawer open and fished out a string of condoms. He ripped one loose and opened the packet with his teeth while she moved to the middle of the enormous mattress.

Watching him roll on the condom sent a jolt to her center, and she knew that for the first time, she was going to come during sex and not alone in the shower later that evening. She was so turned on, so ready, that simply watching him crawl onto the bed, stalking her like a jungle cat had her breath catching and heat shooting through her.

Robert licked her nipple and then settled himself between her spread thighs. After teasing the tight bud with his tongue, he drew the nipple into his mouth and suckled. His fingertips smoothed down her stomach and over her mound before he thrust a finger deep inside her, making her hips rise to meet him.

Beth cupped the back of his head, encouraging him to continue all the exquisite torture. A shock wave went from her breast to her center, making her gulp in a breath. "Now," she said, wanting him joined with her when she climaxed.

Robert rose over her, rubbing his erection between her folds. "You're ready?"

"*Past* ready."

He dipped his head to rest his forehead against hers as he thrust inside her.

Letting out a gasp, she tried to ease the tightness in her muscles to allow the invasion. She hadn't meant to tense up, but when he pushed back on his elbows to give her a concerned frown, she shook her head and pulled him down for a tongue-dueling kiss. Her body relaxed, letting him slide inside, the friction making her close her eyes and hum in happiness.

Robert pulled back, slowly, tantalizingly before thrusting inside her again.

The teasing was making her frantic. She showed him with her hips and her kiss that she needed him rougher, faster.

And he obliged. Together they found a rhythm that pulled her higher and higher until the tight knot deep inside her snapped and she cried out his name. Delightful spasms spread from her center through her being, filling her with a joy she'd never known.

This was what she'd always searched for. This was what she'd sought for her whole darn life. This was the way making love should be.

Robert's movements became frantic, and Beth squeezed her thighs tightly against his hips, putting her palms against his backside again, encouraging him, wanting him to enjoy the same kind of bliss he'd given her.

His body tensed before he buried his face against her neck, groaned, and shuddered, her name spilling from his lips.

It was the sweetest song she'd ever heard.

Chapter 10

Good morning."

A deep, rumbling voice snapped Beth from the last light tethers of sleep. She slowly opened her eyes as she lay on her left side. Dark, laughing eyes greeted her. Robert also lay on his side facing her, a grin on his beard-stubbled face. She ran her fingertips down the sandpaper surface of his cheek to his chin, smiling as she remembered the night. Such sweet memories to hold close to her heart.

When she started to open her mouth to return his sentiment, she suddenly worried about whether her breath would be horrendous. She grabbed the sheet and held it against the bottom half of her face. "Good morning."

His brows knit. "B? Why are you—"

"Morning breath."

He chuckled and jerked the sheet away.

She tensed. Then he kissed her, his lips settling on hers. A simple kiss of acceptance that she felt all the way to her toes.

Easing back, Robert grinned again, so arrogant, probably since her face had followed his. He gave her another quick peck and tossed the sheet aside. After he crawled out of the bed, he wandered around the room, pulling articles of clothing from the open boxes.

The man had no modesty whatsoever. While Beth hastily tugged the sheet to cover her breasts, he just strolled around the enormous master suite as though he were alone. Not that she minded. The view was heavenly.

Time had come to face her day. "We should work on getting our closets organized today." She was mostly thinking aloud about prioritizing the long list of tasks that needed to be done.

Surprisingly, he stopped to gape at her. "What d'ya mean closets?"

She cocked her head. "What did you think I meant?"

"You said *closets*. Not *closet*."

"I don't understand, Robert."

He dropped his clothes on the foot of the bed, put his hands on his hips, and glared at her. "I thought we'd be sharing a closet now."

All she could do was stare at his cock. Even though it wasn't erect, she couldn't force herself to look away. It hung limp, nestled in a patch of dark brown curls, and she found the thing completely captivating. If he really wanted to have a conversation, he was going to have to put on his boxer shorts.

"B?" There was a touch of laughter in his voice. "Hey, lady. My eyes are up here."

A hot flush raced over her face and down her neck. Even her ears grew warm. She would've shifted her gaze to his face if his cock hadn't started to grow. The way it straightened and elongated right before her eyes kept her transfixed, the sight utterly fascinating. And arousing. Heat shot to her core before fanning to her limbs, and she held the sheet tighter against her, dumbfounded.

Robert took the last steps to the bed, picked up her hand, and wrapped her fingers around his burgeoning erection. "After seeing what you do to me, do you really think I'm gonna let you have your own room?"

"I did…this?" She stroked him gently, a little in awe of the beauty of what she held.

He let out a heavy sigh. "No, I get hard smelling the new carpet." Sarcasm dripped from every word.

"Well, you *are* a builder." She stroked him again, loving how he closed his eyes and moaned.

"You make me as hard as that granite you seem to like for countertops. Just seeing you is all I need and—*whamo*—every drop of blood flows south."

While that made her happy, she couldn't help but worry about setting a good role model for her niece—her *daughter*. "What about Emma? She shouldn't see us sharing a room and…and a bed."

"What Emma will see is exactly how wonderful it is when two adults care deeply about each other. It's not like we're gonna parade around naked, B." His gaze dropped to her hand. "But when we're alone in this room, I prefer you naked." With no warning, he snatched the sheet down.

Beth didn't even flinch at revealing her nudity, despite how bright the sunlight was. She was too busy worrying about his demand that she share the master bedroom with him to give much thought to how much of her body he could see.

She wanted what he was offering, for them to be a couple and share their lives. Everything from a bed to a closet to long, loving kisses and where those could lead. To be his roommate in every way would be heaven.

So why was she hesitating?

Fear. Pure, naked terror that one day he'd grow tired of her and want his more typical lithe blonde. Even thinking about the painful, awkward conversation when he would tell her it was time to go their separate ways made her ill.

* * *

Robert waited impatiently, barely keeping himself from clutching Beth's shoulders and giving her a shake. Why couldn't she see how good they were together?

He'd gone from flaccid to erect with enough speed to make him a little dizzy. Just thinking about how great it had been to make love to her had him greedy and ready to share that bliss again.

Without a word, he opened the nightstand drawer, fished out a condom, and tossed it on the surface, almost daring her to say no.

She didn't. Instead, she lifted the sheet to invite him back into bed.

Their bed.

Did she know how much she pleased him? When he tried to cover her body with his own, she stopped him by putting her palms against his chest.

"Wait," she said.

"B?"

"On your back, mister." She gripped his arms and guided him to lie down at her side.

He obliged, eager to see exactly where this would lead.

Beth picked up the condom, plucked it from the wrapper, and slowly, sensuously rolled it over his cock. Then she leaned in, kissing him, gently pushing her tongue past his lips.

He wasn't accustomed to women taking the lead. Most of his lovers liked him to call the shots, so it was a new experience to have the normally shy Beth running the show. He was worried they hadn't had much foreplay, and he sure didn't want to hurt her because he didn't give her enough attention to help her get nice and wet.

She straddled his hips, allowing him to slip his hand between her thighs before she could settle herself on his cock. Moist heat greeted him, making him let out a low growl. To know she was turned on hit him like a shock wave to the groin. Could she be that wet because he'd been parading around naked? Because she'd witnessed his cock growing? Because she'd stroked his erection?

With a smile and a sweet hum, she let her head fall back as he found her tight nub and rubbed it with his fingers. "Feels so good." Her words were akin to a cat purring. "So good..."

Her hips rocked into his touch, and he sped the rhythm, hoping to bring her to climax. She surprised him by brushing his hand away and grabbing his cock. Slowly, maddeningly, she lowered herself onto his erection, closing her eyes and smiling as though she savored every inch sliding inside her tight sheath.

Robert couldn't take her teasing a second longer. Holding tightly to her hips, he thrust the rest of the way inside her.

So tight. So hot. So perfect.

His breath came in choppy gasps, and he couldn't stop himself from driving up into her, setting a fast pace when what he'd wanted was to go slow and savor each sensation. The feel of her pushed all those notions of lingering aside. He wanted to keep thrusting until she took him back to that wonderful place, the one she'd shown him last night that made every cell in his body explode.

And she led him there again, the strength of his orgasm

forcing him to clench his fingers into her soft hips and his body to bow off the mattress. He called to her, wanting her to join him. To keep from leaving her behind, he kept raising his hips, pushing into her and savoring her delighted response.

Her mouth opened as her eyes squeezed tightly shut, a tear leaking from the corner of one. "Robert... I'm... oh..." Then she gasped, and he felt the spasms as her core contracted, squeezing him, making him want her all over again.

After the storm passed, she opened her eyes and gave him a sexy smile.

Robert cupped her face in his hands and pulled her down for a slow, easy kiss. Then he stared into her eyes, losing himself in those dark depths. "So beautiful."

Beth's gaze dropped as she blushed. "Thank you."

"I mean it, B. You're beautiful. And you're the best lover I've ever had."

Her head snapped up. "Really?"

"Really."

A sense of panic flooded his senses, his body. The voraciousness of his own feelings overwhelmed him, pressing down on him like a heavy weight and making him quickly end the tender moment. "Let's get up. I need coffee. Stat." He lifted her until she moved to his side and scrambled off the bed.

Her lips dropped from the breathtaking smile, and he regretted not telling her what was in his heart.

Love. If he wasn't in love with her now, he soon would be. And why that scared the hell out of him, he wasn't sure. All he knew was that his heart had settled on Beth—and Emma—and wouldn't be dissuaded.

It was just too early in the game to let her know that or for him to know how to deal with it.

The best course of action was retreat for a few moments so he could regain his courage.

* * *

Beth tried not to let Robert see her disappointment. He'd gone as cold as a block of ice, and darn if she knew why. With a tight grip on the condom, he rushed to the bathroom.

That action took some of the sting out of his abrupt departure. He wasn't fleeing her; he didn't want the condom to spill. The last thing either of them needed was a "surprise." She'd watched the agony Jules had gone through when she'd found herself pregnant early in her relationship with her husband, Connor. Beth wasn't about to go through that. She had enough on her plate.

She got to her feet and wrapped herself in the sheet. "Robert? You're right. We should share this bedroom." Sticking her head into the bathroom, she tried to see what he was doing, but his back was to her. "Robert? Did you hear me?"

He nodded over his shoulder. "Glad you agree." After tossing the condom in the trash, he came to her and kissed her forehead. "I didn't want to have to fight about it."

"It's that important to you?" At least he wasn't acting cold now. She didn't have the nerve to ask why he kept shifting from loving to aloof.

"Absolutely." Then he opened the shower door and started the water.

"I should probably go on the pill," she said. "If we're going to be, um, intimate so often, the pill would help make sure I don't get pregnant."

"You would do that?" His eyes were wide in clear disbelief.

"Don't look so shocked. I've been on the pill lots of times."

"I just assumed..."

"I know. You assumed that I didn't need to because I don't date much." She sighed. "They keep me from getting acne, and you can stop grinning at me. You know I didn't need them for anything else. But now I do."

Robert checked the water before stepping into the enormous glass-enclosed shower. "You wouldn't mind not having condoms?" he asked before flicking on the multitude of side sprays she'd told him would make the shower a downright religious experience.

"Fine with me."

"Then we'll go get tested sometime today."

Since the master bathroom's shower was more than big enough for both of them, even having two different sets of showerheads, Beth let herself in and turned on the water for her side. "No need. I trust you."

Robert stared at her as he squirted shampoo onto his palm. "Thanks, B. I trust you, too," he insisted. "But it's not a matter of trust. It's a matter of proof. It will ease both our minds, and by going together...well, it's the best way to start a relationship. It's just the right thing to do."

Her head fell back as she let the water wash over her hair. "If you say so."

"I do."

"Then we'll go before we get Emma."

He didn't say another word until they were both wrapped in towels, working on their morning grooming rituals.

After he'd combed his hair, his gaze caught hers in the mirror. "So you'll really share this room with m-me?"

She smiled at the nervous catch in his voice before she set her brush down and thought through the ramifications.

There would be questions from the Ladies, their other friends, the Douglas High faculty. Pretty much everyone. Was she ready for that kind of inquisition?

Then there were her students' parents. Despite the fact that it was the twenty-first century, the small town they lived in remained firmly planted in the morality of the 1950s. Would there be any repercussions with the townsfolk or the school board?

A smile curved her lips. None of it mattered. Her heart belonged to Robert Ashford, whether he wanted it to or not. She might as well enjoy the time they could share for as long as they could share it.

"You win, Robert. Now why don't you help me drag my boxes of clothes in here?"

Chapter 11

Dani kept staring at Beth from across the table. "I don't think I've ever seen you looking so... so happy."

"That's saying a lot," Mallory chimed in. "Because our Beth is usually happy. Now she's downright giddy."

Jules cocked her head and tapped her index finger against her cheek. "Hmm. If I had to guess, I'd say she looks like... I know! A well-laid woman." When Beth gasped, Jules added, "That rascal Robert is proving to be quite a surprise." She clucked her tongue. "And I thought I knew him oh so well." Leaning closer, Jules talked behind her hand as though she wanted to speak only to Beth, which was anything but true considering her volume. "So, Bethany, just how big is his—"

"Enough, already." While Beth normally loved the jovial teasing of the Ladies Who Lunch, she'd usually been the one delivering the barbs. Receiving them wasn't nearly as fun.

Not that she was a bad sport. She loved laughing at herself, but not about this, not about Robert Ashford. Not when her future happiness rested firmly in his calloused hands.

"Beth?" Dani put her hand over Beth's. "You okay?"

She gave Dani a curt nod. "Just tired."

Jules shot her a knowing expression of sympathy. "I know that feeling well. Raising a baby—"

"*Babies* in your case, Jules," Mallory added.

"—ain't easy. I hope Emma sleeps better than Craig and Carter. Those two keep Connor and me hopping all night."

At least the conversation had ventured down a better road, so Beth jumped in. "Emma isn't a problem. Up once a night if at all and usually only because she needs to be changed." She always tried to beat Robert to the punch whenever Emma woke in the night, not wanting him to feel obligated for her care. Yet there were still times he took the responsibility while Beth slept blissfully unaware until the next morning. "At what age do you start to potty train them?"

"Sick of dirty diapers already?" Dani asked. "That's one of the reasons I don't think I'll ever have munchkins. I still gag when I change a smelly diaper." She shrugged. "Maybe it's different when the baby's your own."

"It's definitely different when she's your own." The words slipped out before Beth realized their significance.

In the weeks since she and Emma had moved in with Robert, Beth had effortlessly glided into the role of "mother," of *matka*. If she didn't overthink things, she could picture herself and Robert as parents and Emma as their child. But only if she didn't overthink, which wasn't bloody likely. People were, after all, nothing but creatures of habit. Overanalyzing was every bit a part of her as breathing.

Then again, she was beginning to understand Robert's rapid attachment to Emma. If only Beth could be sure that he cared for her every bit as much as he did the baby.

"About that..." Dani fumbled around in her purse for a

moment and then produced a business card. "This is the lawyer I told you about."

"The custody specialist?" Beth took the card, surprised that it was vivid lavender with a cartoon cat in the background. What kind of lawyer had purple business cards?

The best, according to Dani and some of her college sorority sisters.

"She's the one who helped Maggie Butler and her domestic partner, or wife, or whatever the PC term is," Dani said. "It wasn't an easy process to say the least."

"Their son was Vietnamese, right?" Mallory asked, leaning over to read the card Beth still held. "Alexis Comer, attorney at law."

Dani answered with a nod. "You wouldn't believe all Maggie and Carla had to do to get that baby. But Alexis was there every step of the way. Maggie said she even flew to Vietnam with them to pick Henry up and bring him home."

"After that case, helping me adopt Emma should be a cake-walk." No sooner had she said it than a shiver ran the length of Beth's spine.

"Careful, Beth. Don't wanna jinx yourself," Jules said, which was exactly what Beth had been thinking. At least Jules threw in a wink to lighten the foreboding mood.

"What about Robert?" Mallory picked up her Diet Cherry Coke and leaned back in her chair. "Is he adopting her, too?"

"Why should he?" Beth wasn't sure she was ready to even think about Robert adopting Emma. That would rock the boat, and since the present was smooth sailing, it seemed a silly thing to do.

The Ladies were right. She *was* smiling all the time now. Everything was close to perfect. Robert had been her knight in shining armor. He'd helped her at a time when she had most certainly been a damsel in distress. She'd been given a baby she was ill equipped to care for; he'd taught her the tricks of parenting. Her home had been too small; he'd given her a castle. Loneliness had been making her unhappy; he'd filled her life with love.

One-sided love.

Since when had she become so cynical? Why couldn't she just live in the moment and enjoy what she shared with him before it ended?

"Earth to Beth." Dani gripped her hand. "You know, for someone who was smiling like the Cheshire cat a minute ago, you're frowning enough to make me worried."

"Typical Beth," Mallory added, her tone teasing. "I've never seen anyone who could change moods as fast as you do, sweetie."

"Sorry," Beth said with a shrug. "Just thinking." *Thinking too much, as usual.*

She shoved the business card in her purse, planning on calling the lawyer when she got home from school. "Thanks for the referral, Dani."

"You're welcome. But you still didn't answer my question."

The topic wasn't going to drop, darn it. "Robert hasn't said a word about wanting to adopt Emma. It's not like he wants anything that permanent." *With either of us.*

"I think you're underestimating him," Mallory said. "He loves that baby."

"I know that," Beth snapped before she could stop herself. Then she breathed a sigh. "Sorry. I know Emma means the world to him."

Mallory set her can down and folded her arms under her breasts. "So do you."

"He likes me well enough, I suppose." The way he'd made love to her, she knew there was affection behind his actions. He'd insisted she share the master suite with him. They were telling the world they were a couple. She only wished she knew exactly how he felt.

"Likes?" Dani shook her head. "It's a helluva lot more than that. Robert loves you."

Since she wasn't sure what he felt had—or ever would—become love, Beth only shrugged.

"Give it time." Jules popped to her feet. "Gotta run. As usual." She slung the strap of her enormous purse over her shoulder. Then she leveled a hard stare at Beth. "Do me a favor, Beth?"

"Of course!"

"Trust me on this. I've been Robert's friend since before we were the Ladies Who Lunch, so I understand him better. There's no way he'd have moved you into that gorgeous house if he didn't feel every bit as strongly about you as he does about Emma. I'd expect a ring, and perhaps an adoption request, in the near future."

"You're all moving way too fast," Beth insisted. Jules's words had set her hopes soaring and her heart pounding.

"I think Jules is right," Mallory said with a nod. "It's just easier for him to admit that he loves Emma than it is for him to admit that he loves you."

Beth let out a snort. "He doesn't love me."

"You're the only one who doesn't see it," Dani said. "I think Mal and Jules have it pegged. Guys are scared of talking about their feelings. It's one thing to be so open with Emma. With you...well, he's probably more afraid."

That made no sense. "Afraid? Of what?"

"Of you." Jules made it to the door before she glanced back. "Of how much he feels for you. You might have to tell him first, Beth."

"Tell him what?"

"That you love him." With a wave, Jules left.

* * *

The end of the school day couldn't come fast enough.

Beth's afternoon classes had been nothing short of torture. The students were working on writing essays, which left her with far too much quiet time to get lost in her thoughts.

If what the Ladies said at lunch was true, that Robert loved her, why hadn't he told her so?

Duh.

Fear of rejection.

But Beth had never rejected him, nor would she ever. She'd welcomed him into her life, her body, and her heart with arms wide open. If she was honest with herself, her invitation had been sent a long time ago, from the moment she'd met him. He'd always been the man she compared all of her dates to, and she'd turned to him sometimes before she'd turned to Dani.

Surely he knew what she felt. He'd be blind not to see it.

Then there was Emma to consider. Beth wanted to make things easier for their future. By adopting her, Beth could avoid the discomfort of constantly having to say, "I'm her aunt *and* her guardian." Everything from enrolling her in school to getting her on the school's health insurance plan required a "parent." Sure, she was Emma's guardian, but Beth was sick and tired of having to jerk out the paperwork to prove it.

She needed to be Emma's mother. Officially. End of discussion. Alexis Comer was getting a phone call when school ended.

One question niggled at Beth's brain.

Does Robert want to be Emma's father?

Broaching the subject would be opening up a scary and rather awkward discussion at a way-too-early time in their relationship. Unfortunately, time wasn't on their side. If Beth planned to move forward with the adoption, it would be best if Robert were a part of it from the first moment. Then they would have to talk about adoption proceedings, and the "M" word was sure to come into play.

The last thing in the world she wanted was to have him think he had to marry her to be able to hold on to Emma. If he wanted marriage, he needed better, stronger reasons.

Like he loves me.

Beth feared his feelings for her were so entangled with his feelings for Emma that he could never separate the two. If there was a choice between them, a need to know exactly which of his "girls" he cared for most, Emma would win. Hands down.

A knock on her classroom door drew her back to the world.

"Ms. Rogers. Here." A frowning sophomore with a far-too-large T-shirt thrust a folded piece of pink paper at her.

Beth plucked it out of his grasp and absently said, "Thanks." Not like the kid even heard it. He'd already started hiking back down the long corridor.

It was only when she unfolded the message that her heart leapt to a furious cadence. One word jumped out of the scribblings.

Emma.

"Darn it!"

Every student glanced up from their work at her unusually loud outburst.

"Sorry," Beth said, a hot flush spreading over her face. "Please get back to your essays."

She'd forgotten that she'd silenced her classroom phone while the students were working on a quiz before lunch. Since the kids weren't allowed to have their cell phones during the day, Beth had become accustomed to leaving hers in her purse. A dumb thing to do since Robert had obviously been trying unsuccessfully to reach her.

Good mothers didn't leave their phones in their purses.

The note asked her to call him immediately, so Beth flicked her classroom phone back to life. Despite the twenty-eight adolescents who'd be listening in, she quickly dialed Robert's cell and waited for what seemed like an eternity for him to answer.

"Beth! Finally!" The irritation was plain in his voice.

"What's wrong?"

"What's *wrong* is that I couldn't get you to answer a damn phone. I've been trying to reach you for close to an hour."

In all their time together, way back to when she'd first come to Douglas High School, he'd never taken that kind of angry tone with her. Not even when they'd disagreed over some of her suggestions for one of the houses they'd worked on together.

"I'm sorry. There was a quiz and...I...I forgot to turn the ringer back on after lunch." She sounded exactly like a child making an excuse for having played outside past suppertime. "Why did you need me? The note said to call about Emma."

"I had to take her to Hudson County Hospital. We're in the ER."

"Oh dear Lord. What happened?"

"She fell and hit her head. It's bad. I need you to get down here as fast as you can."

Chapter 12

Robert dragged his fingers through his hair as he paced the concrete just outside the doors of the emergency room, trying to calm his thoughts. It shouldn't take so long for Beth to drive from the school to the hospital. The nurses weren't letting him back into the treatment area with Emma, and he couldn't stop worrying about her. When Beth got there, they'd finally be able to see their daughter.

"Stupid hospital," he mumbled to himself as he paced. "Stupid HIPAA. Stupid CPS."

Child Protective Services. An agency he'd never thought he'd encounter since he'd left teaching. Yet a CPS worker had been summoned not long after Robert was asked to leave the ER room where the nurse and doctor were treating Emma's head injury.

He calmed his unwarranted anger. These people were only doing their jobs. Hell, he was a man with an injured child who wasn't any relation of his. If he was totally honest with himself, he'd admit he'd have reacted the exact same way. They were doing what they believed was best for Emma.

CPS was stepping in because a nearly year-old girl had fallen and hit her forehead against the corner of an open cabinet door while in the care of her aunt's boyfriend. Poor Emma had a nice-sized goose egg above her left eye, and she hadn't stopped crying until the nurse in the ER took her from Robert.

Then Emma had screamed.

Maybe when she was older, he'd be able to look back and laugh as he told the story of how Emma had called his name for the first time when he'd rushed her to the ER and she'd been taken from his arms. Not only had she called for him—*Bobber*—but she'd also damn near squirmed her way out of the nurse's grasp to get back to him.

With her first birthday only weeks away, he and Beth had been worried because Emma didn't talk much. Even when she wanted something, she tended to use her own unique version of sign language to let them know what she needed.

Well, she was damn well talking now.

"Robert!"

He stopped grumbling and pacing to watch Beth jog across the small ER parking lot. He shook his head at his inability to stop watching her breasts bouncing as she moved.

"Where's Emma?" Beth was out of breath, and her eyes were wide with panic.

"She's still in the treatment area."

"Why aren't you with her?"

As Beth tried to step past him, Robert grabbed her arm. "Because we can't go back there. Not yet."

She glared at his restraining hand. "Why?"

Dropping her arm, he laced his fingers through hers. "She got hurt while I was watching her, so they want to investigate if it was an accident or deliberate injury."

Beth blinked a couple of times, the only indication she'd even heard his words. "Are you joking?"

"About this?" He shook his head.

"They can't possibly think you'd hurt Emma on purpose."

"Yeah, well..." He'd been devastated by the veiled accusation, and he hadn't been able to shrug them off. No matter how he tried to justify their actions, those actions hurt him. Deeply.

Hurt Emma?

Not in a million years!

He frowned. "I guess they want to err on the side of caution."

"On the side of ridiculous." Beth tugged his hand, leading him back through the doors and into the ER receiving area. She strode right up to the desk and rapped on the glass window.

The clerk in a navy-blue smock with a Hudson County Hospital patch glanced up, smiled, then hit a button as she spoke into a microphone. "May I help you?"

"Yes, you can. Please open the doors to the treatment area so I can get back there and see my daughter."

"What's your daughter's name?" the woman asked, her fingers poised over the keyboard of her computer.

"Emma Rogers."

The clerk tapped out some information before frowning at the screen. "I'm afraid I'm going to have to ask you to remain in the waiting area until one of the nurses calls your name." She pointed at a set of huge double doors. "Keep an eye on those. A nurse will come talk to you soon."

Beth narrowed her eyes as her face mottled red. "To heck with that!" She rapped on the glass with her knuckles. "Hey, lady. I want to see my daughter. *Now.*"

The clerk let out a dramatic sigh and hit the button again. "Yes?"

"I want to see my daughter."

"Ma'am..."

"Please."

With another weighty sigh, the clerk said, "I'll see what I can do." She hurried out of the cubicle.

Robert winced at the agony in Beth's voice. This was all his fault. Not once in all the weeks Beth and Emma had lived with him had he witnessed the baby on two legs without him or Beth helping her. But she'd come toddling right across the kitchen floor as he'd made her lunch. A big smile lit her face when he'd grinned at her and called her a "big girl," and she'd sped her steps. Unable to handle walking that fast, she'd stumbled and fallen headfirst against a cabinet he'd left open.

"I'm sorry, B," he whispered, squeezing her hand.

"It's not your fault they're acting like buttholes. I have no clue why I can't see Emma. What happened?"

Before he could explain the accident or why the hospital wasn't leading her straight to Emma, the clerk came back and took a seat at her desk. "The nurse will be with you in just a moment to take you back to the treatment area."

"Thank you." Beth brushed away a stray tear.

No sooner were the words out of her mouth than the doors opened. A woman in purple scrubs stepped through. "Family of Emma Rogers?"

Robert hurried over, Beth walking fast enough to beat him there.

"I'm her mother."

The nurse eyed Robert warily. "You're the man who brought her in?"

He wanted to scream that he was Emma's father but bit his tongue. He wasn't. Nor had Beth asked him to be. Not once. "Yeah."

"Follow me."

* * *

Beth's anger burned like a hot coal in her stomach until she saw Emma. Once she stepped through the sliding door to the treatment room and saw Emma, she relaxed. The baby was smiling at a nurse who was talking to her in a low voice and letting Emma play with a fabric book in her lap.

"Hey, Em." Beth approached the bed cautiously, not wanting to startle either of them.

Emma's head popped up. She grinned at Beth, then craned her neck, clearly trying to look past her to Robert.

"Bobber!" Emma clapped her hands, a radiant smile on her face.

Bobber. A baby's way of saying Robert.

Emma's first real word, and the girl had no idea how much she'd wounded her mother.

Robert put a hand on her shoulder. "See? She's got a helluva goose egg."

Of course she saw the big bump on Emma's forehead. What was making Beth crazy was having no idea how a baby who'd only crawled was able to strike her head that hard against anything. "I see it."

"Do you want to hold her?" the nurse said, her gaze shifting between Beth and Robert.

Robert knit his brows. "You're not going to call the CPS worker again?"

The nurse shook her head. "She released her to your care."

"CPS?" Beth felt as though she'd walked into the middle of a movie and was having difficulty figuring out the plot. "They actually called CPS in on this?"

Robert drew his lips into a grim line. "They thought I'd abused her."

Her whole body stiffened in fear. "Are you kidding me?"

He shook his head.

That's all she needed, a file at CPS that contained possible abuse. She'd never be able to adopt Emma now. The need to know the whole story near to drowned her. "What in the heck happened, Robert?"

"Bobber!" Emma squealed.

Robert went to Emma and lifted her. She wrapped her arms around his neck and gave him a sloppy kiss on the cheek that made the nurse laugh.

"She's fine," the nurse said. "The doctor will be in soon to give you discharge instructions." She tousled Emma's hair before she left, closing the sliding door behind her.

Beth rubbed Emma's back, her already fragile heart shattering when Emma arched away from her touch. Choking back the urge to weep, she tried to hide her hurt as she gently brushed her fingertips over the knot on Emma's forehead. "Can you please tell me what happened?"

Why the question made Robert smile was beyond Beth. "Our girl was walking."

"What?"

"She toddled into the kitchen when I was making lunch. I'd left a cabinet door open—"

Beth narrowed her eyes.

"I know, I know. That always makes you mad. Sorry. Anyway, I talked to her, and she tried running. She stumbled and went headfirst into the edge of the cabinet door." He kissed Emma's forehead. "Bobber's sorry, Emma."

"Bobber," the child cooed, laying her head against his shoulder and putting her thumb in her mouth.

As soon as Beth got them both home and could get a moment

to herself, she was going to cry a river. She'd missed Emma's first word and the first time she'd walked. It was also painfully obvious that the baby loved Robert and wanted nothing to do with her new mother. Somehow Beth would have to try harder to win Emma's love, because Emma held Beth's heart in her tiny hands, just as she held Robert's.

Did Emma realize how lucky she was to have a man as good as Robert Ashford love her as deeply as he did? And did Robert realize he was every bit as lucky to have a baby as special as Emma return that love?

"You okay, B?"

"Fine."

"B…Don't lie to me."

Thankfully, the doctor chose that moment to slide the door open and step into the treatment room. "Ah, Emma's parents are here. Glad to see we got everything cleared up."

Since Robert didn't correct him, neither did she. The doctor, who appeared to be so young he might've passed for a senior at Douglas, went through his spiel about caring for a child with a minor head injury, had Beth sign some papers, then told them to have a nice day.

Once they were outside, Robert nodded toward his SUV. "I've got her car seat. Want me to put it in your car?"

Beth shook her head. "Take her home. I'm going to stop to get a few groceries so I can make a nice dinner."

"I thought we were going to Pizza Parade tonight. Emma loves the train that brings the drinks."

"Not tonight. I'll just make us something." The idea of people seeing Emma's injury and then looking at Beth as though she'd caused it turned her stomach. "She needs to rest and relax."

He let out a chuckle. "You know our girl. *Rest* and *relax* aren't in her vocabulary."

No, but Bobber *sure is.* "We can at least keep her doing calm things. You know how much she loves us reading to her."

"Then I'll read to her all night if I have to." He shifted his gaze to Emma. "Bobber's sorry, Em. I wouldn't hurt you for the world."

Emma was practically asleep in his arms and didn't respond to his heartfelt apology.

"We'll see you at home?" he asked.

"Yeah, I'll be there soon."

He brushed a kiss over her mouth, easing some of her hurt. The spontaneous display of affection showed he might really care for her and not just Emma.

The hike to her car was long enough to allow Beth's emotions to take control. By the time she slid behind the steering wheel, a few tears were sliding down her cheeks, falling and making dark spots on her light blue skirt. She fought the need to cry herself out. Robert and Emma didn't need to see exactly how devastated and jealous she was, his kiss all but forgotten. She'd bury her feelings deep enough they no longer showed.

Emma had arched away from her touch. That simple movement was like a knife plunged into Beth's heart. Not only did the baby love Robert more, but she didn't even want Beth to touch her.

She searched for a tissue, wanting to hide behind it so people in the parking lot wouldn't stare at her. She finally found one in her purse and held it to her face. Not giving in to her emotions, she slipped into a numb emotional state accompanied by soft hiccups. Tears wouldn't fix anything.

It truly didn't matter whether Emma loved her or not. Beth

was her mother now. She'd do everything she could to love and protect her. Shoot, there were a lot of girls who didn't appreciate their mothers, so many it was almost cliché.

Maybe love would follow. One day.

She also decided she'd broach the topic of Robert adopting Emma. Whether he wanted to be her father or not, Emma had taken him into her heart and accepted him in that role. He'd be a fantastic father, and he loved her like a daughter.

They might as well make it legal.

Chapter 13

Emma's finally down." Robert stepped into the master bedroom, expecting Beth to already be in bed, if not asleep.

She was in bed, but she was most definitely *not* asleep.

Kneeling in the middle of their king-sized bed, she was dressed in a bit of black lace that could barely be called a nightie. The meager light came from candles she'd scattered around the room, and the sheets had been turned back in invitation. She'd set the perfect seduction scene. Her boldness was belied by the way she nibbled on her bottom lip.

His body's response was damn near instantaneous.

This greeting wasn't at all what he'd expected. Beth had been silent, almost sullen after they'd gotten home from the hospital. She'd brought groceries and made them a nice pot of spaghetti, one of Emma's favorites. While Emma ended up using the sauce more as fingerpaint than food and babbled contently, Beth had picked at her own plate, not even trying to make her usual pleasant conversation.

He hadn't realized how accustomed he was to sharing meals and chats with his new family until Beth had been so quiet. Robert had assumed she was mad about Emma getting hurt, perhaps even blaming him for not watching her well enough. Judging from the way she was beckoning to him now, he'd been wrong.

"B-B? W-where did you get that, um, nightgown?" He swept his polo over his head and dropped it on the floor, not wanting to waste a moment of time before making love to her.

"I've had it for a while, actually. I was just waiting for the right person to wear it for." Her voice was husky, downright sultry.

He whipped his belt from the loops and shoved his jeans and boxers down to his ankles. He almost fell as he tried to kick them off and walk to the bed at the same time. After catching himself against the mattress, he turned to sit and kick off his clothes and socks.

Beth moved behind him, running her warm hands over his back and up to his shoulders. She started rubbing out the tense knots that had formed there because of the day's high drama. Her own pleasant scent mingled with the Dior perfume she favored. She'd definitely put a lot of thought into this interlude.

"You're tight," she murmured, working on the knots as she leaned closer to run her tongue around his ear.

In the month they'd been together, she'd never been the one to initiate sex. Not that Robert had any doubt of her desire for him. She was the most responsive and open partner he'd ever had, and he treasured how she made him feel like the best lover in the world by being so vocal about her pleasure. But he'd always been the one to reach for her first. His ego reveled in this new, daring part of her personality.

She smoothed her palms down his chest as she rubbed her breasts against his back. Her hot breath brushed his ear. "Do you want me?"

Had he not been afraid she'd think he was being crude, he would have led her hand right to his erection. "Oh yeah, B. I want you b-bad."

"Then come to bed." Beth backed away, the mattress shifting as she moved.

Robert had to resist the urge to scramble after her, flip her onto her back, and drive himself right inside her body. He'd never craved a woman like he did his Beth, and that craving grew more intense each time they made love. So different from any other lover. Once or twice in the sack, then he'd grown bored and downright restless.

Beth had him bewitched in a way he knew he might never shake. And he was ready for that. He'd grown weary of playing the field and of worrying about ending up alone—his worst nightmare. She'd given him all the right reasons to finally settle down, from letting him be Emma's surrogate father to the way she filled his life with passion.

She shook her head when he reached for her, grabbing his shoulders and pushing him to the mattress. "On your back, mister. I want to play first."

"That sounds intriguing."

"I sure hope so."

She straddled his hips, leaned down, framed his face in her hands, and gave him the kiss he'd been craving. Her tongue swept into his mouth, stroking his and beginning the dance he loved. Thrust and then parry. Retreat and then surge forward. Kissing her was always so consuming, and he lost himself in the moment, knowing only Beth. Her scent. Her touch. The way she made him burn.

Easing back, she gave him a seductive smile before nuzzling his neck, sending shivers racing over him. She nipped him, soothing each sting with a loving lick. Her lips branded his skin. His collarbone. His chest. His stomach. Then her fingers wrapped around his stiff cock as she moved her face over his hips.

"B... You don't have to—"

Her gaze found his. "I know, but... I want to." She licked the crown and shot him a salacious smile.

Robert fisted his hands in the sheets, a low moan spilling from his lips. He couldn't even find a word to tell her how wonderful she was making him feel.

With a rather arrogant chuckle, she ran her tongue from root to tip before taking him deeply into her warm, wet mouth.

The women he'd slept with had always acted like going down on him was a loathsome chore. That, or they let him know just how much he owed them for the privilege. He'd never make the mistake of comparing Beth to those other women again.

If he was correct in his assessment, she enjoyed the act. The small sexy sounds she made. The smile on her lips whenever he growled or moaned. The way she squirmed, rubbing her breasts against his legs. All of it told him she was almost as enflamed by the act as he was.

And she was talented. She knew instinctively how to keep him on the edge without pushing him over it.

"Stop, B. Please." Robert gripped her shoulders. "I want to be inside you when I come."

"You're sure? I mean, I wouldn't mind..."

"I'm sure." He tugged gently until she rose over him and straddled his hips again. Grabbing the hem of the nightie, he pulled it over her head.

She wasn't wearing any panties.

Slipping his hand between her thighs, he closed his eyes and fought for control. He'd been right. She *had* been enjoying herself. She was so damned wet, so ready.

"Robert?"

The touch of worry in her voice made him smile and open his eyes.

She stared at him, her brows drawn together in concern. "You okay?"

"More than okay." He set his hands against her full breasts, loving how the hardened nipples drilled into his palms. "I want you so bad."

"I want you, too." Beth raised herself enough to hold his cock to help guide him to her core. Before he could thrust up, she'd pushed down, impaling herself until he filled her completely.

He almost came. How could he resist her tight heat or her enthusiasm? He could almost believe she loved him.

* * *

Beth smiled at the pleasure she saw written all over Robert's face. It filled her heart to overflowing. All of her courage had been rewarded. Now she wanted a show-stopping finale. "Fuck me."

His eyes widened. "Did you just say—"

"I said fuck me, Robert. *Now.*" She didn't wait for him to move, raising her hips up slightly before pushing back down. The feel of his thick cock sliding so deeply into her body made her close her eyes and let out a low moan.

Robert squeezed her hips and started a rough ride, thrusting up against her hard enough that they bounced on the mattress.

Her body was wound tight, ready to explode. Going down on him had been one of her fantasies, and she hoped he wasn't shocked by how generously she'd made love to him with her mouth. The silky feel of his skin over the heated, hard flesh beneath was intoxicating. She'd been so intimate with only one man before, and he made her feel as if she had to because he'd bought her an expensive dinner. Robert was different. She gave him her love freely, and the moment she first took his cock in her mouth had been so arousing, her body had reacted, growing hot and wet.

"Bethany." His voice was hoarse. "Come with me." The rhythm sped, Robert slamming into her again and again, somehow knowing she needed it rough and fast.

When the tight knot inside her snapped, she threw her head back, her mouth open, although she tried hard to squelch the way she wanted to shout her delight. Riding the waves of bliss, she felt her body detonate again when he thrust into her one last time and let out a shout as the heat of his seed filled her.

Beth collapsed against his chest, waiting for her rapid heartbeat and breathing to slow. Now that the intimate moment was over, she felt the heat of embarrassment creeping over her face. What would he think of her now? Sweet little Bethany Rogers had just made a snack of Robert's cock and then ridden him like a bucking bronco. Oh, and *the* word. That word. She'd actually said it, hoping he'd find it sexy and not slutty.

His fingers raked through her hair. "Wow."

She couldn't look him in the eye yet, so she kept her face buried against his neck. "A good wow or a bad wow?"

He nudged her face up. "You are something else, B."

Why did all of his attempts at compliments sound double-edged to her, as if they could be interpreted more than one way? Did "something else" mean he'd enjoyed her seduction or had been shocked by it?

He kissed her nose. "We should clean up before we ruin the clean sheets."

Robert. Always so darn practical.

Without another word, Beth rolled off him, picking up the robe she'd left draped over the end of the bed and quickly donning it. While he grabbed some tissues, she hurried to the bathroom, needing a moment to freshen up and try to discard her awkwardness.

After a quick cleanup followed by brushing her teeth, she put on her nightshirt and returned to their bedroom.

Robert was in bed, wearing his typical ratty T-shirt and boxers. "Are you a Gemini?"

"What an odd question." One she hadn't remotely expected. Why wasn't he asking about what she'd done or what she'd said instead? "I didn't know you were into astrology."

He shrugged. "Just trying to understand you."

"What's to understand?"

"Sometimes you surprise me. Makes me wonder if you're really two people in one body. You know, a Gemini or something."

"Good guess," she said as she went around the room, blowing out the candles. "I am."

He clicked on the nightstand lamp. "You definitely shocked me tonight."

Heat bathed her face, spreading down her neck. "Sorry." She grabbed her e-reader and crawled into bed next to him, hoping she could disappear into a book.

"Sorry?" Robert cocked his head and stared at her. "Why? That was probably the most intense sex I've ever had."

"Can we talk about something else?"

"See? A Gemini. One minute you're a vixen. The next? A virgin." He picked up the remote but didn't turn on the television. Instead, he kept watching her. "I'm just glad you're not mad at me."

"Mad? You mean about Emma?"

He nodded.

"Not in the least. Accidents happen. I just wish CPS hadn't poked their nose in it." Since he'd brought up the topic of Emma, Beth summoned her courage and spit out the question she'd been unable to ask all evening. "I called the adoption attorney today. She asked whether you, um..."

No, that wasn't the right tactic. She didn't want him to think her offer was prompted by the attorney, which was actually the opposite of what happened. In their discussion, Alexis had cautioned Beth to consider the ramifications of sharing Emma with Robert, explaining the adoption would be much easier if she petitioned by herself.

In her mind, he'd earned the honor of being Emma's father. She wasn't going to deny him the chance simply because the paperwork might be a little trickier. "Um, I was wondering. Do you want to be Emma's father? I mean, we could both apply for adoption."

"You're serious?" His eyes searched hers.

"Very serious."

"You really want to share custody of Emma with me?"

She hadn't thought about it in that way. *Custody*. That would be exactly what they'd share since they weren't married. And whenever they ended this relationship—something that even thinking about near to killed her—Emma would still belong to both of them. There would be visitations and child-care orders.

Didn't matter. Emma's happiness was tied to Robert now. Beth would give her the best father, one who already loved her completely.

"After what happened today," he said, rubbing the back of his neck, "I figured you'd be madder than a hornet at me. Instead, you're asking me to be Emma's real dad."

Emma's real dad. The only scary hurdle in the whole adoption process. Alexis had warned Beth that they would have to take out ads and do a diligent search to find Emma's biological father and warn him about their petition to adopt her. Not easy tasks considering she didn't even know the guy's name.

One problem at a time.

"I know how much you love Emma," Beth said. "She obviously loves you every bit as much." She tossed him a weak smile. "After all, you're her first word, *Bobber*."

His chuckle eased her worry. "*Bobber* and *Matka*. Quite a pair of parents, eh?"

"If you don't like Bobber, we can teach her to say Daddy or Papa or whatever you'd like."

"Bobber is wonderful. How many girls have a Bobber to watch over them? Makes me feel special."

"Bobber it is." Beth put her hand over his and squeezed his fingers. "It's your choice on what to do. If you want to think about it for a while—"

"I'll do it."

"Just like that? No thought? No talking it over with anyone? This is a big step, Robert. A really big step that will affect the rest of your life."

Leaning over, Robert brushed a kiss over her mouth. "The only person I'd want to talk it over with is you. You're the only one who knows how much this means to me."

"I have an appointment for a consultation tomorrow after school. Want to go with me?" she asked.

"Absolutely. I'll make sure my niece can take Emma so we can focus on what the lawyer says."

He kissed her again, his tongue rubbing against hers in a long, lazy caress. When he ended the kiss, he smiled and then clicked the remote and let the television draw his attention away.

I love you fought hard to escape her lips, but Beth beat the urge down. She'd saddled him with having her and Emma as roommates and was now adding to his burden by asking him to adopt Emma. She wasn't about to make him feel as if he had to return the sentiment.

If anyone was going to say it first, it would be Robert.

Or it would never be said at all.

Chapter 14

Beth tossed Robert a weak smile when he took her hand. He always seemed to know exactly when she needed his strength, and right now was one of those moments.

They sat side by side in Alexis Comer's waiting room. The office wasn't at all what Beth expected. No three-year-old magazines. No boring, backbreaking furniture. No canned music from the 1960s. Instead, the walls were papered in vibrant colors. She and Robert sat on a leather sofa that was every bit as comfortable as the one they had at home. A flat-screen television was tuned to a news channel.

"You okay?" he whispered.

"Yeah. I just want to get this done." She had a case of nerves, but the best thing for the future was to tackle the mountain of legal paperwork required to adopt Emma. She hoped this lawyer would be the right person to guide them through the process. The phone conversation Beth shared with Alexis had been promising.

"We'll go pick up Emma when we're done," Robert whispered. "Then we can all go get some supper. Okay?"

"That would be great," she replied.

Beth was still a little surprised Robert had agreed to being a part of the adoption so quickly. Not that she doubted his commitment to Emma. She'd just figured he'd want to muddy the waters by talking about marriage as a way to make the adoption less difficult. But he hadn't said a word about anything except being Emma's dad, claiming the adoption would ensure that Emma would always be a part of his life, implying he and Beth could eventually go their separate ways.

Perhaps his affection for her wasn't as deep as she'd believed. Or perhaps it was her own insecurity whispering in her ear. She loved him with every ounce of her being, more each passing day, but he might always be more concerned about Emma than he'd ever be about her.

Maybe he didn't like the idea of marrying. Maybe he didn't want to tie himself down. Maybe he didn't care to be bound to *her* for the rest of his life.

Beth tried to shake off that depressing thought by reminding herself he still reached for her almost every night, to the point she spent a good part of her days yawning. Even if he didn't love her, he desired her.

It would have to be enough.

The receptionist sitting at the desk right outside the big oak door answered the buzz of her phone and then called to them. "Ms. Comer will see you now." She swept her hand toward the door to her right.

After a deep, fortifying breath, Beth got to her feet. Keeping a tight grip on Robert's hand, she led him into the lawyer's inner sanctum.

Exactly like her office surprised Beth, so did Alexis Comer. Despite the woman's rather eccentric business cards, Beth figured

Alexis would still dress and act like a stereotypical lawyer, like the attorneys she saw in movies and on television. A no-nonsense suit. Hair pulled into a tight bun. Minimal jewelry.

Alexis Comer was anything but a stereotype. The African American woman wore her dark brown hair, lightly tinted with enough gray to hint at her age, in long dreadlocks pulled away from her round face by a headband with brightly colored flowers. The earrings dangling from her ears were silver with a kaleidoscope of beads that brushed against her shoulders. Her gauzy skirt was the same floral pattern as the headband, and it swirled around her ankles when she rose and came around her desk to greet them.

She shook each of their hands. "Welcome. Come in, come in." She smiled as she gestured at the two chairs opposite her glass-and-chrome desk. "So glad to finally meet you." After sitting back in her chair, she pulled closer to her desk and picked up a forest green file. "Let's get down to business. The good news is the adoption petition should be relatively easy. As I told you, Beth, the only concern is the biological father."

Robert cocked his head. "Since we don't know who he is, why's he a problem?"

"I'm afraid it's not that simple. We have to make an effort to find him."

"Really?" he asked, his tone curious.

"Absolutely," she replied. "We have to show due diligence to notify the biological father that an adoption is being petitioned." Alexis shuffled through the papers in the file. "We'll have to take out ads in the Legal Notice sections of the newspapers in the places Tiffany lived." Plucking out a paper, she laid it on top of the file, a small frown bowing her lips. "Beth, I have something I need you to do that might make this somewhat easier."

Beth nodded. "Anything I can do to help."

"I'd like you to talk to your mother again. When I spoke to her yesterday, she sounded a bit…hesitant when I asked about Emma's father."

"Hesitant? What's to hesitate about? Tiffany never told us his name."

Alexis leveled a hard stare. "May I be frank?"

"Of course," Beth replied.

Robert took her hand again, as though he expected Alexis to say something that might hurt her.

Alexis clasped her hands together, rested them on the paperwork, and leaned closer. "I've been a lawyer for more than twenty years. After all that time, I've developed very good instincts. I usually know when someone's lying."

"Lying?" Beth knit her brows. "Who's lying?"

"I think your mother knows who Emma's father is."

For a moment, all Beth could do was sit dumbly and blink.

"What did she say?" Robert asked, saving her from trying to spit out the words and sounding as befuddled as she felt.

"It wasn't what she said exactly," Alexis replied. "It was her tone and how so much went unsaid." Her gaze found Beth's. "I could be wrong, which is why I was hoping you could get your mother to open up to you. She might be able to make our job a lot easier."

"And the adoption a lot harder," Robert grumbled.

Beth's relationship with her mother had always been a bit… distant. While a part of the blame was Beth's, the larger share went to Carol.

Who was she trying to kid? Carol Rogers was the most judgmental, pessimistic, and critical woman Beth had ever known. To grow up constantly hearing how much about her was lacking in her mother's opinion, Beth had developed an inferiority complex as large as the Grand Canyon. Until she became a teacher and began to hear how good she was at her job and to feel the affection her students held for her, she'd lived life thinking she wasn't worth too darn much.

The Ladies Who Lunch had zeroed in on her insecurity early in their relationship and gone to great lengths to help Beth learn to appreciate herself. Dani especially went out of her way to compliment Beth, to make her feel as though she had value. She'd made great strides in learning to love herself, but somewhere deep inside would always be the timid little girl who was never quite good enough for her mother.

An A minus? I suppose that's a good grade. Not quite an A, but…

Class salutatorian? That's nice. A little more effort and you could've been valedictorian, but…

A teacher? That's a decent job if you don't mind being poor, but…

With Carol, there was always a "but."

"I-I'll try," Beth promised. "Mom and I, well, we don't get along."

The knowing smile on Alexis's face eased some of the hurt that had crept over Beth. "Just remember you're doing it for Emma." Leaning back, she tilted her head. "Now, one more thing. What's up with the two of you?"

"Pardon?"

"You're living in the same house, correct?"

Both Beth and Robert nodded.

"And Robert owns it outright," Alexis said rather than asked. "That actually works both for and against you in an adoption."

"Why against us?" Robert asked. "I'd think the fact that I own the place shows financial security and stability."

"It does," Alexis said. "For you. Not for Beth." When Alexis smiled, she was downright beautiful. "I suppose my next obvious question is why aren't the two of you married? The house is an asset if both of you own it. If it's only Robert, a judge might worry that Emma and Beth could be stranded if he leaves the relationship."

Beth's heart froze before suddenly leaping back to life to pound furiously. This wasn't a topic she wanted broached, especially not in front of someone they barely knew. Everything about what was supposed to be an easy adoption was turning complicated, and Beth felt a knot form in the pit of her stomach. The last thing in the world she wanted was for Robert to feel obligated to do something he simply wasn't ready to do.

Alexis pushed her chair back and stood. "Well, it appears from the way you're both speechless that I've given you some food for thought. I'll be in touch in the next few days, and in the meantime, you get with your mother, Beth. See if you can get her to open up."

* * *

Robert glanced over at Beth, wishing he knew the right thing to say.

Ever since they'd left Alexis Comer's office, Beth had been as silent as a stone. He'd expected her to be thinking aloud like she always did, asking and then answering questions about the adoption paperwork or about Alexis's assertion that Beth's mother knew who Emma's father was.

Or better yet, the suggestion that he marry Beth.

Instead, she just sat there, her hands folded and resting on the manila folder on her lap. Inside the folder were papers they needed to fill out and bring back to Alexis. He knew those didn't bother her. What did were the bombs Alexis had dropped.

He couldn't stand the silence. "Tiffany never told you anything about Emma's father?"

Beth shook her head.

"Not even a hint?"

"Not even a teeny, tiny hint. She always told me that he didn't want to be a father and that she just wanted to forget." She turned her head to stare out the side window. "She confided in Mom, not me."

The sadness in her voice tore at his heart. He wondered if part of the pain was because she hadn't truly had a chance to grieve for her sister. Within days of Tiffany's death, Beth had been back in Cloverleaf and taking care of Emma. Now she had to be hurting that her sister had kept her in the dark about Emma's father. Knowing how much Beth had done for Tiffany, protecting her from their mother's harsh criticism, she had to feel betrayed that Tiffany had turned to Carol with such a big secret.

Robert reached over to take her hand in his.

Beth let out a little sigh. "I made a lot of assumptions, which were obviously wrong, especially if Mom knew."

"Such as?"

She shifted her gaze to his face. "I thought Tiffany might not even know the guy."

"What do you mean?"

"Tiff was kind of, um, wild. If she was in the mood, she'd pick up some guy at a bar and..." Her shoulders rose in a shrug. "It wouldn't have been the first time she'd had sex with a man she didn't even know."

"I see."

"I hate myself for thinking that about her, especially because she'd cleaned up her act."

Robert squeezed her hand, not knowing what to say. Beth had spoken of Tiffany often over the years, usually expressing her concern about her baby sister's self-destructive lifestyle. He could understand why she'd assumed Tiffany might not know Emma's father.

"I'll call Mom tonight," Beth said with a decisive nod. "I need to know for sure. If she does know, we need to convince that guy to let Emma stay with us."

"That's one problem down."

"One? What's the other?"

"The house," he replied.

What Alexis had said about him owning their home as both an asset and a liability to the adoption had hit him hard. He wanted to be sure nothing interfered with Emma being his daughter. If that meant rushing things in his relationship with Beth, so be it. There'd be plenty of time in the future for the two of them to hash out exactly how they felt about each other. The way she gave of herself so freely, both in the bedroom and out of it, told Robert she cared for him. And he'd grown to need her in his life. Without her, there was no reason to face each new day.

Swallowing hard, he jumped into the pool with both feet. "I'm ready to put it in your name, too. Then there won't be a problem with it anymore. We'll both be owners of a paid-in-full home."

There. He'd said it. He'd actually given her half of a five-hundred-thousand-dollar home just to show her how much he loved her and Emma.

So why was she frowning at him?

"B, tell me what's bugging you."

"You're giving me half the house? Just like that. Here, have half of my ultra-expensive, showcase house."

"Yep. I don't want anything to mess up this adoption. Emma is ours. We need to be sure no one has any reason to question whether we'd be good parents."

Robert pulled into the driveway of his sister's home. After killing the engine and shoving the keys into his pocket, he looked over at Beth. She was still frowning the same way she always did when someone had hurt her feelings. Problem was, he had no idea what he'd said that could have been remotely injuring.

"Now what's wrong?" he asked, resisting the urge to throw his hands up in exasperation.

He was never going to understand her. He'd tried. God knew he'd tried. Up until she started scowling at him, he'd thought he'd done a good job of giving her what she needed to be happy.

After all, he'd stepped up to the plate and assumed responsibility for her and for Emma. How many men would do that?

He'd given her a bigger and much nicer home when she'd been in that cramped studio apartment. He'd helped her arrange great child care for Emma during the times when one of them couldn't be with her. And he'd shared himself with Beth in a way he'd never done before—body, mind, and heart.

Anger sparked inside him. Why wasn't she thanking him for all he'd done instead of getting pissed? Why wasn't she excited that adopting Emma wasn't going to be too difficult?

Beth interrupted his inner diatribe. "Did you get a chance to get the stuff we needed at the grocery store? I gave you that list this morning..."

"Stop changing the subject," Robert snapped. Then the answer hit him right between the eyes. The grocery store. Beth's list. "*That* explains everything."

"What are you talking about?"

"The grocery list. I remember everything that was on it, and that explains things."

She threw her hands up. "Oh, well, that clears it all up. For *one* of us." With a weighty sigh, she put her hands on her thighs. "Could you please tell me why remembering the grocery list explains anything?"

"You had me buy chocolate bars."

Her eyes narrowed.

Since he knew what was irking her, he didn't get angrier. "You've obviously got PMS."

* * *

If Beth hadn't laced her fingers together, she would've smacked Robert. But she wouldn't hit him. No matter how much he deserved it. "Why does every man on this whole stupid planet think that whenever a woman's upset, she has PMS?"

"You mean you're n-not close to that time of the m-month?"

His nervous stutter eased some of her annoyance, but she kept her hands squeezed together just in case he said something else stupid. "Did it ever cross your mind that *you* might be the reason I'm upset?"

"Me? What did *I* do?"

You want Emma and not me!

Instead of shouting her frustration, Beth bit her bottom lip and shook her head. "Never mind."

He shook his head. "Nope. You don't get off the hook that easy." When he reached for her hand, she let him take it. "Look,

B. I only want to understand what's got you so upset. Help me understand. Please."

She knew he was frustrated, and the blame lay with her. How could he possibly figure things out if she wasn't honest with him? But how could she tell him how much she wanted him to love her the way she loved him? There was no way she'd put her heart on the line like that. What if she told him the truth, that she loved him, and he said something thoughtless like *thanks*?

None of this would be a problem if she were the kind of person a man like Robert could love.

Would Carol's critical voice ever leave her alone, even in her own thoughts?

Beth tried to focus on the more obvious problem. She wasn't about to let him put her name on that deed. "I can't take half the house, Robert."

He shot her an incredulous glare. "W-why not?"

"I just can't. It's too much."

He pulled his lips into a grim line, lost in thought for a few moments. "So you won't let me put your name on the deed?"

She shook her head. "It's your house."

"It's our house," he insisted. "Yours, mine, and Emma's."

"You're very generous." She squeezed his hand. "And I'm grateful you'd be willing to do that. I can't let you." Lifting their joined hands, she brushed a kiss on his knuckles. "You're such a giving man, Robert Ashford. I thank God every day He sent you to me. To us. It's just not right for me to take that kind of money from you."

The man actually blushed.

"But I do thank you for the offer."

"You really won't let me give you half the house?"

"Nope. No way."

His sigh filled the silence that settled between them. "Well, then… That only leaves us one choice if we want this adoption to work."

This was the most confusing conversation she'd ever had. "One choice? What do you mean?"

"You're just gonna have to marry me, B."

That's it? That's *his marriage proposal?*

Beth closed her eyes, willing herself not to cry. She wasn't normally a weepy person, but it seemed like she'd done nothing but fight back tears since Tiffany's death. When she should be doing backflips because the man she loved had just said "marry" without even stuttering, she was on the verge of wailing in anguish.

There would be no sweet, romantic moment, no image to treasure of Robert dropping to one knee as he asked her to be his bride. Instead, she'd have the memory of the businesslike statement that stole away every ounce of tenderness from the proposal.

Beth gave herself an inner scolding. Reminding herself that she was thirty and that she was long past girlish notions of romance, she tried to focus on the good in the situation. Robert wanted to be Emma's father. That much was crystal clear.

What wasn't nearly as cut and dry was whether he held the same kind of affection for Beth. Desire? Definitely. But love?

Teaching for years had shown her so many different family situations. The marriages that held no love were the easiest to spot. No way she'd let herself be one of those wives who constantly had to look at her husband with a suspicious eye, nor would she be the type of woman who would find herself searching for affection outside her marriage when her husband grew cold.

But Robert wasn't cold. At least not yet. If she loved him, if she kept giving her heart freely and let him know how much he meant to her, couldn't he learn to love her in return?

God help her, she just didn't know.

"B?" He squeezed her hand.

"Can I think about it?" Even though she wanted to shout that she would be his wife, she had to search her heart to see if she could get past his brusque order that should have been a tender question.

He didn't pull away, but the hurt was clear when he turned to look at her. "How long?"

"How long what?" From the moment he'd said they should marry, she'd been drowning in thoughts that ranged from disappointed to elated and back again. Her brain couldn't seem to concentrate on what he was saying now.

"How long do you need to think? I d-don't mean to rush you, but we should get this s-settled before we start the p-paperwork." He tossed her a weak smile. "Otherwise Alexis w-will have to do it all over again with your m-married name."

"Give me a day or two, okay?" she pleaded, despite his clear nervousness. "I just want to think it all through. For Emma's sake."

Robert gave her a curt nod. "Anything for Emma."

Chapter 15

He *what*?" Dani leaned forward, jostling everything on the small table.

Beth knew the question was rhetorical, but she answered it anyway. "He asked me to marry him."

Asked wasn't exactly the right word. More like *told*. Not that it mattered. Even though Beth desperately wanted to be Robert's wife, she wouldn't accept his proposal when the only reason he wanted to marry her was to make Emma's adoption easier.

"Weird," Dani said. "I sort of expected it, but to hear the news is still...surprising. It's just so damn fast."

With a shrug, Beth picked up her glass and took a sip of her sangria.

"I mean, you've known each other a long time, but you've only been a couple since you moved in together. It's been really fast."

"Yeah, it's definitely been fast," Beth admitted. "Trying to adopt Emma pushed things ahead of a normal relationship."

"So what did you tell him?" Dani picked up her own glass, taking a drink of her white wine.

Beth had called to invite the Ladies Who Lunch to a night out, but she needed to talk to her best friend first. When she'd pulled up Mallory's number, ready to call her and Jules as well, Beth couldn't make herself dial. To tell the Ladies—all of them—that the only reason Robert had brought up marriage was because he wanted to be Emma's father would be humiliating.

But Dani would understand and not give her those I-feel-so-sorry-for-you eyes she expected from the other Ladies. Once she was able to talk it through with Dani, then she could confide in the others. So when she finally called all the Ladies, Beth made sure to give her and Dani a window of time to themselves. They'd meet early, and Beth hoped Dani would help her come to a decision before Jules and Mallory arrived. Unfortunately, Dani had arrived twenty minutes late, eating up a great deal of their "alone" time.

A rail-thin waitress came over to set their stuffed mushroom appetizers on the table. "Refills?"

"Not yet," Beth replied. "We're waiting for two more people. Then we can get drinks all around."

"I'll keep a lookout for them," the waitress replied before flitting to another table in the bar.

"Sorry I was so late, but why'd you ask me to meet you before Jules and Mallory?" Dani asked. "I mean, you're gonna tell them about the proposal, right?"

"Like I could keep it a secret." Beth let out a sigh. "I just wanted to see what you thought first."

"What's to think? Yes, I think it's hasty, but then again, you love the guy and have known him for years. He's a great father to Emma. Marry him."

Gathering up her courage, Beth revealed her deepest fear. "He doesn't love me."

Dani dismissed the heartrending statement with a simple wave of her hand.

So much for empathy.

"He doesn't love *me*," Beth insisted. "He loves *Emma*." Finally. She'd said the words aloud. Now someone else would understand why she was rattled by the proposal.

"You're jealous of a baby?" Dani rolled her eyes. "Of course he loves Emma, but that doesn't mean he doesn't love you, too."

"He cares for me. I know that. But..."

"But." Dani shook her head. "With you, there's always a *but*. Shit, I'd love to get my hands on your mother right about now."

"My mother?"

"Yeah. I want to give her a good smack upside the head. Maybe two."

"Why?"

"Because she made you think you're never good enough." After another sip of wine, Dani leveled a hard stare at her. "You are, you know."

This whole conversation had gotten too far off target. Dani was supposed to recognize Beth's fear. Instead, they'd morphed their night out into some kind of therapy session. "I'm what?"

"Good enough. I'd bet my entire retirement savings, pathetic though it may be, that Robert loves you—probably every bit as much as you love him. Everyone else sees it. Why can't you?"

"Sees what?" Mallory asked as she set her hands on Beth's shoulders.

Funny, but the friendly squeeze Mallory gave her, added to Dani's confident tone, made Beth feel a little better.

"That Robert loves her." Dani moved her purse from the chair next to her.

Mallory sat down and waved back toward the entrance.

Whipping her head around to see who Mallory waved to, Beth smiled as Jules came striding into the restaurant, heavy purse in tow and phone firmly in her hands.

What would she do without the Ladies Who Lunch?

After rapidly touching her screen several times, Jules dropped her purse, took a seat, and finally put her phone aside. "Catch me up."

"On what?" Beth teased. "The drinks or the conversation?"

"Both."

The waitress came back as promised. After drink orders were given, Beth figured she should fill the Ladies in on the latest development in the soap opera that was her life.

Dani beat her to the punch. "Robert proposed."

"Congratulations," Mallory said with a genuine smile. "I knew he would."

"Me too," Jules said. "Now that he's finally got you, he's not gonna let you go."

"It's only because of the adoption," Beth said, taking another taste of her drink.

"Bullshit." Jules. Blunt as always. "We all knew he'd propose. He just needed to work up the guts. The guy has had a thing for you for years."

"Ben and Connor wanted to start a pool, but we wouldn't let them," Mallory added. Then she stared hard at Beth. "But you still don't think he wants you, do you?"

"He only wants to be married so the adoption will go smoothly," Beth replied.

"She doesn't believe he loves her as much as he loves Emma,"

Dani said. "Will you both tell her he loves her? She doesn't believe me."

"C'mon, Beth." Jules took her drink from the waitress. "Open your eyes. How can you not see it?"

"Because I'm not anything near the kind of woman he usually likes." The sangria had definitely loosened her tongue.

"Oh, *now* I get it." Jules sipped her margarita before setting it down and shaking her head. "You're wrong, Beth. Robert's changed. Even the guys noticed it. Sure, he might've played the field the last few years…"

"Yeah," Beth drawled. "With lots of skinny blondes."

"So what? He was a single guy," Mallory said. "He was also kind of…immature. I think he's grown up since he went into business for himself."

"Probably 'cause he's not around teenagers all day now," Dani said with a smirk. "Admit it. The men who teach at our school are all a bit juvenile. Part of being a high school teacher."

"They end up like Peter Pan," Mallory added. "They never grow up. But I think Robert's changed."

"You're absolutely right, Beth," Jules said. "He played the field. A lot. But you and Emma mean the world to him. He's ready to settle down now."

Beth tried to let the words sink in, and for the first time, she struggled to look at her relationship with Robert through the eyes of her friends. Hope sparked inside her, and she tried to grab it and hold tight.

She loved Robert so much; how could he not love her in return? How could he make love to her the way he did if his feelings weren't involved? Sure, guys were horn dogs, but she could sense some of how he felt when they were joined. It was more than sex. It was truly making love.

"You can't let your insecurity ruin this," Jules insisted. "If you keep insisting he doesn't care for you, you'll turn things sour. He'll start to think there's nothing he can do to convince you of his sincerity. Besides, you and Emma are a package deal now. You should be celebrating the fact that he loves you both. A lot of guys would run the other way at the idea of a ready-made family. We've all known guys like that or had students from families like that. It's never a good situation. You're lucky. You got one of the good ones to fall for you."

"And he's definitely one of the good ones," Beth couldn't help but point out, feeling the weight lifting from her shoulders.

"Damn right, he is." Dani lifted her glass in toast. "Sounds like you're finally opening your eyes."

"I'm trying." But it wasn't easy.

Yet the more Beth thought about everything Robert had done for her—and not only because of Emma—she started to realize there had already been a bond between them before Emma was thrust into her life. *Their* lives.

Her own attraction to him might be years old, but maybe it just took Robert a little longer to see how good they could be together.

Perhaps she'd been looking at things all wrong. It wasn't that he loved Emma more; it was that he could love Emma freely, with no fear of rejection. He couldn't tell Beth what was in his heart any more than she could tell him.

She grasped hold of that thought and hoped she could squeeze tight enough she'd never let it go.

"You know what?" The smile on her face matched the lightness in her heart. "I think you're all right. He does care for me."

Dani put her hand over Beth's. "He does more than care, but at least now you're getting it."

* * *

Robert breathed a sigh of relief when Dani gave them one last wave before she went inside her apartment.

Since he'd volunteered to be the sober ride home for their Ladies' night out, he'd had to endure the giggles and teasing of Beth's three rather tipsy friends directed right at him. Most was about his marriage proposal, which was a sore spot since Beth hadn't immediately accepted. Not that he could blame her.

As far as romance, the proposal had left much to be desired. The funny thing was that he'd always had such great ideas for how to propose to the woman he finally decided to marry. A hot air balloon ride. A surprise trip to a beach for a moonlit stroll. A Jumbotron proposal when he'd take her to a Chicago Bulls game.

Instead, he'd just blurted out they should get married as a way to make an adoption easier. Beth had to be thinking he was more concerned about Emma than her.

"Dumbass," he whispered to himself.

"Pardon?" Beth gave him a sexy smile and then put her hand on his thigh. She rubbed his leg, easing closer and closer to his groin.

"Nothing." Robert didn't stop her, rather enjoying her being so frisky. The fact that her attention turned his cock hard as a rock made it a bit tricky to drive with great skill, but they were almost home. At least Emma was still sound asleep in her car seat. She probably wouldn't even notice when he put her back in her crib. Now that she slept through the night, there wasn't much that would make her stir once she'd closed her eyes.

Beth rubbed his erection with the heel of her hand.

"B, you're making me crazy here."

"That's the plan." She popped her seat belt and slid closer. "I want to make love." She ran her tongue around his ear.

Heat raced through his veins. "Probably not a good idea right now. Would hate to cause an accident."

"I meant when we get home, silly." She ran his fingers over his jeans, outlining the shape of his cock. "And I think it sounds like a wonderful idea."

"You've been drinking," he said. "I-I don't want to take advantage." She wasn't acting at all like the reserved Beth he knew so well. Sure, she might be a bit of a wildcat in bed, but she'd never been quite *this* insistent.

"I only had three glasses of sangria," she insisted. "I'm not drunk. I just want you."

Her words made his breath catch.

Once he pulled into the garage and killed the engine, Robert gave in to the overpowering need to kiss her. The moment his lips touched hers, she threaded her arms around his neck and pressed her breasts to his chest. Her tongue slid past his lips, rubbing against his. She tasted wonderful, a heady mixture of Beth with a touch of sweet wine. A growl rose from his chest.

Easing back, she smiled at him. "Why don't you put Emma in her crib? I'll go get ready." Before he could say a word, she'd slipped out of the car and was going through the door into the house.

Emma didn't even twitch as he gently unstrapped her from the car seat and carried her up the stairs. He normally liked to watch her as she slept, marveling at how perfect such a tiny creature could be. Tonight, he only stayed long enough to be sure she stayed asleep. His mind and his senses were full of Beth.

She was going to marry him. There was no way she'd be trying to get him in bed if she wasn't ready to accept his proposal. He vowed to make the lack of a romantic proposal up to her, maybe by taking her to Hawaii or somewhere else special for their first anniversary. At the very least, he'd get the Ladies to help make their small, rather quick wedding nice.

Caught between being relieved that Beth had accepted his proposal and being excited at the prospect of making her his wife, Robert had taken only a few steps into the room before he stopped short and gaped.

Beth was standing next to the bed, waiting for him.

Naked.

With no memory of jerking off his clothes, he picked her up and laid her on the mattress. Then he blanketed her body with his. A slight shudder raced through her, echoing the one that moved through him. There was no better feeling in the world than being skin-to-skin with her.

"So you've forgiven me?" he asked as he gazed into her chocolate eyes.

"Forgiven you?" Her gaze searched his as her brows gathered. "For what?"

"For botching my proposal. I should've gotten down on one knee and asked you to m-marry m-me. Instead, I—"

She kissed him, a quick hard kiss. "It's fine, Robert."

"It w-wasn't—"

When she kissed him again, he got the hint.

But he needed to hear her say she'd accept him. "Will you marry me, B?"

"Yes," she hissed a moment before she arched up against him. "If you make love to me. Now."

Whatever the Ladies had done during that girls' night out had freed something inside his Bethany, and Robert wasn't a man to look a gift horse in the mouth. "Oh, no worries there."

He gave her another deep kiss before nuzzling her neck, licking and nibbling at her silky skin. His need for her was so strong he knew this would be one of their quick, rather rough trysts. The way she scraped her nails across his shoulders fired his blood and revealed her need was every bit as great.

Moving lower, he drew one of her tight nipples between his teeth and gently tugged. She replied with a throaty moan and tunneled her fingers through his hair. Shifting to her other breast, he sucked the nipple hard, loving how she started to squirm.

"Robert... now."

"Too soon," he managed to spit out before he pressed his lips against her stomach, moving lower and only stopping long enough to kiss or lick her skin. After teasing her navel with his tongue, he scooted back farther and eased her thighs apart.

"I want you," Beth said. Her words ended on a moan when he slipped his fingers between her folds.

"You're so wet already." He had to taste her.

She let out a gasp when he stabbed his tongue into her. Then she raised her knees, digging her heels into the mattress as he loved her with his mouth. The way she tugged his hair stung, but it only added to the multitude of sensations that were bringing him closer and closer to losing control.

"I love you." Her throaty declaration ended when she cried out in release.

Something inside him snapped. He rose over her and thrust inside her body. Lifting her legs higher up on his hips, he pushed into her again and again, mindless to anything except helping her come again.

And she did. The way her body squeezed his cock set off his own release. His heartbeat roared in his ears as his body shuddered in orgasm.

In the aftermath, his muscles had all the tension of wet noodles. Since he was probably crushing her, Robert broke their connection and rolled to her side. When Beth didn't immediately move into his arms as usual, he glanced over only to find her scrambling off the bed.

"B? What's wrong?"

She shook her head and scurried into the bathroom.

Although he was so sated and content that it was hard to move, he threw his legs over the side of the mattress and got to his feet. After what they'd just shared, he couldn't understand why she'd hurry away like that. "B?"

She'd grabbed her robe off the hook and sat on the closed toilet seat, cocooned in terry cloth. Her face was red, and she appeared close to tears.

Confused, Robert strode over and knelt at her feet. "What's wrong?"

She bowed her head and gave it a shake.

He nudged her chin to get her to look at him. "You just sent me over the moon, but now you're upset. I don't understand."

"I said it first!"

* * *

Beth hadn't meant to shout, but she was so incredibly angry at herself. In that moment when he brought her to sheer bliss, she'd gone and blurted out that she loved him. Just like that. She was mortified.

So why in the heck was he grinning?

"You didn't say it," he said, his tone teasing.

"I did."

He grinned and shook his head.

"I did, too! I said I loved you!"

"You didn't *say* it. You *shouted* it. I think the neighbors heard."

And just like that, Robert's wonderful humor snatched away the self-directed anger. "They'll get over it," she drawled.

"Did you m-mean it?"

As if she could deny the words, especially with the hopeful, somewhat wary way he watched her. It dawned on her he was every bit as nervous as she was, which meant one thing.

The Ladies were right. He cared. Maybe even loved.

So with a deep sigh, Beth confessed what was in her heart. "Yeah, I meant it. I love you, Robert."

He took her hand and kissed the back of it. Then he gave her a heart-stopping smile. "Damn good thing, because I love you, too."

Chapter 16

If you know, Mom, you've got to tell me." Beth tried to temper her tone, knowing if she pushed her mother too hard, Carol would get her back up. "If we don't let the guy know, then Robert and I can't adopt Emma."

Carol snorted. "Why does Robert care anyway? Why would he wanna be saddled with a kid that isn't even his? He hasn't married you yet, and God only knows if he'll follow through on that. Why buy the cow when the milk is free?"

"Robert loves Emma." The heat of anger and hurt rose inside Beth, setting her face on fire.

The cow analogy had always been one of her mother's favorites. Whenever she preached it at her daughters, Beth had winced. Tiffany? She'd started "mooing" before laughing her butt off and then doing whatever the heck she'd wanted.

If only I could find some of Tiff's chutzpah.

"Please, Mom. Don't make me beg," Beth said, even though her tone had already slipped into pleading. Anything for Emma.

Carol released a weighty sigh. "Right after basic training, Tiffany started seeing that Darren kid again. Such a bad influence."

"Darren Brown? Seriously? I figured by now he'd be in prison or something."

Of all the scumbags Tiffany had latched on to, Darren had been the only one she'd claimed to love. Thankfully, he wasn't nearly as bad as some of the guys Tiffany left in her wake. Although he did get arrested for possession of weed back in his senior year of high school.

Beth remembered it well because she and Tiffany had been in the car when Darren was pulled over for having a broken taillight. After the officer took his license and registration, he started shining the flashlight in the car and sniffing deeply. Then he asked why he smelled marijuana and told everyone to get out of the car.

In a gallant gesture, Darren had pulled a baggie of marijuana out of his pocket, handed it to the officer, and told him that the girls didn't even know he had it. No doubt Beth's horrified expression had added weight to his confession.

"Tiffany never said for sure," Carol added. "For all I know, she might not have even known who Emma's father was. The way she carried on and all."

Even though Tiffany was gone, Carol still had to get in one last insult.

"I guess I'll try to hunt him down."

"No need for that," her mother said. "I saw him when we were in Princeville."

"Where?"

"He was working at the Burger Barn in Meadows Plaza."

Beth gave her mother a rather terse farewell, letting Carol enjoy herself by getting in a few acerbic comments about Robert's lack of a romantic proposal before they ended the call.

Exhausted from the uncomfortable conversation, Beth practically fell onto the sofa, thinking about the ramifications of

Darren Brown being Emma's father. No matter what angle she looked from, he was bad news. But could that be good news for her and Robert?

This was supposed to be an easy adoption once she and Robert were married. Tiffany had named Beth as Emma's guardian should anything happen to her while deployed. There was no father mentioned, which was good enough for the army. Evidently it wasn't good enough for anyone else.

The patio door opened, and Robert carried a laughing Emma inside. The days were getting warmer, so he often took her out to push her on the swing. He and Ben had built an enormous playground-worthy swing set that had everything from a slide to swings to a child's version of a climbing wall.

Emma would be one very spoiled young lady. She had her Bobber firmly wrapped around her little fingers.

Beth plastered on a grin even though she felt nothing like smiling. "Did you two have fun?"

"We sure did," he replied. "Emma got to swing."

"Bobber!" Emma gave him a kiss on the cheek after he took off her coat and hat. Her smile lit up her entire chubby face. "Seen!" Her way of saying "swing."

She'd gone from being entirely silent to babbling constantly. Her first birthday was in a couple of weeks, and Beth had already made plans to have the Ladies, their guys, and Jules's twins over for a small party. If the weather cooperated, Robert wanted to use his new gas grill. The thing was bigger than Beth's first car.

After he helped Emma wash her hands, Robert got her a sippy cup of milk and sat her down in her playpen. She set the drink aside and promptly jerked off her shoes as he laughed.

"I'd rather be barefoot, too," he said, tousling her curls.

Plopping down on the sofa next to Beth, he draped his arm over her shoulder. "So what did your eternally pleasant mother have to say? Was Alexis right?"

Beth nodded. "I've got a name. Can't guarantee he's the father, but it's as good a place to start as any."

He gave her a squeeze. "I know you're worried, but we have to do this. It's the only way to adopt Emma. Besides, whoever he is, the guy deserves to know if she's his. I'd want to know."

"His name's Darren Brown. He and Tiff dated most of high school." Beth told him the story about the traffic stop and how Darren had to serve some time in juvenile detention for the possession charge—one of a handful of times he'd been caught doing something against the law back when Beth knew him.

"He wasn't eighteen?" Robert asked.

"A few months shy. Saved his butt, because it wasn't the first time he'd been caught with drugs."

"Drugs? More than just weed?"

Beth shook her head. "Only marijuana, according to what Tiff told me." She knit her brows. "What's it matter anyway? Drugs are drugs."

"We might have to agree to disagree on that, B."

She gaped at him. "Are you serious?"

He nodded.

"I don't understand. Marijuana is a *drug*."

"It's no worse than tobacco."

"Did you smoke dope?"

His exaggerated sigh was as good as a confession.

"You really smoked dope?" Her tone was bordering on hysterical. The Robert she knew might have been a bit of a player with the ladies. But drugs?

No. No way.

He heaved a sigh. "A lot of people don't consider pot a big problem. Some of the guys in my frat smoked it, so I did, too. It wasn't a big deal, B. I only got in trouble once. J-just a misdemeanor for p-possession. At least give this Darren a chance."

* * *

Robert couldn't believe his own ears. Why in the hell was he defending the guy when he hadn't even met him and knew absolutely nothing about him? If Darren Brown was Emma's biological father, he might have the power to take Emma away from them.

Sure, Tiffany had made things crystal clear in all of the military paperwork, naming Beth to be Emma's guardian. But Alexis had explained that the biological father's rights might supersede Tiffany's wishes, especially since he'd never been informed of Emma's birth.

Losing Emma would be a blow Robert might never recover from, and it would be worse for Beth. He scrambled to think of scenarios that would give them joint custody with Darren, any way to save a part of Emma's life for themselves.

She belonged to them. They were a family now.

"I can't believe you're telling me this." Beth shrugged his arm away and jumped to her feet.

He'd been so lost in thought he needed a few moments to realize what she was talking about. "You're pissed because of my smoking a little weed back in college?"

She stomped to the kitchen and started slamming cabinets and pans, probably getting things ready for supper. The whole time, she muttered to herself. He caught words like *irresponsible*, *stupid*, and *idiot*, which told him this wasn't going to be the nonissue he'd hoped it would be.

A single arrest for possession, one that was expunged years ago, wasn't something to get worked up over. Sure, his attitude about weed was rather laid back, especially as a former teacher. But a lot of people saw it as a venial sin, something not all that bad. Hell, some states had even made it legal.

Emma had finished her milk and picked up one of her stuffed toys, but once Beth had begun her little tantrum, for want of a better word, Emma had dropped the toy and now stared at Beth with wide eyes.

Robert got up, went over to Emma, and rubbed her back. "It's okay, squirt. Matka's just upset with Bobber."

Her brown eyes shifted from him to Beth and back again. The intelligence in those eyes never ceased to amaze him.

He picked up the stuffed pony she'd dropped and handed it to her.

She grabbed it and babbled some of her baby talk at the pony. That storm calmed, he went to soothe his other girl.

Beth was attacking some ground beef in a big glass bowl, stopping every now and then to add a few more ingredients before going back at the mixture with the long-handled wooden spoon.

With no warning, the handle snapped off.

"Damn it!" She tossed the part in her hand into the sink and then stared at the food, her hands on her hips.

Robert came up behind her and wrapped his arms around her waist. Although she was stiff as a crowbar, he pulled her back against him and rubbed his chin on top of her head. "I d-didn't mean to disappoint you, B. I'm human. I make m-mistakes."

She sighed and nodded, bumping his chin. Then she sniffed hard a few times as though fighting back tears.

He turned her to face him, lifting her chin with his finger

so he could look into her eyes. "This is more than my youthful indiscretion. Tell me what's wrong."

"What if someone finds out you were arrested and tries to use that against us so we can't adopt Emma?"

"It was a misdemeanor. I paid the fine. The thing got expunged. Think about it. I was able to teach, right? It didn't stop the state of Illinois from giving me a teaching license."

"Oh. I hadn't thought about that." She drew her lips tight. "I still can't believe you smoke pot."

"*Smoked*. Ancient history. I s-swear." He held up three fingers. "Scout's honor."

At least he got a hesitant smile from her.

Robert brushed a quick kiss over her lips. "How 'bout I finish supper while you give Alexis a call?"

She frowned. "I need to tell her about Darren."

"Yep, you do. Wonder if he'll be hard to track down?"

"Not according to my mother. Evidently, he works at the Burger Barn back in my hometown."

"How does she know that?" Robert asked.

"She saw him there when they were in town for the funeral," Beth replied.

"That's great!"

She cocked her head. "Why?"

He grinned, hoping to give her some of the confidence that had filled him at learning where Darren worked. "What judge would take her away from a married couple who own their home outright and have great jobs to give her to a guy who smokes dope and flips burgers for a living?"

Chapter 17

Robert picked up his spatula, tossed it end over end, and caught the handle in midair. He was feeling pretty cocky since the birthday barbeque had gone so well. Why not show off a little?

And there was even more to come.

Beth and her Ladies were all sitting back, sipping their drinks. Ben and Connor were sprawled over deck chairs, rubbing their stomachs and grumbling about being too full. The children had eaten huge portions of the special foods Robert had prepared for them, and they were now napping in the nursery with Aubrey watching over them.

"I'm gonna pop the button on my pants," Connor teasingly complained. "You put on a mighty fine spread, Robert, my man."

"Hey!" Beth protested. "I made most of the side dishes."

"They were delicious," Connor added. "But your guy knows how to grill the perfect medium-well rib eye."

"Amen!" Ben raised his beer in salute. "I feel like I'm going to explode."

"Compliments to the chef," Jules added, lifting her drink in salute.

The day had been perfect, the fickle Illinois weather cooperating for once, which would make Robert's surprise come off even better. Nothing worse than trying to get people to stand outside in the pouring rain.

But sunshine was in abundance, and the air held the scent of spring after a winter of far too much snow and below-zero wind chills. Beth had even been able to put out some flowers, although she was running out of time to decide exactly what she wanted to do with the landscaping. She'd have to choose soon, because spring had finally arrived.

Robert closed the lid on the grill and set his spatula aside when he heard the first of the sounds he'd expected. A trumpet-trilling reveille pierced the air.

"What the heck?" Beth set her drink aside and scurried down the deck, hurrying to the fence gate.

"Wait for me!" Afraid she'd make it to the front of the house before him, Robert leapt over the railing, drawing a confused frown from Beth. Taking her hand, he turned back to his guests. "C'mon, everyone! I've got something special planned!"

"Robert, I don't understand." Beth stumbled to keep up with him.

He slowed his pace, not wanting to drag her to the driveway. He just couldn't contain his excitement. Planning this event had taken far longer than he'd anticipated, but it was finally here.

His heart was pounding, although he had no idea why. She'd already accepted his proposal. Surely she wouldn't change her mind now.

So why the nerves?

Because Robert owed her this gesture, and he wanted her to know exactly how much she meant to him. The fear that she might change her mind about committing to him was there, niggling at him. Her declaration of love should have silenced that negative voice, but it had been there his whole life. Three little words, no matter how deeply they touched his heart, weren't going to send that pessimism packing.

Beth clenched his hand when they reached the concrete driveway.

The Douglas High marching band was in formation on the street, the two drum majors standing atop small stepladders at the end of the driveway. The band director, Marty Bourne, gave Robert a wave before nodding at his drum majors. The young man and woman nodded in return, lifted their batons, and launched the band into their private performance.

"Robert?" Beth knit her brows, and although she asked something more, her words were lost in the volume of the band.

"Just listen," Robert said, raising his voice in hopes she'd hear him.

The students played "Marry You," a Bruno Mars song he'd often heard her singing when she thought she was alone. He'd never told her he could hear her, not wanting her tendency toward being an introvert to silence such a beautiful voice. Besides, sitting quietly to listen to her happiness made him happy, too.

Robert let his gaze wander, glad to see Connor and Ben grinning. Mallory's eyes brimmed with tears, while Jules and Dani were laughing as though watching a Monty Python movie. Aubrey had come out to the front porch, holding a wide-eyed Emma against her hip as the equally amazed twins stood on either side of her. Most of their neighbors had spilled out into their driveways to watch the band's performance.

The only person not smiling was Beth. Standing next to him, still clasping his hand, she pressed the fingers of her other hand against her lips.

He frowned as he stared down at her, afraid he'd gone too far over the top in an attempt to show her that he could be romantic and that she meant enough to him to deserve a grand gesture.

* * *

Beth couldn't look at Robert. If she did, she'd burst into tears. As it was, she held only a tenuous grip over her rioting emotions, just enough that she wouldn't make a fool of herself.

Ever since Tiffany's death, Beth had felt the need to control herself, especially where her feelings were concerned. Bottling them up was easier than dealing with them, something that seemed akin to opening Pandora's box. She simply didn't have time to be emotional anymore.

She didn't need Robert to tell her this gesture was all his idea. The song the band played said it clearly. She also knew why he'd gone to so much trouble in arranging this serenade. How many times had he apologized because he thought his proposal hadn't been at all romantic? It didn't seem to matter how often she told him she wasn't disappointed. He wouldn't get it through his thick skull. Even though she'd assured him the proposal was fine, he'd gone ahead and arranged this performance. *How very like Robert…*

When the song ended and the drum majors lowered their batons, Robert squeezed her hand and turned to face her.

Everyone was staring at them, and her cheeks were on fire. It was one thing to hold her class's attention when she was teaching, but to be the focus of so many people? That embarrassment, added to her tumultuous emotions, pushed her close to the brink of breaking down.

Holding her gaze, Robert dropped to one knee as his free

hand fished around in the pocket of his jeans. He was really going to do this—propose again in front of her friends and students.

Beth choked back a sob. She didn't want to burst into tears in front of all these people, especially the band. Her heart was overflowing, and if she moved her fingers away from her lips, she'd be bawling like a starving baby.

Robert produced a navy-blue velvet box and held it out to her. His hand shook. "B-Bethany Michelle Rogers? Will you do me the honor of b-being my wife?"

All she could do was nod like a jostled bobblehead doll.

The students broke out in a deafening cheer, raising their instruments in the air as they high-fived each other.

Despite her best efforts, a tear slipped from her eye, tracing a wet path down her cheek. He held the box out to her again, so she finally pulled her hand away from her mouth to take the offering from him. No sob bubbled out, but she was trembling from head to toe and couldn't utter a coherent sentence to save her life.

Instead of giving her the box, Robert opened it, plucked the silver ring from inside, and dropped her right hand to take her left in his. Then he slid the ring onto her third finger—or at least he tried to. The thing was so big it slipped right back off.

He caught the ring before it hit the ground. "I guess w-we'll have to get it resized." He held it out to her. "What do you think?" he shouted above the noise of the crowd.

She grasped the shiny ring between her thumb and index finger and stared at the beautiful and far-too-large diamond. "It's gorgeous." Her voice wasn't louder than a mouse squeaking.

"What?" Cupping his ear, he leaned closer.

"It's gorgeous!" she shouted above the din, finally able to speak.

The band was still whooping it up, as were Jules, Mallory, and Dani. Connor and Ben both came over to cuff Robert on the shoulder in manly congratulations.

A hand settled on Beth's arm. She spun around to find a grinning Alexis. She'd called earlier to tell them she'd be late to the barbeque. Robert had invited her, telling Beth he wanted her to see how happy Emma was with them so she'd know she was fighting the good fight to help with the adoption.

"Congratulations." Alexis pulled Beth into a quick hug. "I'm happy for you two."

Beth swiped at her cheek with the heel of her hand. "Thanks."

At least the band was dispersing, heading down the street in both directions, undoubtedly to find their ways back to their cars.

"Sorry I'm late," Alexis added. "But at least I got here in time for the big show."

The band director came striding up to them. "What did you think, Beth?"

"You're the best, Marty," she replied, giving him a quick hug. "The kids were wonderful."

Robert shook his hand. "I owe you one."

"My pleasure." Marty left with a saucy salute and a sassy grin.

"How about we all adjourn to the deck?" Beth suggested, taking the velvet box Robert handed her. She tucked her engagement ring inside and let him put the box back in his pocket.

She was still overwhelmed with emotions, making the proper introductions difficult. If she herded everyone out back, she could take a few precious moments to get herself under control.

After brushing a quick kiss over her lips, Robert led the way to the backyard. Aubrey gave Beth a smile and nod and took the children back inside through the front door. The Ladies and their men followed Robert while Beth walked slowly with Alexis at her side.

Once everyone was settled on the deck, Alexis seemed reluctant to speak.

Beth tried to put her at ease while Robert got a plate of food for her. "These are our friends," she told Alexis. "If you know anything about the adoption, you can speak freely in front of them."

Alexis frowned. "Are you sure?"

Beth gave her lawyer a quick explanation of how important the Ladies Who Lunch were, even pulling her shirt aside enough to reveal the pink ribbon tattoo, an action Jules and Dani mimicked.

"Thank you," Alexis said as she took the full plate from Robert and set it on the table next to her chair. "So here's the story... I talked to Darren Brown. To say he was shocked when I told him about Emma is an understatement. He says it's possible he's her father, that the timing is right. He's also willing to take a DNA test."

Beth's heart started slamming in her chest hard enough that a wave of nausea hit her.

The pessimist who made a home in her brain already knew what that test would show. Darren was Emma's father, and he would use the results of that test to snatch Emma away from her and Robert.

"Don't look so down," Alexis said. "It's only the first step. Darren wasn't positive. He said it was possible but not a sure thing. He told me Tiffany never even hinted she was expecting. The breakup wasn't good."

"Let me guess," Beth said, resigned to yet another of her sister's fiascos. "They argued about something and Tiffany up and left without a warning."

"Bingo. There's one more important thing you should know. He doesn't work at the Burger Barn," Alexis said.

"He's unemployed?" Robert's tone was downright hopeful.

Alexis shook her head. "He *owns* the Burger Barn, which means we need to start preparing for what to do if he's Emma's father."

"Preparing?" Robert asked. He stood behind the chair Beth had sat in and rested his hands on her shoulders. The slight tremble in his touch told her he was also shaken by Darren's situation.

Owns the restaurant? Darren?

He'd definitely come up in the world.

Comforted by Robert's touch, she reached up to put her hand over his. "We're prepared, and we'll do whatever else we have to do, anything you think will help, Alexis."

"Well, then…" She rubbed her hands together. "When's the wedding?"

Beth glanced back at him. "We haven't set a date."

"I only now proposed properly," Robert teased.

"How soon could you arrange it?" Alexis asked.

"Soon," Robert said with a decisive nod. "How about spring break, B?"

Dani hopped into the conversation. "But that's only a week away! We need time to plan."

"No plans." Beth gave Robert's hand a squeeze and then dropped her own hand back into her lap. "We want something small. Maybe a justice of the peace or something."

"Not easy to find," Alexis said. "Despite what movies portray, it's actually really hard to get a justice of the peace. But a judge? That, I could help with."

"We won't even have time to get a proper bachelorette party together." Dani shifted her gaze from Beth to Jules and then Mallory as though seeking support.

"We can always have a party after," Jules consoled. "Since when do the Ladies need an excuse for a raunchy night out on the town?" She winked at Beth.

"Illinois only has a day wait after you get the license," Alexis said, picking up the plate of food and putting it on her lap. "Just let me know when, and I'll set up a nice civil ceremony. You can bring your friends. I'd keep it under ten people, though. The judge doesn't like people crowding the courtroom."

"I'd bring the Ladies," Beth said.

"Connor and Ben," Robert added. "Maybe my oldest brother if he could get here to be my best man."

"Perfect!" Alexis took a bite of the Asiago cheese dinner rolls Beth had made. She closed her eyes and hummed.

"They're heaven, aren't they?" Robert patted Beth's shoulder. "So, B? How about we get the license next Friday and have the ceremony the Monday of spring break? Maybe my sister could keep Emma for a couple of nights, and I'll take you to Chicago for a short but sweet honeymoon. You love the museums."

The man thought of everything. Only one thing stopped her from telling him it was a wonderful plan.

She didn't want to leave Emma behind.

But who took their kid on a honeymoon?

They might as well drag her along. Nothing else about her relationship with Robert had happened at all like Beth had dreamed, so why not screw up the honeymoon, too?

When she was a little girl, she'd thought a lot about how her wedding would be. Perhaps the elaborate fantasies helped her get through a childhood full of her mother's disapproval and her father's negligence, or perhaps they were the thoughts of all hopeless romantic girls.

The wedding would be in a church strewn with pink flowers, looking a lot like the Pepto-Bismol wedding for Julia Roberts in *Steel Magnolias*. She'd have at least six bridesmaids and an adorable flower girl, and her father would have to pay attention for once as he walked her down the aisle. The train on her lacy dress would stretch at least five pews behind her, and people would *ooh* and *aah* when they saw her.

"I might as well wear jeans," she muttered before mentally kicking herself.

"Jeans? You want to wear jeans?" Robert asked.

She hadn't meant to say that aloud. But now that it was out there, she nodded. "Why not?"

"Beth, no." Dani's frown was fierce. "You wanted a big—"

Not about to let Dani make Robert feel bad that this wedding wasn't what she'd told Dani she wanted, Beth interrupted. "It's fine, Dani. We'll keep it low-key."

"But you said—"

"It's fine. Leave it be. Please."

"Then it's settled," Alexis announced.

Robert came around to stand in front of Beth. He took her hands and pulled her to her feet. "Can we talk? Alone?"

Great. Now he thought he'd disappointed her again. She wasn't about to make him think he had to give her a showy wedding, especially after going to so much trouble with improving his proposal. "Sure."

Once inside the house, he led her to the sofa. They sat side by side.

"B, I don't want you to settle."

"Settle?"

"For a crappy wedding."

"It won't be crappy. It'll just be...fast. That's all."

When he wrapped his arm around her shoulder, she leaned against him, laying her cheek on his chest. "It might be in a courtroom, but we can still dress up," he suggested. "It can still be a nice wedding."

"Sure, Robert. Whatever you want."

"No, it's whatever *you* want. Guys don't care about the wedding." He kissed the top of her head. "All they care about is the wedding night."

She chuckled, glad he could find humor in any situation. He was right. She could have a nice wedding. Small didn't have to mean her dreams had to die. "Maybe Dani and I can find a nice wedding dress that works for a courtroom ceremony."

"That's my girl." He rubbed his chin on her head. "Are you sure you won't be disappointed with a civil ceremony? No white dress. No bridesmaids. No big reception with dancing and gifts and—"

Beth brushed her lips over his. "None of that matters. Truly. The Ladies will help me make it a nice wedding. Besides...all that matters is that we're married and that we can keep Emma."

"Don't worry, B. I won't let anyone break up our family."

Chapter 18

Beth checked herself in her grandmother's cheval glass mirror, one of the precious things Robert had helped her retrieve from storage when they'd moved into the house. Even though this was an impromptu wedding, she still looked like a traditional bride. The minute the date had been set, panic hit her hard. This small wedding was going to be anything but austere.

Dani took Beth on the hunt for the perfect dress. Both took a personal day from school so they could hightail it to Chicago for some serious shopping. Four chain stores and at least a dozen dresses later, Dani led Beth into a small vintage clothing store just off the Miracle Mile.

Flipping through the racks of dresses mostly from the twentieth century, Beth stumbled across an ivory sheath. It was satin with a simple cut—square neck with short, capped sleeves. The entire dress was covered in a layer of Chantilly lace that ended right below the knees. A quick check made her heart skip. It was her size. Once she tried it on, she knew she had her wedding dress.

Dani stepped up beside her. She wore the A-line dress she'd

bought on the Chicago trip. The deep purple complemented her light hair and eyes. "You're beautiful!"

"You're my best friend. You have to say that. But I appreciate the compliment."

"Since it's your wedding day, I won't scold you for your lack of self-esteem."

"Thank you for the restraint."

"Nervous?" Dani handed Beth a nosegay of violets that matched her own.

Beth shook her head. "Not one bit. I'll admit I thought I would be. I'm just…not."

"Why'd you think you'd be nervous?" Dani asked. "The groom's supposed to balk, not the bride."

"Because I'm still not entirely sure he loves me."

The derisive snort seemed out of place coming from such a pretty blonde. "Then you're the only one who isn't sure. Has he told you he loves you?"

"Yeah, but—"

"Is Robert a guy who lies?"

"No, but—"

"You don't get to 'but' this time, Bethany Rogers-soon-to-be-Ashford. For once, you're going to look at this without your mom's voice in your head." Dani nodded at their reflected images. "Are you happy with how you look?"

Beth considered her image again, trying hard to push aside any negativity about herself. How odd that she could be so positive about everyone else and so pessimistic where her own appearance or actions were concerned.

The dress was a flattering cut for her body type, making her appear slender. She had to admit she wasn't truly fat, no matter what Carol often said about hiding a pretty girl behind a layer of padding.

Beth's hair was longer than it had been since high school. Today, Dani had helped her sweep the thick mass into a French twist, leaving a few loose curls on each side of her face and against the back of her neck. Then Dani held it all in place with a pearl-accented comb and sprayed the whole thing with hairspray that added a touch of sparkle every time the light caught Beth just right.

Jules had done Beth's makeup, putting emphasis on her eyes, which Beth considered to be her best feature. She'd been powdered and pampered, and she looked like a model ready for a photo shoot.

Beth smiled at her reflection. "I'm…pretty."

With an enormous smile, Dani patted Beth's shoulder. "By George, I think she's got it."

Someone knocked before the bedroom door opened. "It's not Robert," Mallory called as she came inside. "He and Ben already left for the courthouse." Her gaze caught Beth's in the mirror, and Mallory stopped so quickly Jules ran into her back.

"Geesh," Jules said, stepping back. "You need brake lights, Mal."

"Beth." Mallory hurried to her. "You're gorgeous. That dress is amazing."

Jules came to stand next to Dani. "Robert won't know what hit him."

* * *

Robert had never been a nervous pacer. He'd watched more than his share, mostly anxious customers waiting for their real estate closings. He'd always thought walking back and forth was a sad waste of energy, probably because patience was his only virtue.

That virtue had abandoned him. Now he was the one taking sixteen steps to the end of the corridor and sixteen steps back. Each time, he passed by the carved wooden bench where his oldest brother, George, and Ben Carpenter sat waiting for Connor to chauffeur the Ladies to the courthouse.

Both George and Ben grinned at Robert each time he strode past, but they had the decency not to say anything, especially not to indulge in teasing him. He wasn't in the mood for it, and until Beth arrived and took her vows, he was likely to jump down the throat of anyone who pushed his buttons.

The funny thing was that he knew Beth loved him. At least he thought she did. She wasn't a woman who toyed with people's feelings. The fear that she'd change her mind shouldn't plague him. But it did.

The next time he found himself in front of the bench, he stopped and looked at Ben and George. Both were married men, which he hoped meant they could help. "Were either of you this nervous?"

"Hell, yeah," Ben replied.

"A lot worse than you," George added.

"Why?" Robert rubbed the back of his neck. "I mean, you love your wives. I love Beth. Why am I so damned worried?"

"Because," Ben said with a smirk, "you're not doubting your love for her. You're asking yourself why such a great gal would want to marry a guy like you."

George nodded. "Exactly. Until that preacher—"

"Judge," Robert corrected.

With a roll of his eyes, George said, "Whatever. Until you hear her speak the vows, you'll be scared she'll get away."

"Here comes the bride!" Dani's singsong voice echoed down the corridor.

"Thank God," Robert muttered, hurrying over to the small group climbing the ornate marble staircase.

He took Beth's hand as she came up the last step. His gaze swept her from head to toe, and any words he might have uttered froze in his throat. She'd never looked as lovely as she did at that moment. He was the luckiest man on the face of the planet. "Wow."

"I'll take that as a compliment," she said, brushing a quick kiss on his cheek and then using her thumb to smooth away the lipstick she'd left behind.

"You're absolutely gorgeous. Where'd you find the dress?"

"On the Chicago trip."

When Beth had finally decided not to play their wedding low-key, Robert had been relieved. He'd feared that she'd regret letting it pass without something special to mark the day. Even if they wouldn't have a church strewn with flowers and candles, they would have a wedding day to remember.

Ben went with Robert to buy new suits since neither thought anything they owned fit the importance of the event. Now that he saw Beth in her lace dress, her hair and face the picture of perfection, he was glad he'd gone with Ben's suggestions for his suit, shirt, and tie. New shoes were even a part of the package.

"B, you are gorgeous," he said, taking a tight hold of her free hand.

She dropped her gaze as a blush bloomed on her face.

Jules cuffed her lightly on the shoulder. "For pity's sake, woman. Learn to take a compliment."

Connor adjusted his lapels as he stepped up to his wife. "Well, if that's not the pot calling the kettle—"

"Shut up and tell me I'm beautiful," she ordered.

He obliged. "Prettiest woman I've ever been married to."

"I'm the only woman you've ever been married to, smartass."

Ben had risen to go to his wife and waited nearby with an arm draped over her shoulders. "I will never understand why women don't want to hear guys tell them they're pretty."

"Oh, we *do* want to hear that!" Beth said.

"We just don't believe it," Dani added with lopsided smile.

Giving his head a shake, Ben said, "No matter how old and wise I get, I will never understand women."

"Oh, please," Mallory said with a chuckle. "You know me better than I know myself."

He gave her a mock gasp. "No way. You're like a computer with a hundred tabs open at the same time."

Connor nudged him with his elbow. "Like Juliana always tells me, the only things women need are for us to tell them they're beautiful and then hand them some chocolate."

The banter was great, something Robert had begun to truly enjoy, but he wanted this wedding done. He needed Beth to be tied to him. Permanently.

"Feels weird, doesn't it?" Beth asked softly.

Robert cocked his head. "Getting married feels weird?"

"No, being here without Emma."

"I know what you mean," Jules added. "I keep looking around for the twins, wondering where they've disappeared to now."

"Aubrey's got them all," Robert reminded the women. "They're fine."

"I know," Beth said. "It still feels weird. I love that little bugger so much."

"Me too." He gave her a quick kiss.

Thankfully, the door to the courtroom opened, and a man in a sheriff's uniform stepped out. "Are you the weddin' party?"

A ridiculous question considering the men were in suits, Beth was dressed like a bride, and the women were all carrying flowers. "That's us. Is the judge ready?" Robert couldn't even keep the impatience from his voice.

"Are you all right?" Beth asked. The way she'd knit her brows in concern, he half expected her to put the back of her hand against his forehead the same way she did whenever she was worried that Emma might have a fever.

"I'm fine. I'm just ready to get this over with."

Her features softened despite his poor choice of words, and she squeezed his hand and tossed his words back at him. "Me too."

"If you'll follow me." The deputy opened the door and waited as Robert led Beth into the courtroom, the Ladies and their guys right behind.

Robert didn't know Judge Layton. Thanks to Alexis, the man had agreed to stay late to perform the wedding ceremony. He appeared to be close to Robert's age, which came as a surprise. Weren't all judges supposed to be ancient, silver-haired founts of wisdom?

The judge held his hand out to Robert. After they shook hands and Robert introduced himself, Judge Layton nodded at Beth. "The bride, I presume?"

"Yes, sir," she replied, her voice a whisper.

"You don't have to keep your voice down," Judge Layton said with a wink. "Court's not in session now."

Her cheeks flamed.

"If the two of you will stand in front of me, we can begin." The judge's gaze shifted to the entourage. "If you ladies will stand next to the bride and the gentlemen will join the groom, we'll get the knot tied for these two."

There was a bit of a Southern drawl to his voice as he read from a small black book he held. There were none of the religious admonitions. No words of faith. Blessings weren't offered. Instead, the judge spoke of love, fidelity, and promises for the future. The words were more moving to Robert than any that a preacher could have spoken, especially when Judge Layton uttered words of commitment.

Robert had never expected to pledge his life to one woman. He'd always enjoyed playing the field, even if the field in Cloverleaf was a bit limited. The chase had always excited him, while boredom kicked in almost immediately after he caught the woman who'd captured his fancy.

But that was before Beth. In some ways, he'd been faithful to her from the moment they started working together. He'd dated less and less, and his sex life had rapidly dwindled until it went into full hibernation. The days he could spend with her as she helped decorate the homes he built were what he looked forward to, even finding reasons to call or meet with her that were downright frivolous. Hell, he'd lived for whatever time she could fit him into her busy teaching schedule.

Yet he'd never told her, he'd never found the balls to ask if she wanted to try for a relationship. It had taken Emma coming into Beth's life to finally get him to realize all he could have with Beth. With them both.

Just looking at her now made him feel as though someone were squeezing his chest too tightly for him to breathe. How he'd managed to get a woman like her, someone so beautiful in mind, body, and heart, to fall in love with him was still confusing, but he thanked God every day she'd looked past his flaws and loved him for who he was.

Judge Layton loudly cleared his throat, drawing Robert out of his meandering thoughts.

"Sorry." Heat spread across Robert's face.

"Will you, Robert Stuart Ashford, take this woman as your lawfully wedded wife?"

"I will," Robert replied in a strong, steady voice.

The judge gave him a grin; then he glanced at Beth. "Will you, Bethany Michelle Rogers, take this man as your lawfully wedded husband?"

* * *

Beth clenched the nosegay in her hand so tightly some of the stems snapped. A couple violets broke off and tumbled to the floor as the gravity of the situation slammed into her.

She wanted to say the words, but they'd stuck in her throat and refused to budge. Doubt crowded out all the reasons she should be taking these vows with Robert. Uncertainty about whether he truly loved her. Doubt about what the future would be if Darren Brown was Emma's father. Doubt about whether Robert would want to be tied to her if Emma wasn't a part of their lives.

He'd hesitated, had been lost in his thoughts when Judge Layton had asked "the" question. What had Robert been thinking? About whether he really wanted to do this? About whether they were rushing into marriage?

If only she could read his mind.

The judge cleared his throat again, the same way he'd gotten Robert to stop standing there, daydreaming. It didn't have the same effect on Beth. Instead, she only worried more as she wondered exactly what had seized Robert's thoughts so tightly he'd forgotten he was in the middle of getting married.

Dani stepped closer and leaned in to whisper in Beth's ear. "Beth, you need to answer the judge."

Beth gave her a brisk nod, but she couldn't spit out the words.

"If you don't want to do this," Dani began. "We can—"

"We need a moment, please," Robert said as he took Beth's elbow and pulled her away from the judge and their friends.

Beth hurried after him as he marched several steps toward the door. Then he abruptly stopped, turned to face her, and grabbed her shoulders. "Why don't you want to marry me?"

There was no anger in his voice. Instead, she heard fear and a note of hurt. Those are what she reacted to by wrapping her arms around his waist and resting her cheek against his chest.

"Please, B. I need you. Marry me."

Her hesitation wasn't fair. She was embarrassing him, shaming him in front of all these people. "I'm so sorry. I was just... worried."

"What are you worried about?"

She wasn't about to tell him her concerns. Her heart wanted him. Emma needed him. There was no turning back. "It was only cold feet."

"Do you want to marry me?"

Easing back, she looked him in the eye. "I do."

"Try saying that for the judge now," he teased, dragging her back to the gaping folks who'd come to see a wedding.

"I'm sorry," Beth said to Judge Layton. "May we please continue?"

"If that's what you'd like to do," the judge replied. The concern on his face made her pat his arm.

"It is. It's exactly what I want."

"Will you take Robert as your lawfully wedded husband?"

Beth nodded and stated clearly and loudly, "I will."

Chapter 19

All Beth could do was stare at the computer printout and wonder why the results of one stupid little test could have the potential to destroy her life so thoroughly.

Just as she'd feared, Emma was Darren Brown's biological daughter. DNA said so. According to the laws of the state of Illinois, it also gave him the right to contest the adoption and perhaps take Emma away.

The normally optimistic Beth couldn't stop herself from dreaming up sinister reasons Darren might fight for custody. The one she finally settled on was money.

Tiffany's life insurance policies provided a rather large sum of money for her daughter. Beth had sunk all the funds into secure investments to earn interest as Emma grew. Once she was of age, Emma could use that money for her education or to buy a home. There was nothing that required Beth to do so because there were no rules for Emma's guardian on what to do with the money. Darren would surely see it as a windfall.

"Don't look so down," Alexis said, dragging Beth back into the present.

Robert frowned. "Why not? The guy's her father."

"*You're* her father." Alexis drummed her fingers on her glass desktop. "He was just the sperm donor. Doesn't mean the fight is over. Not by a long shot."

"I thought it was a done deal," he said, looking as upset as Beth felt. "Biological fathers always get custody in court, don't they?"

"Not at all," Alexis replied. "First off, I haven't had a chance to talk to him yet, at least not at length. Just a quick phone chat to get some pertinent facts. He hasn't retained a lawyer, either, which means he hasn't decided exactly what he wants to do."

Beth's heart leapt at that news. If she had just discovered she had a daughter, she'd be hunting down a modern-day Clarence Darrow to start whatever needed to be done to get her home. And she sure wouldn't spare a thought for the people who tried to keep her from her true mother.

I'm a hypocrite.

She tried to switch tactics. Maybe Darren didn't want kids. Why hadn't she thought about that sooner instead of wallowing in worry? None of the guys Tiffany hung around were exactly "dad" material. With Darren's past, he might not even want Emma around. He had a business to run; he didn't have time to care for a child.

"He wants to come here," Alexis announced. "We have an appointment next Monday."

"Here?" Beth's voice cracked. "He's coming *here*?" So much for him not wanting Emma.

"He's driving to Cloverleaf with his girlfriend—his pregnant girlfriend."

Even better! Why would he and his woman want Emma when they were starting a family of their own? Unless…

What if they thought Emma belonged in their growing family?

"Beth?" Alexis's voice was soft. "You're very quiet today. What's on your mind?"

"Worry," Robert replied. "She's worried, and so am I."

Alexis shook her head. "It's too soon to be concerned. The game's just beginning."

"Game?" Beth clenched her hands into fists. "You think this is a *game*? I could lose my daughter." Even saying the words hurt.

"Easy," Alexis said. "I wasn't making light of your situation. I promise you that I take it every bit as seriously as you and Robert do."

"Then why call it a game?"

"Because that's how I view the law. It's a chess game, a matter of finding the right strategy and seeing it through until there are no moves left." A smile lit the lawyer's face. "I promise you this—I'm a pro at it. I'm going to do everything I can to keep Emma with you two. I've seen how great you are and how she's already found her family. Darren might have helped create her, but Robert is her father. And you're her mother, Beth."

Robert took Beth's hand and gave it a squeeze. "Hear that? You're Emma's mother, B. Never forget that."

"I guess I just don't understand why Tiffany's wishes aren't being considered. Shouldn't the court follow what she wanted for Emma?" Beth asked.

"I'd be dishonest if I told you we weren't fighting an uphill battle," Alexis replied. "Despite Tiffany's wishes, biology has the upper hand in the law, especially since Tiffany never told Darren about Emma. Legally, he has the best chance at custody. But I intend to make a sound argument about what's in Emma's best interests. As an officer of the court, I believe staying with you is what's in her best interests. If Darren fights for her, the court will also appoint a guardian ad litem whose only concern is what is the right thing to do for Emma."

* * *

It wasn't until after supper that Beth was able to find the time to think hard about the future. She'd been too busy all evening being a wife and a mother. Making their meal. Doing a couple of loads of the never-ending laundry. Picking up the things Emma always discarded around the house.

Sometimes she was surprised just how quickly she and Robert had settled into married life. Like any couple, they had spats. But most of the time, their relationship went as smoothly as a well-choreographed dance. They each had chores they performed without complaint, and they balanced their time with Emma so that she knew how much she was loved.

Marriage seemed to agree with Robert. With the exception of when they were discussing the possibility of losing Emma, he was usually in a good mood. He smiled. He whistled. He still gave her hugs and kisses whenever they'd been apart, even if for only an hour.

She loved him to the depths of her soul.

With a half-smile, Beth hung up the jacket Robert had thrown over the end of the couch when he'd come home. God love him, her husband was a slob. Beth never scolded him for dropping his shoes wherever he'd been when he kicked them off, nor did she complain about the wet towels he left on the bathroom floor or the fact that he constantly left the toothpaste resting on the sink, next to the cap he'd forgotten to put back on.

Little things like that didn't bother her. If she was honest with herself, she'd admit she found his habits endearing, probably because she loved him so darn much. And he always returned the "ignoring" favor.

Robert never mentioned how she left the books she loved to read all around the house or how she'd taken up a heck of a lot more than half of the master closet. He also overlooked her rather obsessive need to buy toilet paper, paper towels, and tissues in bulk quantities.

They complemented each other, and their passion burned bright. All he had to do was fix those eyes on her and her blood turned hot. Perhaps that was only because they were still newlyweds, but she wasn't going to question such a wonderful gift.

Almost ready to turn in for the night, Beth crossed her arms under her breasts and leaned her shoulder against the door frame, watching Emma sleeping in her crib. Although she was in perpetual motion from the moment she opened her eyes each morning, she always slept like a rock. She looked so peaceful, her lips parted as she breathed slow and even. The perfect little angel, and Beth loved her with every piece of her heart.

It took all of her restraint not to go over, gather Emma into her arms, and hold her tight. A tear slipped from the corner of her eye at the thought of her daughter being snatched from the only stability she'd ever enjoyed and thrust into a world full of people she didn't even know. How much psychological damage could that kind of jarring change create?

Strong arms snaked around Beth's waist before Robert pulled her back against him. He brushed a kiss against her cheek, sending shivers racing over her skin. "I got tired of waiting for you to come to bed." He nuzzled her neck, making a small giggle bubble up.

"I was watching Emma." All of the warmth inside her vanished. "I love her so much."

Robert squeezed her tightly and rubbed his chin against her temple. "So do I, B."

"We can't lose her."

"Have some faith. Alexis is the best. Let her do her job and keep hope in your heart." He turned her in his arms, and she looped her arms around his neck. "You know it's the thing I love most about you."

She searched his eyes, trying to make sense of his comment. "What is?"

"How you never give up hope."

Beth tried to drop her gaze, ashamed he didn't see her as she truly was. He was wrong. Each passing hour stole a little more of the confidence she'd held her whole life that things happened for a reason. What reason could justify Emma losing her mother—and then losing her second mother? In what world was that fair?

With gentle fingertips, he lifted her chin until she was looking into his eyes again. "I'm right here, love. You don't have to go through this alone."

Tears filled her eyes, but these were tears of joy rather than sadness. She rose on tiptoes to press her lips to his.

* * *

Desire flooded Robert's senses. His emotions were running hot, and he needed Beth right now in a way that felt downright primitive. In one quick move, he swept her into his arms and strode to their room, gently kicking the door shut behind them.

As was her endearing habit, she took a quick glance at the tiny screen on her nightstand—the monitor to the technological eye that kept watch over Emma whenever she was in her crib. He'd often awaken in the wee hours of the morning to find Beth awake as well, watching their daughter sleep.

Robert captured Beth's mouth for a kiss, growling in impatience. He slid his tongue past her lips, and she returned the ferocity of the kiss, cradling his face in her cool hands as her tongue mated with his.

After setting her on the bed, he lifted her nightshirt over her head and tossed it aside. Then he stumbled out of his boxers, trying to keep staring at his sexy wife and undressing at the same time.

As Beth lay back, he stretched over her, loving the heat of her smooth skin as it touched his. It was probably a good thing she wore lacy panties. Otherwise he'd be fighting the overwhelming urge to immediately thrust inside her. He kissed her again, thinking he should slow things down a little.

Beth wouldn't allow it. With her hands against his chest, she lightly pushed him away before she wriggled out of her panties. Falling back against the mattress, she opened her arms in welcome.

Robert answered her invitation, blanketing her with his body and kissing her again, a mating of their tongues until he thought he'd go mad for want of her. Moving to his side, he stroked up her thigh until he was caressing her core, seeking the spot he knew would drive her wild.

Her hips bucked when he found the sensitive nub, and she drew in a sharp breath. He tormented and taunted and gave her no quarter. He kissed her neck, teasing her with nibbles as he worked his way to her chest. After pressing a reverent kiss to the valley between her breasts, he closed his mouth around one tight nipple and suckled.

A low moan escaped her lips. Arching her back, she raked her fingers through his hair.

When he slid his fingers deep inside her, Beth's body clenched around them, telling him she was close. He shifted to her other breast, laving the nipple before pulling it gently with his teeth.

"Robert. I need you inside me. Please." She tugged hard on his hair.

His need was every bit as desperate as hers, so Robert answered her call, moving over her and using his knee to push her legs farther apart. Before he could guide his cock inside her, she grasped it and led him home.

One thrust found him deep inside his wife's warmth, and the feeling was so sublime he had to close his eyes and breathe deeply to maintain his self-control. Before he could start to move, Beth wrapped her legs around his hips and pulled him as deeply inside her as he could go.

He was lost, mindless to anything except giving her pleasure and seeking his own. Again and again he pushed into her, each thrust a little harder until she caught her breath and held it. Then her thighs squeezed his hips as she moaned his name, the sound of her pleasure hitting him hard and forcing his own orgasm as he poured his essence into his wife.

Robert was so spent, he could barely hold himself up on his elbows to shelter Beth from his weight. She lazily trailed her fingers up and down his back, humming softly. Another of her endearing habits.

After reluctantly withdrawing, doing a hasty cleanup, and then slipping his boxers back on, he slid beneath the sheets. As she went into their bathroom, he waited for her to join him.

When she flipped off the light and crawled into bed, he pulled her into his arms. She laid her hand on his chest, pillowed her head against his shoulder, and let out what he hoped was a contented sigh. "That was... amazing."

He gave her a quick squeeze. "Damn right it was. You're a wildcat, B. And it's dark in here, so don't even bother blushing."

She pushed herself up enough to check the monitor before dropping her head against his shoulder again. "She's still asleep." Her body tensed. "I'm afraid, Robert."

"I am, too."

"What can we do?" she asked, her voice barely a whisper.

Her fear was understandable because he shared it. Every time he thought about them losing Emma, he bordered on a panic attack. His chest would become heavy and tight, as though everything were pressing in on him. To have his daughter raised by another man, even if that man was her biological father, seemed wrong. Darren might have contributed his DNA, but Robert was her *Bobber*, the man who chased away the monsters from under the crib. The man who read to her every day, who pushed her swing while she squealed in joy. No one could love her as much as he did.

"Robert? Are you okay?"

Having not realized he'd tensed, he eased the tight hold he had on his wife. "I'm fine."

"You still haven't answered me. Should we squirrel away some money and, I don't know, try to hide?"

He shook his head. "We can't run away from our lives."

"I need you to help me with this," she insisted. "What are we gonna do?"

After a moment of searching to find the right things to say to calm her fears, he decided honesty was the best thing he could offer her. “We can trust Alexis to do her job and hope things turn out right.”

“If we lose Emma—”

“One day at a time, love. Instead of driving ourselves crazy with worry, let’s just take things one day at a time.”

Chapter 20

The moment Beth saw Darren, the past came rushing back. In her eyes, he was still that kid who liked to stir up trouble, the bad boy who Tiffany claimed to love. The good times and the bad were right there, plain as day.

How could Tiffany have hidden his child from him? Why was her sister too afraid to tell him about Emma? What did Tiffany know that Beth didn't? Or was it something Tiffany feared?

The unknowns were the hardest to fight, and Beth would drive herself insane thinking about them before this whole ordeal was over.

Darren was still a good-looking guy, although he'd cut his long hair into a short, businesslike style. His youthful skinny body had bulked up, his arms muscular and his waist trim. Had she not been so desperately in love with Robert, Beth might even have been attracted to him.

He'd dressed in expensive clothing, and she recognized his loafers as Gucci. Clearly he was a success now, and she'd have to stop thinking about him as a kid who'd done stupid things. He owned his own business and had made something of himself.

A young woman walked by his side as they came up the carpeted hallway of Alexis's office suite. Alexis had chosen the location, wanting there to be some formality and control in the affair. The girl was blond, her build slender. Her clothes and shoes had to be designer as well, and she was clearly pregnant. The rock on the third finger of her left hand was about two carats bigger than the engagement ring Robert had given Beth.

In her fear, all Beth could think was that Darren and this woman were having a baby of their own. Why would they need to take away hers?

"Wow." Darren gave Beth a weak smile. "You haven't changed a bit, B."

Robert scowled at him, probably at the use of his pet name for her.

She'd forgotten how Darren used to tease her, almost unmercifully, and how he'd always called her B. It had bugged the heck out of Tiffany, who often gave him a playful punch in the arm whenever he joked with Beth.

"You sure have," Beth said. "Changed, that is. A lot." She wasn't surprised to hear the tremor in her voice. Then a flush heated her face. "Sorry. I didn't mean—"

"It's okay," Darren said with a lopsided smile. "I *have* changed, and I'm damned proud of it." His features sobered. "Losing Tiffany was a big wakeup call for me. I wanted to be the kind of man she deserved. So I picked myself up, dusted myself off, and made something of my life. Took me years to get where I am, and I was so happy when we connected again. But…"

Beth could easily finish the story. "But she ran away. Again."

Darren nodded. "Took me a while to find out where she was, but by then she'd gone to Afghanistan and…"

She had to glance away.

"I-I'm sorry about what happened. For your loss."

Beth nodded, trying not to get choked up. The grief over losing her only sister was still too new, too raw. "Thank you." Then she looked at Darren again and patted the baby's back. "This is Emma."

Darren leveled a hard stare to where Emma lay sleeping with her face pillowed against Beth's chest. "She's really mine?"

"That's what the test says."

Alexis jumped into the conversation. "Why don't we all get a little more comfortable? I have a nice social room we can use."

As if on cue, her assistant rose and picked up a large silver tray full of coffee cups, a large carafe, several pastries, and pieces of fruit. She carried them through an ornate door and set them on the large table by the seating area.

The room was bathed in neutral tones, so different than the vivacious Alexis and her office. Beiges and browns were set off by light teal as accent on the two sofas' throw pillows. A large abstract painting that reminded Beth of a Pollock work was the only art on the walls. Alexis no doubt used the room as a place to have what probably were heated discussions, hoping the muted tone would help lessen the strong emotions of any clients.

After helping Beth to her feet with a welcomed hand on her elbow, Robert, still frowning, followed the receptionist. Beth cradled Emma against her, hoping the baby wouldn't wake up. Emma was getting heavy, but although Beth's arms ached, she couldn't make herself ask Robert to take her. As long as Emma was in her arms, she was safe. Someone would have to hurt Beth to get to her baby.

Robert waited until Beth sat on one of the couches before he dropped down at her side. She tried to make herself comfortable in what was sure to be one of the most uncomfortable moments of her life. He draped an arm over her shoulders, and she gave him a gentle nudge with her elbow to try getting him to ease up on the glare he was shooting at Darren.

"Be nice," she whispered.

Robert didn't reply.

Darren sat next to the blonde on the other sofa. He leaned forward, resting his forearms on his thighs and clasping his hands as he studied Emma.

Beth had to fight the urge to grab a blanket from the diaper bag and toss it over the baby, as though she could shield Emma from her biological father's penetrating perusal. As though Beth had any control over what was going to happen.

"She looks more like you than Tiff, B," he finally said. "That hair is pure you."

The comments were so close to her own thoughts that they took her by surprise. She didn't want to smile, but the corners of her mouth rose anyway. Even though her fear of losing Emma nearly choked the air from her lungs, she also saw how in awe Darren was of his daughter and how overwhelmed he was at seeing her for the first time. He couldn't seem to tear his gaze away.

Alexis nodded at the blonde. "Beth, Robert, let me introduce you to Kelly Dalton, Darren's fiancée."

Kelly smiled and gave them a little wave. "We're getting married in June." She held up her left hand to show off the enormous solitaire on her third finger.

"Congratulations," Robert said drolly. "When's the baby due?"

Beth jabbed him with her elbow again, hoping he'd get the snide tone out of his voice. "Be nice," she whispered again.

"August," Darren replied, shifting his eyes to Robert. "You must be Beth's boyfriend."

"Husband." Robert's tone shifted, but instead of softening, he now sounded angry. "I'm her *husband*."

Beth was tempted to haul him out into the reception area and scold him the way she often did with rude or disrespectful students. "We were married over spring break."

"That's so sweet," Kelly said. Her voice was high-pitched, so much so it made Beth wonder if she'd considered a career doing cartoon voices.

Alexis stood and went to the tray her assistant had carried in. "Where are my manners? My mama would be horrified." She smiled and held up the carafe. "May I offer any of you some refreshments? Coffee? A pastry, perhaps?"

Everyone declined, so Alexis poured some coffee into a cup, dropped in a couple of sugar cubes, and then took her beverage to her high-backed chair. The leather groaned in complaint as she sat back and sipped her coffee, but there was no relaxation seen in her features. She watched them all intently, yet she said nothing.

Beth stared at her in stunned silence. Shouldn't Alexis be doing something? Shouldn't she suggest that Darren take a good look at how happy and healthy Emma was? Shouldn't she push him to think about how much work raising a child could be, even point out that two babies would equal double that already challenging task? Shouldn't she demand that he give up his paternal rights right this flippin' moment?

That was the problem. They couldn't—probably shouldn't—*demand* anything from Darren. The poor guy was clearly stunned over this whole situation. Forcing his hand wouldn't get them what they wanted, and it might even make him dig in his heels and refuse anything they asked.

The reality was that Tiffany had lied to him by never telling him she was pregnant. A lie of omission was still a lie. Darren had every right to blow his stack, to tell them to hand over his daughter, and to march right out of there with her.

Thank God he didn't.

Emma stirred, pushing herself back and looking up at Beth. Blinking sleepily, she smiled.

Robert reached for Emma at the same time she shifted to reach for him. "You're up, squirt."

"Bobber!" Once he had a good grasp of her, she stood on Robert's thighs, clapping and bouncing happily while he held her around her waist.

Darren's gaze had followed his daughter. The moment she was in Robert's arms, a frown darkened his features.

"Her name's Emma, right?" Kelly asked.

Emma stopped moving and turned her head to peer at the other people in the room. Robert let her swivel around; then she plopped onto his lap, leaned back against him, and stuck her thumb in her mouth.

She hadn't sucked her thumb in weeks, which meant she'd probably picked up on the tension in the room. That, and she didn't cotton much to strangers. Despite the fact that Darren was her biological father, he was still a stranger.

That notion made Beth sad and helped her understand a little of what the poor man was going through.

"When's her birthday?" he asked.

Robert replied before Beth could. "Last week. The sixteenth."

"We could plan a belated birthday party," Kelly said with a naïve grin. "Cake. Balloons. Maybe a clown." Darned if she didn't clap her hands just like Emma had.

How old was she anyway? Twenty? Twenty-one? It was as if she was oblivious to the antagonism shooting between Robert and Darren. All her ridiculous offer did was make the men glower more deeply.

"No, thanks. We had it covered," Robert said with a shake of his head. "We had a family celebration."

Kelly knit her brows. "I'm confused." She cocked her head as she looked to Darren. "I thought you said we'd take her—"

"Kelly, stop!" Darren barked like a drill sergeant.

Alexis spoke a moment before Beth could push aside her incredulity at what Kelly was clearly going to say and find her tongue. "You'd take her *where*, Mr. Brown?"

Kelly kept shifting her gaze between Emma and Darren. "We're taking her home, right? That's what you said, bunny."

Ice water ran through Beth's veins. Fear raced roughshod over her with such intensity she almost doubled over in pain.

After jumping to his feet, Robert turned his back to Darren as though he could shield Emma exactly as Beth had wanted. He glared at Darren over his shoulder. "You're not taking my daughter anywhere."

Darren narrowed his eyes. "She's my daughter, and I can take her home if I damn well want to."

Rising, Alexis said, "Gentlemen, please." She strode between the two men. "Losing your tempers won't help the situation." She directed her gaze at Darren. "Mr. Brown, I understand your desire to be with your daughter—"

"She's m-my daughter," Robert muttered loud enough it was obvious he intended to be heard. His eyes fell on Beth. "I knew this was going to happen."

The accusatory tone hurt. Beth wanted to shout at him that it wasn't her fault and that he should settle down. Unfortunately, that would only aggravate the escalating situation. She knew Robert well enough to understand he was lashing out because he was hurting at the thought of losing Emma, exactly like she was. She could easily forgive him, but they had a bigger problem on their hands.

Alexis gave Robert a censuring look. "As I was saying…we sympathize with the situation you're in, Mr. Brown. However, we should all get a strong hand on our emotions and discuss both the legal ramifications of the DNA test results as well as what decisions are in Emma's best interests. I can guarantee you, those will be the only factors a judge and a guardian ad litem will consider."

Emma clung to Robert in a manner rivaling the most tenacious ivy. Her bottom lip quivered, making Beth reach for the diaper bag to fetch the blanket Emma dragged with her everywhere. Beth handed it to Emma, who snatched it out of her hands, held it against the side of her face, and stuck her thumb back in her mouth.

"That's really bad for her teeth, you know," Kelly scolded, sounding a lot like Betty Boop.

Beth wanted to snap back that it wasn't any of Kelly's business what Emma did or didn't do, but that might not be true. Kelly could very well become one of Emma's caregivers.

Tears threatened. Beth swallowed hard and forced them back. Her heart feared her worst nightmare was playing out right before her eyes and there was nothing she could do to stop it.

"Legally," Alexis said, "Emma must stay with the Ashfords. Beth was appointed her guardian and has control over all decisions where Emma is concerned."

Darren jumped to his feet. "That's bullshit!"

"No," Alex countered, "it's merely the law. I'm sure the Ashfords would be glad to have you come and visit Emma. I assure you, they don't want to keep you away from her, but they're the only family she's ever known. You can't expect—"

"I'll get a lawyer," Darren insisted, his face turning ruddier by the minute.

"You have every right to do so, but do you truly want to spend the kind of money it would take to wage a court battle over Emma?"

Darren scoffed. "I'll do what I have to do for my daughter. Money's no object."

"Just look at her." Alexis swept her hand toward where Robert held the baby against his chest, gently stroking her dark curls. "Do you want to put that innocent child in the middle of what could turn into an ugly tug-of-war?"

Moving to Darren's side, Kelly took his hand. Although she didn't say anything, there was a note of worry in her eyes, almost fear.

What did she—or Darren—have to hide?

"The Ashfords are quite willing to offer liberal visitation rights," Alexis assured.

Beth nodded, hoping Robert wouldn't ruin the progress Alexis might be making by contradicting her.

"They can visit. At our home," Robert insisted. "She's n-never out of our sight."

"Robert." Alexis put a gentle hand on his arm. "Please." She didn't need to say anything more. Robert had to understand the lawyer's plea for his silence. "Mr. Brown, we can assure you—"

"Don't bother!" Darren gripped Kelly's hand tight enough his knuckles whitened. "Your assurances obviously don't mean shit." He tossed his head in Robert's direction. "That man seems to think he needs to protect my daughter from her own father." His hand trembled as he stabbed his fingers through his hair;

then he put his hands on his hips. "If any of you think I'm just gonna walk away from my own kid, my own flesh and blood, you're fucking crazy. I'm going home and hiring a lawyer—the best shark I can afford. C'mon, Kel. We're getting outta here. I've got phone calls to make." He stomped out of the office just as Emma let out a shrill scream.

Kelly dropped Darren's hand and cautiously approached Robert. "Is she okay?"

When she reached out and patted Emma's back, Emma screamed again. "Bobber!"

She wanted her father, the only father she'd ever known, to protect her from a stranger.

Withdrawing her hand, Kelly sighed.

"Kel!" Darren shouted. "Now!"

She left without another word.

Silence reigned. Robert had calmed Emma simply by holding her close and rubbing her back.

The moments ticked by slowly until Alexis sighed, sat back down, and picked up her coffee cup. After taking a sip, she let out a rueful chuckle. "Gee, that went well."

God help her, Beth laughed.

Chapter 21

Robert gave up trying to get Beth to listen to him a couple hours after they got home.

The woman was a pro at giving someone the silent treatment. Although he'd trailed after her like a faithful puppy, apologizing, promising to hold his temper next time, and telling her how much he loved her, Beth had stoically gone about her chores. Feeding the family. Folding some laundry. Even emptying the dishwasher, which she'd probably done simply to get to him since it was normally his job.

Now she sat quietly rocking Emma to sleep, another task that usually fell to him. Robert didn't even consider stepping in. Beth probably needed to hold Emma. He understood because right now he wanted to hold his daughter close and never let her go.

He'd fucked up. Royally. Instead of letting his protective instincts prod him into antagonizing Darren Brown, he should've tried a little empathy. It was what his mother always told other kids whenever they'd teased him about his youthful stutter.

Put yourself in his shoes.

Robert hadn't even tried to understand Darren. For God's sake, the man just found out he'd fathered a child he hadn't even been told about. He'd already missed so much. Watching her birth. Hearing Emma's first cries. Seeing her open her eyes to a brand-new world. Choosing her name. Seeing her roll over or crawl for the first time. Her first word had been another man's name.

At that moment, he felt like the biggest jerk in the whole world.

No matter how much they wanted to keep Emma to themselves, he and Beth needed to realize that Darren was going to be a part of her life. Working together, they could make that a good thing. Two sets of adults to give her love and to watch over her as she grew.

Life nowadays was tough—tougher than it had been when he grew up. There were so many temptations being tossed into kids' paths. Easy sex. Drugs. Violence. They could turn Darren and Kelly into allies to help guide Emma through that obstacle course. Instead, Robert had all but turned them into enemies.

He had to fix this somehow.

With a heavy heart, he went to the bedroom, stripped down to his boxers and T-shirt, and stretched out on the bed. It seemed like forever until he was able to find something decent to watch on TV, and he grumbled to himself about how much he paid for satellite and how it sure wasn't worth it considering the shitty choices of programs. After settling on a sitcom he didn't care about, he waited for his wife to join him. Then they could finally talk.

Beth sitting on the side of the bed woke him, which came as a surprise. Since they'd begun sharing a bed, he had difficulty falling asleep unless he was pressed against her back or she was snuggled up to his side. Blinking the sleep from his eyes, he tried to gather his thoughts so they could address the fiasco that had been meeting Darren Brown. Every night, he held her in his arms and they shared the ups and downs of their day. He needed her.

"Hey, B." Robert flipped off the TV, dropped the remote on the nightstand, and held up the covers. "It's been a rough day. Why don't you turn out the light and come to bed?"

She sat there with her back to him and shook her head. It wasn't until he saw her shoulders shaking that he realized she was crying.

He immediately crawled across the mattress. When he sat beside her and tried to wrap his arms around her waist, she pushed him away. "B?"

"I warned you, Robert. Before we left, I *warned* you to keep your temper." Beth stood and started pacing.

Another nervous pacer. He'd never noticed that about her before. Or perhaps he'd just never seen her this upset.

"Darren was trying to be nice," she went on. "No wonder he wants a darn lawyer now. The poor guy probably feels like we're keeping him away from his own kid."

Unfortunately, that was exactly what Robert wanted to do, schmuck that he was. He loved Emma so much, and the notion of sharing her affections with Darren cut him to the bone. Sure it wasn't fair to the guy. But no matter how hard Robert tried to make himself feel bad about that, he couldn't.

Right now, though, he had a bigger problem. His wife looked mad enough to pick up something heavy and start beating him over the head with it. "I t-told you I was sorry."

Beth shot him a piercing glare. "Being sorry doesn't change anything. You know what he's probably doing right now?"

"I dunno... calling a lawyer?" He sounded like an idiot.

"Exactly. And he's going to do everything he flippin' can to take Emma away from us."

"Alexis said—"

"Alexis can say anything she wants, but she doesn't know Darren. I do. He's like a pit bull when he wants something. Look how he turned his life around to try to win Tiffany back. He went from nothing to a successful businessman. He's tenacious when he sets his mind to it. Thanks to you, he wants Emma."

"That's an awful lot to p-put on my shoulders," Robert insisted. "He wanted her before I lost my temper. Remember what Kelly said?"

"Like I could forget." Her sarcastic tone was a one-eighty from the Beth he knew. "They thought they'd waltz out of there with my daughter." She sniffed hard. "You didn't help one bit."

While all he wanted to do was gather her in his arms and soothe away the hurt, he couldn't. He was the one who'd ruffled her feathers. That anger, added to her fear for the future, probably meant he'd be sleeping on the couch tonight.

Then he realized exactly what was happening. A fight. They were having a fight, and Beth was still being polite and holding her tongue. Darn, not damn. Flippin', not fuckin'. It was so quaint and so...funny. No matter how hard he tried to push it down, a laugh slipped out.

Beth clenched her hands into fists and stared at him open-mouthed. "You're laughing about this?"

Holding up one hand, he put the other over his mouth, trying to stop himself from laughing again. It didn't work.

"You...you...jerk!" She stomped her foot.

"I'm t-trying to stop."

The fact that this was their first fight wasn't even that funny, but ever since he'd been a kid, he'd had this problem. If he tried to keep too tight a rein on his feelings, something would "set him off," as his mother used to say. He'd start laughing and simply couldn't stop himself, like some valve had been opened and couldn't be shut again until the pressure had been released.

Although he wanted to apologize, Robert couldn't catch his breath. He was laughing so hard his side hurt.

Beth stomped back to the bed, holding up her fists as though she was ready to deck him. Instead, she grabbed her pillow, tucked it under her arm, and stomped out of the bedroom. She slammed the door behind her.

* * *

"Jerk," Beth said as she pulled the fuzzy blanket over her. "Stupid butthole."

She'd bedded down in the soft chair she'd chosen when she'd decorated Emma's room. It was large enough that when Emma grew, she could still sit next to whoever was reading to her. At least it made a good makeshift bed. Beth had curled up on the chair sideways, drawing her knees up and leaning against the back. Although she was comfortable, there was no way she was going to be able to sleep. Not for a long time.

After punching her pillow again, she finally laid her head down. Thankfully Emma hadn't awakened when Beth slammed the master bedroom door. She hadn't even stirred when Beth came into the room, fumbling around to make herself a place to sleep. Emma slept peacefully, giving a sleepy sigh from time to time and looking like an absolute angel.

The guest room had a perfectly comfortable bed, but Beth had needed to see Emma before going to bed. Her gaze had settled on the big chair, and she'd curled up on it without another thought.

The fuzzy blanket that always lay over the chair offered more than enough warmth.

The only light came from the small night-light and the touch of moonlight that slid through the slats of the wooden blinds. The nursery had an ethereal glow, the toys looking as though they were various shades of gray and blue. Even Emma seemed supernatural in the low light.

Beth watched her daughter sleep, wondering if she could survive losing her. In a short time, Emma had permanently planted herself in Beth's heart. Her eyes filled with tears again, but she took a few deep breaths to banish them. Not only did she hate the idea of waking up Emma, but she wasn't one to wallow in self-pity.

But the reality of the situation refused to let up, weighing on her as though she were Atlas trying to hold up the whole stupid world. While she was sitting there, wondering whether Darren was going to swoop in like a thief and steal her daughter, where was Robert?

Laughing his butt off.

What exactly was so darn funny?

Anger accomplished what fear hadn't by making a few tears spill over her lashes. Her heart was wounded, but she couldn't seem to indulge in a cathartic cry. She flipped the pillow over to the cool side, punched it again because it felt good to do so, then laid her head back down. Closing her eyes, she let her exhaustion scatter her thoughts until Robert's face sabotaged them.

There wasn't any anger left in her, which was why she had an epiphany. Robert hadn't been laughing at their dire situation; he'd been laughing the same way Beth had been crying. Because he needed the release. She'd seen it before. Many times. Students who got the "giggle fits" for absolutely no reason. Heck, it had happened to her once or twice. Like at her great-aunt Agnes's funeral.

She and Tiffany had sat listening to the minister ramble on and on about Agnes's rather boring life. Their gazes connected, one of them sputtered, trying to hold in the building laugh, and then…boom. Two adolescent girls were laughing uncontrollably, gasping for breath and holding on to each other.

Everyone had stared at them until Carol snapped at them to go outside. They'd both been grounded for a month after that, and Carol had made them write apology notes to Agnes's daughter. That had been worse than being grounded.

Beth let out a heavy sigh. She should go back to bed. With her husband. About to toss the blanket aside and go to her own bed to tell Robert she forgave him, she heard the quiet footsteps. The mountain had come to Mohammad.

Robert crouched next to the chair. "You're s-still awake," he whispered.

"Yeah."

"I couldn't sleep, either." He put his hand on her leg and stroked gently. "I'm sorry, B. I d-didn't mean to laugh. I—"

"I know. I overreacted."

"I can't sleep without you."

"I was just coming back to bed," she admitted. "And I'm sorry, too."

She tossed the blanket off and stood. After handing him her pillow, she folded the blanket and put it on the chair's back. Then she took Robert's hand and led him back to the bedroom. Instead of crawling between the covers, she sat on the edge of the mattress and pulled him down beside her. She didn't let go of his hand.

"D-do you know what made me start laughing?" he asked, stroking the back of her hand with his thumb.

Beth shook her head.

"We were having our first fight."

"That made you laugh?"

"It just seemed so…absurd. Hell, B, we've known each other for so many years, but we've never had a fight before."

That statement made her think hard. Surely they'd quarreled over one of the houses they'd worked on together. Yet not a single argument came to mind. "You're right."

"It just struck me as weird that we've only been married a couple of weeks and we were already squabbling, but you still wouldn't cuss."

"Your sense of humor is bent, Robert."

"So I've been told more times than I can remember." He let out a heavy sigh. "We shouldn't be fighting. Not about this."

"Not about anything."

A rueful chuckle slipped out. "Two people living in the same house are bound to fight, B. That's inevitable. There'll be times, lots of times, you want to smack me just like you wanted to tonight. If you think we can be married and never quarrel, you're going to be disappointed."

Having grown up with parents who fought more often than most playground bullies, Beth nodded. She'd wanted to believe her marriage would be perfect, but even her optimism had its limits. Being optimistic was one thing; being naïve was something altogether different.

"But we shouldn't fight over this horrible, scary situation." Drawing her hand to his lips, Robert brushed a kiss against her knuckles. "When things get tough, we need to learn to depend on each other, to lean on each other. We shouldn't push the other away."

What he was saying made perfect sense. "We've both been on

our own for an awfully long time. Sometimes it's hard to remember that I don't have to do this alone."

"It's weird, isn't it? Having to always think about what someone else thinks?"

This time it was Beth who chuckled. *Weird* didn't even come close to describing how much different her life was now that Robert was in it. Everything was topsy-turvy, and although she often felt as though she were riding a whirlwind, she was exactly where she wanted to be. With her husband.

"B?"

"Yeah, honey. It's weird." The sadness of the day threatened again, bringing with it that fear she couldn't seem to escape. She leaned her head against Robert's shoulder. "I can't lose her."

He kissed the top of her head. "I know. I promise to be Mr. Nice Guy from n-now on. I promise you this, B. We're gonna do everything we can to keep her. I don't care how much it costs."

Chapter 22

You should be smiling, Beth!" Dani handed her a grape. "This is the last day we have to see kids. Then we get two months of freedom!"

"I know. I just..." Beth shrugged. She didn't want to turn into a whiner, but she couldn't stop thinking about Emma.

They hadn't heard a peep from Darren since that April meeting. Now it was the end of May, and all Beth could do was worry. Who in her right mind wouldn't be concerned with nothing to do except waiting for the bomb to drop?

Robert tried to keep her spirits up, and Alexis was doing everything she could to push their adoption petition forward, but Darren was the obstacle that kept anything from being permanently decided.

She tried a smile.

"You look like someone just told you your mother was in the office to see you," Dani teased.

"Gee, thanks, Dani." Beth took the grape and popped it in her mouth.

Mallory gave her a sympathetic look. "We just want to see you smile. I know things are rough."

"What's the latest gossip?" Jules said as she breezed into the room. After dropping her heavy purse on the floor, she set down a large brown bag. "Put away that healthy crap, Ladies. I brought gyros from Acropolis!"

"Wow!" Mallory opened the sack. "I can't imagine they're still warm after coming all the way from Greece."

"Smartass." Jules jerked a pile of napkins from the top of the bag, set them aside, and started passing out foil-wrapped sandwiches. As she set one in front of Beth, she said, "Heard anything yet?"

Beth shook her head and picked up a couple of the napkins. She and Robert had been playing their cards awfully close to their vests, but she needed to open up to her friends. Their love and support meant everything to her.

She told them what she knew as she spread out the napkins and opened up her lunch. "Alexis is trying to find out what's going on. Darren hired a real shark, or so Alexis calls him. Is that an insult to lawyers?"

Jules sat down and fiddled with her own sandwich. "Not an insult, per se. More of a comment on a lawyer's morality—or lack thereof."

Dani nodded. "It means they go for the win no matter what."

"Great," Beth grumbled.

"I don't think you need to worry," Mallory said. "Shark or not, there's nothing bad he could possibly say about you or Robert. You're great with Emma. She's so happy and so healthy. She's got a great home with two parents who love her. What's to criticize?"

"You make us sound like saints."

Dani spoke through a mouthful of gyro. "You're close."

"Aside from a few nights I've seen you tipsy," Jules said, "mind you I said *tipsy* not *drunk*, on strawberry daiquiris, I can't think of anything you've ever done that anyone could use against you."

Neither could Beth. Her life had been nothing but conformity. Following rules and doing what she was supposed to. So unlike her sister.

Although she'd never have told Tiffany, sometimes Beth admired her. Her baby sister wanted something, she went for it. Sure, she got in trouble. A lot. Yet there was no doubt she lived her short life to the fullest, and Tiffany was never one to have any regrets.

No, she left that for others. Like the bind she'd left her daughter in.

Beth had to be honest about one other thing. Tiffany might have done exactly what she wanted to do, but she often left heartache in her wake. What kind of conscience could she have had to care so little about the people she hurt as she grabbed what she wanted like some kid in a candy store?

The teachers at Douglas High often groaned whenever they heard one of the students saying, "YOLO." *You only live once.* The motto a lot of kids in this generation lived by, and one that was ruining society as far as Beth and her colleagues were concerned. Well, Tiffany had been the queen of YOLO, and she'd died not even knowing what a hornets' nest she'd stirred up. Unfortunately, the person who could suffer the most was Emma, the one person Tiffany should have protected.

"I'm not perfect," Beth muttered.

Dani laid her hand on Beth's arm. "No one's perfect, Beth. We just wanted to reassure you that no matter what Darren's lawyer tries to find, there's nothing he can use against you."

"Robert's every bit as squeaky clean," Jules said. "You two have nothing to worry about."

"Besides," Mallory added, "everyone in Cloverleaf is behind you two. And you know the Ladies are always in your corner. If there's anything we can do to help, we're there."

The door to the lounge opened and the principal, Jim Reinhardt, walked in, followed by a burly sheriff's deputy.

The deputy held folded papers with a blue jacket, and Beth's heart leapt into her throat. On every legal drama show she watched, anytime a character was served with a summons, it was exactly like this. She had no doubt Darren was finally making his move.

"Ladies," the principal said, "I'm sorry to bother your lunch, but this officer has something for Beth." He inclined his head toward her.

The officer strode over. "Are you Bethany Rogers Ashford, ma'am?"

She nodded before grumbling, "I'm too young to be a ma'am."

He held out the papers. "Consider yourself served." At least he had the decency to look a bit contrite when she let her eyes find his.

It was hard to be mad at the guy since he was only doing his job. With a trembling hand, she took the papers. She couldn't even find her voice to utter a polite "thank you."

Turning on his heel, the deputy left through the door the principal opened. Her boss looked back at Beth. "I'm sorry. I wouldn't have let him come up if he hadn't insisted."

"It's okay, Jim. It's not your fault." Besides, it really didn't matter where she was served with papers. The result was still the same. They would have to fight for Emma.

She stared at the folded papers, wondering if she should read them and try to make some sense of them. To her, reading legalese was akin to trying to decipher hieroglyphics.

"May I?" Jules asked, holding out her hand. "Connor and I have dealt with a lot of legal paperwork, and that's what you've got there."

Beth gave her a curt nod and handed them over as her cell signaled a text from Robert. The message wasn't at all surprising.

just got served papers. you?

Since she wasn't sure if he was with customers, she didn't call. She merely typed back *yes* and waited while Jules flipped through the pages.

And the verdict is…

"These are different than real estate papers, but from what I gather, Darren is seeking full custody of his daughter."

Beth hung her head. "Damn."

* * *

"Remember," Beth scolded. "Keep your temper."

Robert deserved the scolding, so all he did was nod. He wasn't sure why he needed the caution, considering they were going to talk to Alexis. Darren was nowhere near. If he were, Robert would need a whole lot more than scolding. He'd need someone to hold him back so he didn't put his fist right through the guy's face.

Empathy, Robert. Beth had said it a million times. It was just too damned hard to dredge up empathy for a man who was trying to take Emma away from them. After reading and rereading the papers, Robert was fairly sure Darren wasn't even offering them a crumb like visitation rights. He wanted Emma all to himself.

The door to Alexis's office opened. "Come in, come in."

Robert put his hand on the small of Beth's back, guiding her to the doorway. She hadn't said more than a dozen words all day, so lost in thought he wondered if she had lapsed into some kind of catatonia.

Despite the heart-to-heart talk about sharing the sorrows as well as the joys, Beth had pulled into herself and wouldn't lean on him. This was too much for her to handle alone. Hell, it was too much for *him* to handle alone. He needed her, but she was shutting herself off, keeping herself at a distance that made him worry not only about losing Emma but also about what would happen to his marriage if they lost their daughter.

The assistant had followed them into the office. She hovered near the chairs where he and Beth had sat. "May I get you some coffee? Water?"

"No, thanks," Robert said, looking to his wife.

She merely shook her head.

As efficient as ever, the assistant shut the door behind her when she left.

"So," Alexis began, "it's worst-case scenario. Darren Brown wants Emma to himself and to cut you two out of her life. Now, what I'm here to tell you is that he's not going to get everything he wants. Not when I'm on your side."

"What can we do to help?" Beth asked, her voice tremulous.

"Right now, just be honest with me," Alexis replied. "I need to know anything and everything that their private investigator can turn up."

"They've got a PI?" Robert shook his head. "Where'd Darren get that kind of money? Is he selling drugs?"

Beth let out a low hiss. "Stop it."

"Yes, Robert," Alexis continued, "he's got a PI. Trust me, he can afford one. His business is very successful. I prefer not to spend your hard-earned money, at least not until after depositions. And only then if something comes up fishy. Something looks promising, I might hire one to take a deeper look."

"Depositions?" Beth asked.

"Questions under oath," Alexis replied. "Which, by the way, are scheduled for next week. You're off school now?"

Beth nodded.

"Then you and Robert can finish before Darren arrives. I'm going to depose Kelly as well since they're getting married in a few weeks. Although..." After opening the green file, Alexis plucked out a paper and set it aside. "According to his attorney, Darren isn't going to add Kelly to the petition. Seems a bit odd."

It did to Robert, too. Why would Darren not want to share his daughter with his wife? Or was it because Kelly didn't want to be a mother to Emma? Either way boded ill for Emma's future.

At least there was one big thing on their side. Beth. "Good luck to them trying to dig something bad up on Bethany. She's as pure as the driven snow." He gave her a smile she didn't return.

Folding her hands and setting them on the desk, Alexis leveled a hard stare at Robert. "And what about you? Anything you've tucked back deep in your own closet that you forgot about?"

"He smoked pot," Beth blurted out.

Alexis picked up a pen and dutifully noted it on the notebook that always rested to her right.

"Now wait a minute," Robert protested. "It was only a few times. They'll never even know about it anyway. Shit, I was just a kid."

"You'd be amazed what a good investigator can uncover." Alexis's gaze shifted to Beth. "Any drug use in your history?"

"Not me," Beth replied. "But Darren used drugs. A lot, if I remember right."

Alexis nodded as she set her pen aside and fished around in the green folder again. "His juvenile arrest record shows that clearly, but I'm not sure whether it will help us."

"Why the hell not?" Robert asked. "Shows he's a user."

"It all depends on how you look at it. A judge could see that his adult record's clean and see Darren as a man who has matured and learned from his juvenile mistakes. He turned his life around to become a success. Rags to riches."

He couldn't believe what he was hearing. This should've been a slam dunk. He and Beth had made a great home for Emma, and Tiffany wanted Beth to raise her daughter. The girl was thriving. Why did a stupid DNA test have to change everything?

Robert couldn't help but point out another of Darren's sins. "He knocked up Kelly. Just like he did Tiffany. He's reckless."

Once again, Alexis countered. "He and Kelly are going to marry. His lawyer will argue that he would've married Tiffany if she hadn't concealed the pregnancy from him."

"What is Kelly anyway?" Beth asked. "Nineteen?"

"Twenty-three."

Beth's mouth dropped open. "Seriously?"

This smile was the first Alexis had offered that day. "Seriously. That voice, right?"

"Yeah," Beth said, the corners of her mouth hesitantly forming a grin. "That voice."

The lawyer's features sobered. "Now, here's where I'm brutally honest with you. I'll move heaven and earth to help you keep

Emma home, but you need to understand that our chances are fifty-fifty at best."

"Why so bad?" Robert reached for Beth's hand. It was cold as ice.

"I was hoping we could make a good argument that Tiffany wanted Emma with Beth and that the two of you have given her an excellent home. But Darren is turning out to be a decent human being, not the type of father judges would refuse rights to his own daughter. He's got biology on his side. You're going to have to resign yourself to one big truth."

Robert's gut tightened. "And that truth is?"

"Whether you like it or not, Darren Brown is going to be a part of Emma's life."

Chapter 23

The courtroom was much smaller than the one she and Robert had been married in. Beth hoped the cozier atmosphere, one less austere and foreboding, might mean good things for today's outcome.

Heck with it. Now she was grasping at straws.

Today, they faced the family court judge, the woman who would decide for now where Emma would live. The best she and Robert could hope was that Emma would remain in their custody while the judge considered Darren's suit for paternal custody and the adoption petition she and Robert had filed.

Only a couple of weeks had passed since the depositions. Darren's lawyer had been able to get a fast hearing, too fast for Beth to prepare herself. Alexis told them not to worry. The judge was most likely going to keep things status quo. Emma would remain with them, but Darren would get some kind of visitation.

Beth had resigned herself to Emma spending time with Darren. Alexis had prepared them well, and the day she'd told them to accept him in Emma's life, Beth had done just that. Emma was his biological daughter. He deserved to get to know her, to be there as she grew up, and to learn to love her. Beth's only anguish over the scenario was that she wanted him to do all that only once a month. Unfair, she supposed. Her heart didn't care. Emma belonged in her home, with her Matka and Bobber.

Darren, dressed in an impeccable suit, came into the courtroom. Following right behind was a heavyset man in a well-tailored charcoal suit. The man guided Darren to the table on the right side of the judge's bench.

Robert took her hand, but Beth found little comfort from his touch. His frown told her he knew she'd been pulling away. The problem was that she didn't know how to stop herself. Ever since they'd sat in Alexis's office, hearing how their shot at keeping Emma was fifty-fifty, Beth had felt as if she were a tiny rowboat tossed into a roiling sea. There was nothing to ground her, and all she could see for miles and miles ahead were rough waters.

Her husband should've been her anchor in the storm. Instead of leaning on him, holding tight, and letting his strength help her, she'd taken a step back. And then another. They hadn't made love in days, and she'd started snapping at him whenever he left things around the house.

This morning, she'd been so sad about the court hearing, she'd barely been able to force herself out of bed to take a shower and get dressed. If she hadn't been concerned the judge would be assessing her appearance, she wouldn't even have bothered with makeup.

As if putting on mascara would keep the judge from yanking Emma right out of her arms…

Alexis strode into the courtroom, a gray leather bag slung over her shoulder. Instead of her normally flamboyant shirts and skirts, she wore a dark blue business jacket with a pencil skirt.

Only the silver jewelry, especially the geometric earrings, displayed her outgoing personality.

She set her bag on the left table and signaled Beth and Robert to join her.

Beth's joints locked. Even with Robert tugging at her, she couldn't make herself stand up and go to the table. If she did, that meant the hearing would begin. As long as she sat on her butt, nothing would change.

She needed to hold Emma, but her daughter was playing with Jules's twins today. This wasn't the place for her, and as sensitive as she was, no doubt she would pick up on all the tension.

"B?" Robert stared down at her with gathered brows. "Alexis wants us. The hearing's gonna start soon."

Letting her gaze shift to Darren, Beth wondered why he'd come without Kelly. As though he knew he was being watched, his eyes found hers. For a few seconds, she saw the young man she'd known, the one who'd been out to have a good time and just enjoy life. Then he scowled, and what she saw was the determined man, the one who'd scraped together every dime he had to buy himself a restaurant in hopes of impressing Tiffany—the woman who'd lied to him and kept him from his daughter.

Beth glanced away, willing herself to stand.

Robert led her to the table, pulled out a chair for her, then took a seat beside her.

Alexis busied herself with fishing things out of her bag, but the grim look on her face said it all. After she took a seat, she finally turned to Beth. "Are you ready?"

No. "Yeah."

"Robert? Are you ready?"

He tossed her a terse nod.

"All rise," the bailiff barked as the door to the judge's office opened.

Although Alexis had told them the judge was a woman, Beth had erroneously pictured a Judge Judy clone. Instead, she got Jessica Lange. Tall and svelte, she'd swept her blond/gray hair into a severe bun. Her wise blue eyes were framed in laugh lines, but the beauty was still there. She carried a stack of manila folders under her arm, and the tortoise-shell glasses hanging from a gold chain around her neck bounced against her chest.

The judge sat behind the bench, prompting the bailiff to announce, "Please be seated."

After what Beth assumed were perfunctory parts of any hearing, such as swearing everyone in, they all sat at their tables, waiting to hear from Judge Alicia Ramsey.

Judge Ramsey put her glasses on and read from the file for a moment. "I see both the adoption and custody petitions have been joined for this proceeding. I'll hear from the minor's aunt and uncle first."

Alexis rose, smoothing her hands down the front of her skirt. "Thank you, Your Honor."

Beth lost herself in listening to the story of how Emma came to be with her and Robert. What great parents they were. The home they'd given her. Their plans for the money left by Tiffany's insurance policies. How much they both loved her.

"And so, Your Honor, I submit that the Ashfords have given the minor a stable home, the first one she's ever known. While we acknowledge that Mr. Brown is the minor's biological father, and will be happy to grant liberal visitation rights, the court should consider what's in the best interests of this child and grant the petition for adoption. No child should be taken from her loving home and dropped into a world of strangers.

Imagine the damage to her happiness and sense of trust. Please leave her where she belongs, with the woman the minor's biological mother chose, and with the couple committed to making a good life for her." With an incline of her head, she finished with, "We thank Your Honor for her time."

The judge nodded and took several notes. A leftie, she scribbled on an old-fashioned yellow legal pad. "I have a few questions for the petitioners before we proceed. Mrs. Ashford?"

Alexis tugged on Beth's elbow until she stood at her side. "Yes, ma'am?"

"Mrs. Ashford, I see you're a teacher."

Not sure if that was a question or a statement, Beth replied, "Yes, ma'am."

"Who cares for the minor during the school year while you're working?"

"My husband is with her a great deal of the time, and his sister runs a limited day care. She watches Emma, um, *the minor* when we're not with her."

"You married Mr. Ashford only this April?"

Beth nodded.

A woman in a blue cardigan who sat at the judge's right whispered something to the judge. She gave a nod in reply. "Please state your answer for the record, Mrs. Ashford."

"Yes, ma'am. We married in April."

"To strengthen the adoption petition or did you have plans to marry before the minor became your ward?" The judge looked over the rims of her glasses.

Beth had a flashback to her fourth-grade teacher, a somber woman who used to try to intimidate the students by glaring at them over reading glasses much like the judge's. Since she was under oath, Beth replied, "We only married to strengthen the petition."

* * *

Robert winced. His fear from the beginning of the relationship had always been that Beth didn't need him the way he needed her. It shouldn't hurt to hear her state the truth. But it did. She hadn't married him for love or desire. Just for Emma.

Perhaps the same had been true for him in the beginning, but it wasn't any longer. Beth was his wife, so much a part of him that even the thought of losing her felt like a knife to the gut. Now that they faced losing Emma, he couldn't tamp down his fear that if his daughter left, so would his wife.

Sure, she said she loved him. He just couldn't make himself stop thinking that a woman as special as Beth could do so much better than a middle-aged guy who stuttered.

The judge's voice pierced his thoughts. "Mr. Ashford?"

Robert rose as Beth took her seat. "Yes, Your Honor?"

"Did you marry Mrs. Ashford merely to strengthen the petition for adoption?"

Beth's gaze captured his, but he looked away. If he was going to say this, he needed to shield himself from her stare. "I w-wanted to be Emma's d-dad." He swallowed hard, trying to slow down so his stutter would be under better control, but before he could tell the judge how he'd wanted to be with Beth for the longest time, Judge Ramsey shifted her attention to Darren Brown.

Fearing she'd think he was rude if he interrupted, Robert sat back down. He'd have a chance later, maybe in someplace more private, to let Beth know everything that was in his heart. She had to understand that Emma or no Emma, he needed her. He loved her. He intended to spend the rest of his life with her.

"Mr. Brown, I understand you're engaged to be married?"

Darren rose. "Yes, ma'am."

"I'll admit I'm curious as to the reason your fiancée isn't also petitioning."

Darren's lawyer rose. A man in his late fifties, he looked very relaxed and in control. "Your Honor, Mr. Brown would like to keep his petition as uncomplicated as possible for the court. Since he and Ms. Dalton will marry shortly, there was no need for her to be added. She will become the minor's mother upon marriage."

Beth fumbled for Robert's hand, and he laced his fingers with hers. She trembled, but it would probably be against decorum for him to drape his arm over her shoulders while they were in court. He tried to will some strength her way, knowing it had to hurt her to hear Kelly being called Emma's "mother." Beth already filled that role quite well, and Robert wished he could tell the court so.

Alexis had sat when Robert did, but she jumped to her feet again. "Your Honor, we have some information about Ms. Dalton we'd like to share with the court."

"I object," Darren's lawyer said. "Ms. Dalton isn't a part of this proceeding, and any information about her is irrelevant."

"I beg to differ with Mr. Lindstrom, Your Honor," Alexis said. "Ms. Dalton might not be a part of the petition, but she *will* have an impact on the minor's well-being."

Judge Ramsey frowned before nodding. "I'd like to hear what Ms. Comer has to say."

"Your Honor, I—"

"Mr. Lindstrom, I've made my ruling quite clear. Ms. Comer?"

Alexis's smug smile came as a surprise. What did she know that she hadn't told him or Beth?

"While we understand that Mr. Brown has a biological tie to the minor," Alexis said, "we have some concerns about him marrying Ms. Dalton, considering her employment."

The judge flipped her hand as though impatient for the other shoe to drop.

"Ms. Dalton works at the Black Stiletto, a gentleman's club. I believe she was employed as a stripper—"

"Exotic dancer," Mr. Lindstrom interjected.

Alexis gave him a chilling smile. "My sincere apologies. She was an *exotic dancer* and now that she's expecting Mr. Brown's child, she waits tables. As far as I've been able to determine, she has plans to go back to her, um, dancing career after the birth."

No wonder Darren hadn't wanted Kelly to be part of the petition.

Lindstrom swept his jacket aside and set his hands against his hips. "If we're lowering ourselves to slinging mud, then what about Mr. Ashford's history of drug use?"

Beth gasped and snatched her hand back. She faced him, wide-eyed, as her cheeks reddened.

"Your Honor," Alexi said, sounding disgusted, "Mr. Ashford doesn't have, as Mr. Lindstrom so tactlessly phrased it, a history of drug use. We freely admitted in deposition that Mr. Ashford made the mistake of socially using marijuana when he was a member of his fraternity in college. To compare that with Ms. Comer's stripping naked for men to ogle and stuff bills down her crotch—"

Lindstrom interrupted. "And what about CPS being called in when Mr. Ashford injured the minor? She had to be rushed to the ER and—"

The judge grabbed her gavel and banged it hard against a wooden block. "That's enough hyperbole from both of you. This is only a preliminary hearing, and to see you sink to the level of slander..." She shook her head. "I won't have it my courtroom."

Both lawyers uttered apologies that didn't sound at all sincere.

After several moments of the judge shifting through and reading papers from the file, she finally folded her hands and rested them on top of the paperwork. "I'm ready to make my decision on temporary custody of the minor."

Chapter 24

Beth shoved a few more of Emma's clean outfits into the duffel. At the rate she kept adding things, she'd never be able to zip the bag closed. How much did a one-year-old need to spend a week with her biological father and his stripper girlfriend?

An unkind thought, but Beth honestly didn't care. She glanced over to where Emma slept in her playpen, wondering if the baby would awaken if she picked her up and rocked her. Right now, she wanted to hold tight and never let go.

"Beth?" Dani's voice echoed from the foyer. "We're here."

"In the family room," Beth replied, not even softening her voice. If Emma woke up, so be it. Then she wouldn't have to feel guilty about picking her up.

Dani and Mallory strolled into the room, dressed in their comfortable and rather skintight yoga clothes. Beth had blown off yoga today. Hard to relax and stretch when her life had just been turned upside down.

Mallory flopped into Robert's recliner. "We missed you at class."

"Derrick led us," Dani added, sitting on the sofa and giving a quizzical look at the small piles of clothes. "I swear all I want to do is watch him instead of participating in class."

"That ass is sublime," Mallory drawled. "It's just begging to be squeezed."

Beth just snorted at their banter, wishing all she had to worry about was how cute their yoga instructor's butt was in tight pants.

Dani's eyes wandered the room. "What's with all the baby clothes? Did you hit some yard sales?" She gave the air a delicate sniff. "The whole house smells like Downy, so I assume you just did laundry."

What was obviously Dani's attempt to get Beth to laugh fell flat. There was nothing in the whole world that could make her happy at that moment.

"We heard from the judge," Beth replied, her tone flat despite her roiling emotions.

Mallory gasped and scrambled to her feet. "You didn't tell us!"

"Yeah, well...you were both at yoga and Jules was with clients. Figured your phones were off." She shrugged. "You were all coming for lunch anyway."

Lunch. Since she'd been so busy packing, she wouldn't be able to offer them anything more than cold-cut sandwiches and salad. As frazzled as she was, if she tried to cook something she'd probably burn the house to the ground.

"Beth? Mal? Dani?" Jules had arrived.

"In here," Beth called. Part of her wanted the Ladies to leave her alone to mourn in peace; another wanted them to hold her hand and tell her everything would be all right.

But that would be a lie. Beth might be packing for Emma to visit Darren for a week, but she knew things had changed permanently. Soon she'd be sending her daughter to live with him forever.

She sniffed hard, willing herself to stay strong and not give in to the urge to wail like a banshee at the unfairness of things. Life wasn't fair, and she'd been nothing but an utter fool to always think things turned out for the best, that everything happened for a good reason. How could losing Emma ever be "for the best"? What "good reason" could steal a baby from her home?

"Well?" Jules said. "What's the skinny? Other than Mallory?" She tossed her friend a wink.

"The judge made her ruling today," Dani answered.

"Today?" Jules asked. "I thought she was going to rule Friday. Don't you have another court date?"

"Not anymore," Beth mumbled, mostly to herself.

Jules put her hands on her hips. "So is anyone going to tell me what she said? Or are we going to play Twenty Questions?"

"We're still waiting for Beth to tell us," Mallory replied. Then she inclined her head at the stuffed duffel. "Although I think the fact that she's packing says it all."

Beth stopped shoving Emma's clothes into the duffel and let her shoulders droop. "Since Darren's new baby is due in two weeks, Judge Ramsey said he should have this week to spend with Emma."

"What's that supposed to mean?" Dani asked. "That she's only vacationing with him for a week and then she's coming home?"

Beth shrugged. "Alexis says it's only a temporary measure. After the week's over, the judge will schedule us all back in court again for another hearing."

Mallory folded her arms under her breasts and drummed her fingers on her bicep. "Is that good or bad news?"

All Beth did was shrug again, zip the duffel, and toss it next to the tote full of Emma's favorite toys.

Dani went to her and put her arm over Beth's shoulders. "We're here, Beth."

"I know. I just..." The words to explain her fear about giving Emma into Darren's care wouldn't come. Once he had her, he'd probably never give her back. Court or no court.

"You're worried," Dani said. "Totally understandable."

"You haven't lost her for good," Jules added. "This is just a visit. Right?"

"That's what Alexis said," Beth replied. "One week with Darren, then back to us." But she knew better. The simple fact that the judge pushed for this extended visit so darn quick spoke volumes.

Darren would eventually be granted full parental rights, and she and Robert would be demoted to the aunt and uncle who only got to see Emma from time to time.

Mallory looked around before knitting her brows. "Where's Robert?"

"Tracy Barrett's in town," Jules replied before Beth could. "The closing on the house Robert built for her is tomorrow, so he's doing the final walk-through with her and Connor."

The house was Robert's masterpiece—a true mansion. Cloverleaf's first. The CEO of Barrett Foods was in the process of building a new manufacturing plant close to town, and Jules and Connor had chatted Robert up to Tracy to help her build the kind of home she wanted but could never find in a town the size of Cloverleaf.

Beth had chosen all the fixtures based on pictures Tracy and Jules e-mailed her. She was very proud of how it had turned out, but her heart was too heavy to even care what Tracy thought when she saw the place. Nothing mattered except holding herself together until Beth could surrender her daughter to Darren later that afternoon.

"He should be here," Mallory said.

Beth shook her head. "This is too important to blow off. Tracy has sent him a lot of work."

"She not only hired him for her house," Jules added, "but he's building several for her executives as well."

Business had picked up considerably with the warmth of May, and Robert sometimes worked sixty hours a week now. That hadn't been a problem since Beth was on summer break. They'd even talked about her taking a year off to just be with Emma while she was still a baby. Money wasn't a problem, something they'd hoped would strengthen their adoption petition.

None of it mattered now. They'd see Emma a couple of weekends a month for a while. Then she'd have friends and activities, and she'd eventually realize she didn't have enough time for Aunt Beth and Uncle Robert. Just like Robert would have less and less time for Beth once the child he'd considered his daughter was no longer a part of their lives. Maybe he was already pulling back by working so many hours a week.

His own words condemned their marriage. He'd stated in open court that he'd only married her to help with Emma's adoption. Once Emma was gone, the marriage would end. Beth wasn't about to hold Robert to a commitment he'd made for all the wrong reasons. No, she would set him free. Even if it tore her heart out. Words of love uttered in the heat of the moment didn't hold anywhere near the weight of those spoken under oath in a courtroom.

She'd been honest with the judge when she'd said they'd

married to strengthen the adoption petition. Had the judge questioned her further, Beth would have acknowledged that she'd loved Robert for the longest time. But she'd never had the opportunity.

The normally optimistic Beth would've thought that her husband might have had the same problem—being constrained by the limited amount of time to answer the judge's questions. But all her optimism had evaporated.

"Beth, stop." Dani squeezed her shoulders. "I can see how much this is killing you, but you've got to try to look on the bright side."

Anger rose up inside Beth, and she lashed out. Jerking out of Dani's hold, she leveled a hard glare at her friends. "Bright side? Where is the fucking *bright side* here? He's taking my daughter and there's not a damn thing I can do about it!"

Emma woke with a start. She sat up and blinked a few times before her bottom lip began to quiver.

Beth scooped her daughter into her arms. "I'm going to change her diaper and get her ready to go now." She didn't want to order the Ladies out of her house, but she hoped they'd get the hint when she stomped up the stairs to Emma's room.

* * *

Robert sat in Alexis's waiting room for what seemed like the millionth time. So much time spent hoping they could truly make Emma their daughter. All of it wasted.

Beth was supposed to be bringing Emma here to hand her over to Darren. Despite the constant mental reminders that Emma would only be gone a week, Robert was having problems controlling his panic. He was responsible for Emma's safety and well-being. Turning those jobs over to someone else made his stomach lurch.

Emma needed him, just as much as he needed her.

And what about Beth? How devastated would she be to lose her daughter, the only part of her dead sister she could hold on to?

Alexis hadn't arrived yet. Her assistant had offered him a drink, but after he'd snapped at her, she'd retreated to her desk and stayed quite busy. He couldn't blame her. He'd been an ogre. Hearing Beth's voice in his head, scolding him, he'd offered her a muttered apology. From the lack of reaction, the woman hadn't even heard him.

After checking his watch yet again, he let out a weighty sigh. Although Tracy had been very pleased with the way her house turned out, Robert hadn't taken the time to absorb her praise. Once Beth had called to tell him about the judge's unusual ruling, he'd been obsessed with getting to her and Emma.

The outer door opened, and Alexis strolled in. "Robert," she said with a nod. "I'd say it's good to see you, but I'm afraid you'd see right through me. C'mon into my office." She handed her bag to her assistant. "Please transfer the Hart deposition into his file. It's on the pin drive."

"Yes, ma'am," the assistant replied.

Robert followed Alexis into her office, sitting himself down on one of the client chairs opposite her desk. She slipped behind the desk and plopped onto her chair.

"Beth's on her way," he said, hating the silence. The only thing that had been missing to make the wait sheer torture was a loud clock ticking away the seconds.

"Good. I checked my voice mail after I parked my car. Darren and Kelly should be here soon as well."

Since she seemed to be in a talkative mood, he couldn't help but ask the question that had bugged him from the moment Beth called. "Why?"

Alexis cocked her head. "Why what? Why this sudden visitation?"

He nodded.

"To be honest, I haven't the faintest idea. The timing seems... odd. But I learned a long time ago Judge Ramsey has a method to her madness. I just haven't figured out what she's trying to accomplish with this particular bout of insanity."

The door to the office opened, and Beth came in. Emma was awake. When her gaze caught Robert's, she started squirming and reaching for him. "Bobber! Want Bobber!"

Robert stood and reached for her when Beth came to him. "Hey, squirt." It felt damned good to hold her. How was he ever going to find the strength to surrender his daughter to Darren Brown?

"Alexis," Beth began, "I don't understand this at all. What exactly did the judge say?"

"When I talked to her, she seemed to think Darren would have his hands full when Kelly delivers. She said that Emma deserved to spend some time getting to know her biological father without him having to spend an inordinate amount of time with his newborn." With a sigh, Alexis added, "I'll be honest with you both. I've never heard of a ruling like this before, especially when Judge Ramsey didn't so much as hint about what she's decided about permanent custody."

Shifting Emma to his hip, Robert shook his head. "You're wrong. I think she spoke loud and clear about this. She's giving all consideration to Darren and none to us."

"Not necessarily," Alexis countered. "She told me she needs

more time and a chance to hear from the CPS home investigator before she'll decide anything permanent."

"CPS was at our place days ago," Beth said, passing Emma's blanket to Robert. "They haven't been to Darren's yet?"

Alexis shook her head. "They'll go sometime in the week Emma's in his care. They need to see the environment he's providing for her and how they interact with each other. Then they'll file both reports with Judge Ramsey."

Robert focused on soothing his girls. Emma was clingy today, not a surprise considering the tension in the room. Beth, on the other hand, seemed as cold and stiff as a block of ice.

Keeping a steady arm around Emma, he tried to drape his other arm across his wife's shoulder, but she shrugged him away, as if his touch bothered her instead of strengthened her. While he wanted to whisper words of comfort, he had none. They were both hurting and should be leaning on each other. Instead, their new rift grew by the minute. So did his frustration. And his anger at the way his wife was shutting him out.

"I'm s-sick of that bastard," Robert said, his voice rising with his emotions. "Absolutely sick. I wish we could stop all this n-nonsense and raise our daughter in peace."

* * *

Beth frowned at Robert. Couldn't he see the anger in his voice was disturbing Emma?

This situation wasn't any easier on her than it was on him, but she hadn't been reduced to shouting every word. Alexis wasn't to blame for this, and she didn't deserve his disdain. "Stop it," Beth scolded.

His eyes narrowed at her. "Stop what? Trying to keep my

daughter with me?" He tossed his head at the duffel she'd dropped on the floor. "Looks to me like you're already rolling over and playing dead. Hell, you've sent enough for her to m-move permanently instead of a week."

Clenching her hands into fists, she refused to let him yell at her just because he was upset. "I sent enough in case they don't have a washer or dryer. I didn't want them to have to go to a Laundromat for Emma. I'll wash her stuff when she gets home." The fact that he didn't even look contrite made her angrier. "I don't want her to go, either. But you don't hear me screaming at Alexis as if this is her fault."

"I wasn't screaming."

"Beth. Robert." Alexis gestured to the chairs. "Why don't you both have a seat and calm down?" She pulled her chair closer to her desk and folded her hands, resting them on the glass surface. "I know how hard this is on both of you. You know I'll do everything I can to maximize your time with Emma, and I still have some hope that Judge Ramsey might put her with you as guardians. But for Emma's sake, you can't take out your hurt and anger on each other—or on Darren when he arrives. We need to keep things civil."

Beth nodded, although she wasn't surprised that all Robert did was growl.

The door to the office opened, and Alexis's assistant led Darren Brown inside.

"Mr. Brown." Alexis stood and strode to greet him with a handshake. "Isn't Kelly with you?"

"She's waiting at home." He shifted his gaze to Emma. "Is she ready to go?"

"Her car seat's in my car," Beth said. "I can go get—"

"I've already got one."

Beth lifted the heavy duffel. "I packed a lot of clothes. You don't need to worry about washing anything. Just send them home with her next week and—"

"My maid can handle her laundry. I've got this."

Why was he being such a jerk? "I really don't mind. She tends to get a rash if you use—"

"I said I can handle it." Darren strode to Robert. "Give me my daughter."

Emma was gripping her blanket with one hand and sucking on her thumb. Until Darren reached for her. Then she let out a shrill scream, dropped the blanket, and started squirming against Robert as though climbing him like a tree. "No!"

"C'mon, Emma," Darren coaxed, finally easing his rough tone. "Come with Daddy."

Hearing Darren call himself that was as dissonant as nails dragged down a chalkboard.

Emma had developed a rather severe stranger anxiety, and the harder Darren tried to grab her, the more she clung to Robert. It wasn't as if Robert was making it any easier for Darren, but Beth couldn't fault him for his need to protect her.

"Are you going to give her to me?" Darren asked Robert. "Or do we have to play tug-of-war for her?"

Eyes brimming with tears, Robert gently pried Emma's chubby fingers from his shirt. As he helped guide her into Darren's arms, he swallowed hard.

"Bobber!" Emma screamed as Darren held tight and snatched up her duffel. "Want Bobber!"

Robert put his hand over his eyes and turned his back.

Emma's panicked eyes caught Beth's. "Matka! Want Matka!"

"Em…" Beth took a step closer. "Come to Mat—"

"No!" Darren ordered. "You'll just make it harder." He

stomped to the door, which suddenly opened. The assistant, no doubt. "She'll be fine once you're both out of sight." And then he stepped out of the office.

Emma's voice rang loud and clear one last time. "Want Matka!"

Chapter 25

Beth was getting sick and tired of Robert staring at her as if he thought she was about to explode, especially since he was the one more likely to blow up. All she felt was numb. Resigned. Dead.

They'd barely said a word since they got home, which was probably a good thing. Their emotions were running high, and words spoken in anger would be more destructive than constructive. Perhaps withdrawing was how Robert handled rough situations. Even though they were married, they really didn't know each other well at all.

She put the supper dishes in the dishwasher after she'd packed away the remaining food. She'd only picked at the stuff they'd bought at the Chicken Shack. Their extra-crunchy chicken tenders were one of her favorite guilty pleasures, but nothing she tried to eat had any taste tonight. That, and her stomach was tied in nervous knots as she worried about Emma. If she ate anything, she'd probably just throw it right back up.

Her daughter's screams still echoed in Beth's mind. A remorseful chuckle slipped out at the thought that Emma had finally called her *Matka*, but it had been on the worst day of Beth's life. A hollow victory at best.

Robert grabbed a beer and then shut the refrigerator door. He popped the cap off the longneck bottle and took a pull of his Budweiser as he rested his shoulder against the fridge and just watched her.

After drying her hands, Beth set the dishtowel aside and turned to face him, folding her arms over her chest and leaning back against the counter. His close scrutiny made her uncomfortable, so she stared at the floor. Seconds clicked by with agonizing slowness.

Had it only been a couple of hours since they'd lost Emma? Seemed like years.

"I'm sure she's fine," Robert said before taking another swig of his beer.

Beth just nodded, although she wasn't sure of anything, especially whether Emma had eaten a decent supper, or if someone was checking her diaper, or if she'd even stopped crying yet. Would Darren or Kelly know how to comfort her? Would Emma even allow herself to be comforted? She hated strangers, and despite the biological connection that had let Darren take Emma away, that's all the two of them were to that beautiful little girl. Strangers.

An elephant stood between Beth and Robert in the gorgeous kitchen they'd designed together. Since he wasn't mentioning the obvious, she wouldn't, either. But ignoring it wasn't going to make the agony disappear. The fact they had absolutely nothing to say to each other now proved what Beth had feared all along. Without Emma, there was no marriage.

"If you don't need me, um, I was going to go out with B-Ben tonight," Robert said. "We want to see if Charlie Barker's got anything n-new this week."

Charlie Barker. Cloverleaf's guru of resale. Robert and Ben relied on Charlie to supply hard-to-find items, everything from claw-foot bathtubs to antique chandeliers. The man scoured everything from estate sales to junkyards to find items that builders and contractors could use. Buying stuff from Charlie had saved Ashford Homes a lot of money, and Robert relied on him. Besides, going to his place was probably a great excuse for Robert to get away from the overwhelming tension of the day.

But she needed Robert. Here. Now. How could he not know that? Or did he assume she wanted to be alone because he did, because he didn't need her?

If she kept thinking this hard, her tension headache was going to bloom into a full-blown migraine.

Beth had never felt more alone in her whole life. If she admitted exactly how much she wanted him to hold her right now, she'd be baring her soul to a man who'd already put one foot out the door. Unable to speak without revealing her churning emotions, she simply nodded.

"We'll probably grab some w-wings after." He dragged his toes across the tile floor, looking like a little boy asking his mother for permission. "If that's okay with you..."

Heck with that. She wasn't about to start bossing him around. Or begging for him to love her. He wanted to escape the nightmare for a while, fine. She'd bear it all alone. "Go."

"You're sure, B? You don't need me to stay or anything?" Robert pushed away from the fridge and took a couple of tentative steps toward her, like a hunter trying not to spook his prey.

What she wanted was for him to quit hesitating, gather her into his arms, and tell her he loved her as much as she loved him. That if Emma was gone forever, he'd still love her and still want her to be his wife. Instead, she heard his voice from back in the courtroom, saying something much, much different.

I w-wanted to be Emma's d-dad.

"Go see what Charlie's dug up," she forced out before coughing to cover the way her voice broke.

She wasn't going to cry. Not in front of Robert. No way would she manipulate him like that. Guilt wasn't a good foundation for a relationship. A marriage needed love.

Oh, who was she trying to fool? This marriage had no foundation. It had come about as a way for her to keep Emma close and for Robert to fulfill some weird midlife crisis. He'd wanted to be a father, not a husband. If what she feared became reality, if Emma was given to Darren permanently, Beth wouldn't hold him to his marital vows. He deserved better than a union kept together by pity.

"Okay, then." He put the mostly full bottle down next to the sink. "You sure you d-don't mind?"

She shook her head. "I'm just going to read." One thing she wasn't able to fake was a smile, not as depressed as she was. So she didn't even try.

He gave her a quick peck on the cheek that didn't deserve to be called a kiss and headed out the garage door.

Beth went upstairs. Knowing it was a stupid thing to do, she headed straight to Emma's room anyway. Her heart was breaking, and each step felt as though she were walking on broken glass. Stopping in the doorway, she looked around the nursery. The room still bore Emma's scent, a cross between baby and talcum powder. She saw so many things in her mind's eye. Emma sleeping. Emma playing. Emma smiling. Things Beth would probably never see again.

Her daughter wouldn't be her daughter anymore. Sure, the

judge had yet to make a permanent ruling, but the writing was all over the wall like some kind of grotesque graffiti. This week would become more weeks until Judge Ramsey finally awarded Darren full parental rights and relegated Beth and Robert to superfluous relatives.

Unable to bear seeing Emma's things a moment longer, Beth went to the master bedroom. That room was every bit as painful as the nursery. Here, she saw what she'd shared with Robert—from brushing their teeth side by side to making love.

Never would she love another man the way she loved Robert Ashford, but she could no longer trust his declaration of love. As Carol always preached, *actions speak louder than words*. Robert ducking out of the house tonight—a time when they should've been supporting each other through such a devastating event—showed just how little he really cared for her.

She went through her evening routine on autopilot. Washing off her makeup. Combing her hair. Putting on her nightgown. When she was done, she barely had the energy to crawl into bed, pull the blankets over her head, and lie there in the dark with nothing but her torturous thoughts.

Sleep was her only reprieve.

* * *

The house was quiet when Robert returned from Charlie's shop. The man had found a veritable treasure trove of stuff, but Robert hadn't been able to focus on anything Ben or Charlie showed him. No doubt he'd missed a lot of great opportunities for the future houses he would construct, but he honestly didn't give a shit. When the other guys had gone out for wings and beers, Robert told them he needed to go home.

He should never have left Beth. Every moment of the evening, he'd thought of her. Of Emma. When he'd asked Beth whether she wanted him to go, he'd hoped she'd tell him she needed him. He'd hesitated, literally dragged his feet, but she'd snapped at him to go in a voice that screamed that she wanted to be alone.

After kicking off his shoes, he stopped and stared at them as they lay at odd angles on the rug by the kitchen door. Why couldn't he learn to put the damn things away? Beth never complained about him being such a slob. She usually just smiled and put things away. She never griped about him working late or bitched about him leaving the toilet seat up or forgetting to replace the empty toilet paper roll. She did loads and loads of laundry and sinks full of dishes and not once did she nag at him about helping.

Beth took damned good care of him. And of Emma.

His eyes flooded with tears, but he gave his head a shake. Then it dawned on him that Beth hadn't cried, either. He would, but only when he was alone in the shower. It wasn't masculine to weep. Grown men didn't cry in front of people. They sucked it up, manned up, and moved on. Besides, his wife needed him to be strong for her.

Or did she? Beth had handled the drama in the office much better than Robert had. He'd clenched his hands into tight fists to keep from snatching Emma right back. Her screams had reached his soul, making him feel as if he were the biggest failure ever. He'd been her father, her protector. Yet he'd been powerless to stop another man from taking her away.

No wonder Beth didn't need him. She was a wonderful woman who deserved a man of equal strength and character. Instead, she'd married *him*.

After putting his shoes in the coat closet, Robert headed

upstairs. The lights were out except for the night-lights Beth had put in the hallway that lit the entire length like an airport runway. He stopped himself from going in Emma's room. He could barely keep from weeping now. Seeing his daughter's crib and toys would shatter what slim control he now kept over his emotions.

All he could see of his wife was the shape of her body under the blanket. His melancholy eased when he saw that she'd turned the ceiling fan on. Even if it might seem odd that she needed both the fan and the thick blanket, he found it quirky and more than a little endearing.

She'd brought so much warmth and happiness into his life. And how did he repay her? He'd let her down when she needed him, just like he'd let his daughter down. No wonder Beth had wanted to be alone tonight.

After stripping out of his dirty clothes, which he put in the hamper for once, he eased under the covers on his side of the bed. Beth was sleeping, judging by her slow and even breaths. Robert carefully pressed himself against her back, draping an arm over her waist and letting her sweet scent soothe him.

He wanted to make love to her, to promise her that he'd move heaven and earth to get their daughter back where she belonged. But Beth was sleeping so peacefully after such a draining day, he didn't want to be selfish and wake her up so they could talk. At least now he was holding her.

There was one idea he wanted to share with her, something that he'd only recently decided would be something good for their family. Now wasn't the time. When things settled down and Emma's visit with her father was over, then he would tell Beth his brilliant idea.

Robert wanted to have a baby with her. Only then could he be sure that she'd never leave him.

Chapter 26

Robert blinked against the sunlight streaming through the bedroom window. He mentally scolded himself for forgetting to shut the blinds before he crawled into bed.

They'd survived the first night without Emma and the world hadn't ended. Whatever he and Beth faced, they could survive—if they helped each other through.

He rolled over to wake his wife, hoping he could convince her to make love. He needed the connection. With a little luck, she would finally let her walls down and would let him back in. She'd been so emotionally closed off yesterday, so he'd given her space. Now he wanted to bridge that gap, to make their marriage stronger and to show her how much he truly loved her. Her doubts about him were far too easy to see, and the time had come to bury those doubts.

She was gone. "B?" No sounds came from the bathroom. He tried again, loud enough to be heard downstairs. "Bethany?"

There was no response.

Robert threw the covers aside and padded down to the kitchen. There weren't any dirty dishes in the sink, which meant she'd probably skipped breakfast again. He opened the doors to the deck and stuck his head out. "B? Where are you?"

Grumbling to himself, he slammed the door and headed to the garage. Her Beetle was gone.

Rubbing his hand over his face, he cursed himself for not waking up when she did. When they were first married, her mere movement in bed would jar him awake. After weeks of sleeping by her side, he'd grown accustomed to her, which was bad news for him now.

Before going back upstairs to get ready to face the day, he searched around for a note. Nothing. Not a single clue as to where she'd gone. Just a missing phone and purse that screamed she'd flown.

He texted her three times while he shaved and dressed and received no reply. Shifting from irritated to worried, he texted Dani.

B with you?

On a normal day, her replied sarcasm would've made him smile.

Did you lose your wife?

Tired of texting, he called her. After four rings, he was ready to hang up since it would be humiliating to tell her he had no idea why his wife had left. Dani answered before he could disconnect.

"What's up, Robert?"

Too worried to search for the proper words, he blurted out, "Bethany's g-gone."

"What do you mean 'gone'?"

"When I w-woke up, she wasn't here. Did she call you?"

"It's eight in the morning on a summer break day. She knows better than to call that early. So should you."

"Sorry." Every instinct inside him was screaming that Beth needed him, but he wasn't sure where to even start searching for her.

"You really don't know where she is?" Dani asked.

"Not a clue."

"Hold tight. I'm throwing on some clothes and coming over there."

Since he knew "right over" meant at least thirty minutes in Danitalk, Robert wolfed down some cereal and resorted to nervous pacing until she pulled into the driveway. She honked the annoyingly cute horn on her Prius, so he snatched up his phone and sunglasses and went outside.

"Is she back yet?" she called through the open window.

"Nope."

"No call or text?"

He shook his head.

"Then get in," Dani ordered. "I know some places we can check."

* * *

Robert was heartsick. Three hours of searching what seemed like every square inch of Cloverleaf yielded not a single clue as to where Beth had gone. Frustrated enough he wanted to pull his hair out, he weighed the idea of calling the police to get their help. Problem was that he'd heard cops wouldn't get involved in missing person cases until at least twenty-four hours had passed. If he waited that long, he'd go insane.

Where was she? He'd used up most of the juice in his battery texting and calling her. If she had her cell phone with her, the insistent playing of the song "Anyway" had to be driving her nuts.

God, she loved that song. Beth always talked about how it said so much of what she felt in her heart, that even if the chances of success weren't good, a person should always try anyway. It was a song of hope and optimism. Pure Bethany.

Why couldn't she see that the battle for Emma wasn't lost, not yet at least? Why couldn't she reach deep down for that optimism, that hope, she needed? He was here for her, ready to fight right alongside her.

So why the disappearing act? There was no answer to be found, not in his own mind or from the Ladies Who Lunch. They'd joined the search about an hour in because Dani insisted the two of them needed help.

His heart leapt when his phone rang, and he fumbled to unclip it from his belt. "Damn it," he muttered when he saw the caller ID. With a weary sigh, he answered the call. "Hey, Alexis. Now's not a good time."

"I'd say not," she said, a note of anger in her tone. "Do you want to explain why Beth asked me to start annulment proceedings?"

"What?"

Everyone in the supermarket parking lot where he and the other searchers had met turned to stare at him. No wonder, considering he'd shouted loud enough to wake the dead.

"You didn't know?" Alexis sounded as confused as Robert felt.

"N-no." He swatted at Dani, who was gripping his elbow and trying to get him to let her hear the conversation. "Is she there w-with you?"

"No. She left a message about an hour ago with my receptionist. I just now got back to the office and immediately called you to see what in the hell had happened."

"Did she say where she is?" Robert asked.

"She's not with you?"

"No." Now he had to brush all three of the Ladies away. "Stop it," he scolded. "Give me some room."

"Pardon?" Alexis said.

"Nothing. Look, I haven't seen Beth all day. Her friends and I have looked absolutely everywhere. Did she say where she was?"

"No, I'm sorry but she didn't. My assistant said Beth sounded a little…odd. She said Beth also mentioned dropping the adoption petition. I'm really worried about her, Robert."

"So am I. If you hear anything, p-please call me."

"I will," Alexis promised. "And please let me know when you find her. You know, I've been thinking hard about Judge Ramsey insisting on this visitation, and if I'm correct, it weighs in our favor."

"What's that mean?"

"What if she's giving Darren a huge dose of reality by having him take care of Emma so he can see how hard it is? She might especially want him to know how much harder it'll be when they bring the newborn home, too."

"You think the judge would d-do something like that?"

"Judge Ramsey? Absolutely. Look, go on. Go find Beth."

"Thanks. I'll be in t-touch."

Ben pulled up in his truck only a few moments after Robert ended his call with the lawyer. He jumped out and hurried to the group. "Anything yet?"

"N-no," Robert snapped. He was so upset he couldn't get the

stutter under control. Never in his life had he feared for someone so deeply. In the back of his mind, he worried that Beth had sunk into a deep depression and might even be suicidal.

No. Not Beth. No way she would consider taking her own life. She might be feeling a bit beat down by the world right now, but her heart was too full of joy, of life, to ever think about suicide. That was his panic talking.

"What do we do now?" Mallory asked, throwing up her hands.

Everyone else started talking at once. Except Dani. She stood there, lost in thought.

Robert tried to listen to his friends' suggestions, but all he heard was noise much like the adults in the Charlie Brown cartoons. He kept staring at Dani, and he saw the moment she had what looked like an epiphany. Her eyes widened and she let out a soft gasp.

"W-what?" he asked, barely able to keep from grabbing her arms and giving her a shake to get her to spill. "What did you figure out?"

"I think I know where Beth is."

He flipped his hand, trying to hurry her up. If she knew where Beth was, he wanted to be there. Now.

"Have any of you noticed that Beth hasn't cried lately?" Dani asked, her gaze shifting from person to person.

"Of course she's cried," Robert insisted.

Dani's eyes settled on him. "Has she? Really? 'Cause I haven't seen it. Not at her sister's funeral. Not over this adoption battle. Not at all!"

"You're right," Mallory said with a nod; then she knit her brows. "But Beth cries over everything."

"Movies. Songs. Even cute puppies," Jules added. "I'm with Mal. I didn't see her do more than wipe away a few tears at the funeral, not even at the graveside service. Her only sister died, and she hasn't cried?" She gave her head a shake. "That's not the Beth we know."

"Exactly," Dani said. "She hasn't mourned Tiffany. Not really. One minute she's at the grave; the next, she's taking care of Emma. She never had a chance to decompress and let go of the grief."

Robert found some of his patience and actually listened to what had just been said. The more he thought about it, the more he realized they were all right. Beth hadn't grieved for her sister. There might have been a tear or two, but that was it. They were also correct in saying that was unusual for his wife.

Beth had an enormous heart, and she wore it on her sleeve. At graduation, the Douglas students could pick their most influential teacher to hand them their diplomas. Beth always had the most kids, and there were always tears streaming down her cheeks as she said good-bye to her seniors.

Yet she hadn't wept over her sister. Add to that the endless stress caused when Darren Brown had been named Emma's father and then stolen her away. Beth had to feel like a ticking time bomb that was ready to explode.

"You're right, Dani." He rubbed the back of his neck. "But what does that have to do with where she is now?"

"She's with the only person who can help her through this," Dani announced.

Since he figured that person was him, he shook his head. "She's not here."

"You're her husband," Dani said, "but you're not who she needs right now."

"Well, then you're her best friend," he tossed back.

"She doesn't need me, either."

"Then who?"

"Tiffany. I'll bet my last tube of lipstick she's with Tiffany."

* * *

The grave finally looked acceptable, but it had taken a lot longer than Beth had expected.

She smoothed her hands down her jeans, then winced. She was a mess, covered in mud and grass stains. She easily dismissed her sorry condition. It was worth it to look disheveled since she'd gotten that way fixing Tiffany's grave.

Weeds. The darn thing had been covered with weeds. The headstone was in place, but with nothing but a slab of gray granite with her sister's name to mark where she lay, there was no way Tiffany would rest in peace in a place so grim.

Beth had jumped right back into her Beetle and hightailed it to Walmart, where she'd bought a ton of supplies. Once back with her sister, Beth had worked on the grave like a madwoman. Clearing the weeds. Planting the flowers. Putting up a shepherd's hook.

Then she'd tackled the area adjacent, a small piece of land covered in white rocks with a stone bench and a statue of an angel. Weeds were overgrowing the rocks, and the statue had a light covering of moss. She'd had to weed and scrub the bench and statue. The whole time, she'd complained to herself about the poor care the cemetery took of the grounds and vowed to find the caretaker and give him a piece of her mind.

Now she stood with her mud-caked hands on her hips and was pleased with what she'd done. The grave was now marked by a border of purple and yellow pansies, Tiffany's favorite flowers. The weeds were stuffed in the empty gray sacks for Beth to toss in the trash can when she left. The bench and statue gleamed, and the rocks were cleared of the annoying weeds.

Then her smile slowly fell. All the hard work was done, which meant she had to start thinking again. Although the thoughts were painful, she could no longer block them.

When she'd awakened that morning, she'd lain there, staring at Robert as he slept. Even with bed-ruffled hair, the man was so handsome. So masculine. Part of her wanted to reach out to him, to let him comfort her through the heartache that seemed too much to bear.

But then she'd remembered that he didn't love her, not really. His declaration had been nothing but empty words, a point proven when he was under oath. He'd been a good man and stepped up to marry her when she'd needed to strengthen the adoption petition. Now there was nothing to hold that marriage together. Emma was gone, and she wasn't coming back.

Beth still loved him. More than anything in the world—including Emma. Emma might be the daughter of her heart, but Robert was so much more. He was her mate, the man she wanted to spend this life and eternity with, and she had to let him go. She wouldn't use guilt to keep him. The time had come to set him free.

The act of calling Alexis had been painful. Sniffing back tears, she'd asked the lawyer's assistant to start an annulment so Robert could get his life back. The reason for the marriage no longer existed, not since Darren had taken Emma away. So while Beth was at it, she left a message for Alexis to drop the adoption petition. Why should she keep ripping her heart out over and over to fight a battle that was already lost?

Lost. That was exactly how she felt. *Entirely lost.* Adrift with no buoy in sight. Everyone she loved was leaving her. Her husband. Her daughter. And her sister.

The grief slammed into her, so strong she sank to her knees and let out a wail that sounded harsh to her own ears. Tiffany was dead. Up until that moment, Beth hadn't accepted that fact. Her sister was gone. She was never ever coming back.

Folding her arms across her waist, Beth cried in big, choking sobs. All the memories assailed her. The way they'd played as children. How they'd shared so much as adolescents. The love they'd had for each other as women. The agony was too much to bear.

Not only had she lost her sister, but Emma was gone, too. She was going to be raised by a man who didn't know her instead of the aunt who loved her with every piece of her heart.

And Robert. Even thinking about walking away from him renewed her pain until all Beth could do was rock and cry.

Tiffany. I need you. But you left me.

* * *

How much time had passed? Seconds? Minutes? Hours?

Beth opened her eyes, letting the sun that warmed her face into her heart for the first time in what seemed like forever. Weeping had been exactly what she needed, a way to expel the grief, the bile that had smothered her for far too long.

How many times had she advised a troubled student to let her feelings out so that she could think clearly? Seemed as though she'd finally taken her own advice.

Arms still wrapped around herself, Beth thought hard about where she would go from here. It was as though suddenly the path was crystal clear. The real Beth, the one who loved life and tried to find good in everything, talked to her now, whispering until that voice rose to a shout.

Emma was still her daughter, would always be her daughter. Beth might not be able to see her every single day as she wished, but she wasn't going to allow Darren to keep her away from Emma. Not by a long shot.

Nor was she going to walk away from Robert Ashford. The reason they'd married might have changed, but they'd exchanged vows. He might not love her. Not yet. Didn't matter. She was determined to try to make a good marriage with him. She loved Robert, and there was no way he could make love to her the way he did without a depth of feeling that approached love. No, he might not love her now. But he would. She'd make sure of it.

Her biggest problem was where to start. *Ah, yes.* Another phone call to Alexis. Beth could plead temporary insanity and ask for the lawyer to forget everything she'd said this morning. There would be no annulment, and that adoption petition was still in play. Until the court said Emma didn't belong to Beth, she did. And Beth would enjoy every darn minute of time they had together.

She needed Robert. She needed Dani. She needed the Ladies. Life might be a steep uphill battle for a while, and there was no way Beth could fight it by herself. She needed allies. She needed friends. And she needed her husband.

She lifted her head and spoke from her heart. "I can't do this alone."

A hand settled on her shoulder. "Then don't."

Chapter 27

The moment he opened the passenger door, Robert had heard Beth crying. No, not crying. Wailing as though she were in the worst pain of her life. His first instinct was to sprint across to her where she knelt on Tiffany's grave.

Dani slid from behind the wheel and hurried to him. She held him back by grabbing his upper arm. "Wait. Just give her a minute to let it out first."

He glared at her. "She needs me."

"Of course she does. But what she needs first is to get rid of the grief. If you go running to her before she can do that, she'll just bury it again, probably deeper than before."

"Why?"

"Because she'll feel like a burden to you if she cries on your shoulder. That's just how Beth is. She's strong for everyone else, but she never wants anyone to be strong for her."

"That makes absolutely n-no sense," Robert insisted. "I'm her *husband*."

"And I'm her best friend." Dani gave him a pinched frown he had a hard time deciphering, a cross between angry and empathetic.

"Look, Beth might've married you, but she hasn't accepted you as her husband. Not really. She's depended on herself for so long that she can't stop cold turkey. Let her work through this; then we'll all be there for her."

His gaze went back to his wife. She was crying and rocking on the cold ground. He wanted to go to her so badly. "Stop talking in riddles, Dani. I'm going to Beth."

"She loves you." Why did her words sound like an accusation?

"I love her."

"She doesn't believe that."

The news didn't come as a surprise to Robert. Beth had shown him in a lot of ways that she thought he'd only married her for Emma. The fact that the judge had cut him off before he could add to his stupid statement in court must have made Beth doubt him even more.

Well, he hadn't married Beth just to be Emma's father. It was damn well time to make her understand that!

Dani let go of his arm. "Look at her. *Now*, you can go."

He glanced back to his wife, and he immediately saw the change. Instead of appearing so damned defeated, Beth had risen on her knees. Although she still had her arms wrapped around herself, she'd turned her face to the sun. There wasn't a smile on her face, but the pain was clearly gone. If he judged her mood right, she had found a shred of hope and was holding it in a death grip.

Robert strode across the grass, for once not showing the proper respect by skirting around the graves. He needed to get to Beth, to let her know he would never agree to an annulment and to try to get her to continue the fight for Emma. Most of all, to let her know exactly how much he loved her.

Just as he reached her, she said, "I can't do this alone."

His heart swelled with love. She hadn't given up. Far from it. He set his hand on her shoulder. "Then don't."

Beth gasped and whipped her head around. "Robert!" She scrambled to her feet and threw herself into his open arms. "I'm so sorry," she whispered in his ear.

Every inch of her seemed to be covered in dirt. He didn't care. He pressed his lips to her temple and squeezed her tightly. "You've got n-nothing to be sorry for. I'm the one who's s-sorry."

Leaning back, she gathered her brows as she searched his eyes. "You? Why? I'm the one who disappeared on you. I'm the one who... If you only knew what I'd asked Alexis to do—"

"I know."

"You do?"

He nodded. "I talked to her when I was looking for you. She t-told me you wanted an annulment and that you were giving up on Emma's adoption."

"I didn't mean it, Robert. I didn't. None of it. I love you. I love Emma. I'm not giving up on either of you."

He cupped the back of her head and tugged until she laid her cheek against his shoulder. A cowardly thing to do, but he didn't want her to see the tears blurring his vision. "I'm not giving up on you, either, B. Ever."

* * *

Beth watched the scenery go by with little interest. Her impatience to have some privacy with Robert made her wish he'd break every speed limit. They needed to clear the air much the same as shedding her grief had helped her see the true world again.

After assuring the Ladies she was fine and had finally crawled out of the black hole of depression she'd sunk into, she wanted nothing more than to be able to talk openly and honestly with her husband. As always, they'd understood. At least the Ladies had. Ben and Connor kept giving her strange looks as though they weren't sure if they should put her on a suicide watch. She'd spent more time explaining her grief to them than she had Robert. There were a lot more things she was ready to say to him, most of which needed to be said in private.

Once everyone had left, Robert and Beth got into her car. He drove Beth to a service station close to the cemetery so she could clean up. Although there were still stains on her clothes, she'd been able to shed most of the dirt and scrub her hands and face clean.

The drive back home seemed to take forever. Robert drove, but he spent the whole trip back to Cloverleaf holding her hand. He didn't say anything, perhaps because he felt the same as she did, wanting to be able to stare her in the eyes as he bared his heart. She sure hoped that was what he was ready to do, because she was going to give him total honesty.

A late-model sports car she didn't recognize was parked in their driveway. When Robert pulled up alongside it, Beth gasped at seeing the driver—him, and a car seat. "It's Darren."

"And Emma." Robert killed the engine and opened his door.

Beth scrambled out of the car, hurrying to where Darren was pulling Emma from her seat. She looked so sad until her gaze caught Beth's. "Matka!" She extended her arms and kept twisting her hands and stretching her fingers toward her. "Matka! Matka!"

Tears pooling in her eyes, Beth took Emma into her arms and hugged her tight. Emma tangled her fingers in Beth's hair and clung to her like chewing gum on the bottom of a shoe. "I missed you, Em."

Emma finally settled down, laid her head against Beth's shoulder, and stuck her thumb in her mouth. Until she saw Robert. Then the acrobatics started all over again. "Bobber! Want Bobber!"

Beth surrendered Emma to Robert, and she wasn't at all surprised to see tears in his eyes as well. She'd been right in thinking the fight for their daughter was far from over. This bond wasn't going to be broken. Even if they couldn't have Emma with them all the time, they'd find ways to share her with her biological father.

She turned her attention to Darren, a bit surprised to see him staring at the ground, his hands in his back pockets. It was an expression an experienced teacher knew well—one of contrition. "Why are you here? Emma's supposed to be with you all week." Then she thought of Kelly and wondered if Darren brought Emma here out of necessity. "Did Kelly go into labor or something?"

"What Kelly did was leave," he said, finally letting his eyes meet hers.

"Leave? You mean she walked out on you?"

He nodded.

"Why?"

He heaved a sigh. "She'd had enough of me, said she didn't even know me anymore."

"I'm sorry."

"No, I'm the one who's sorry. I shouldn't have taken Emma away. I was just pissed, okay? I mean"—he dragged his fingers through his hair—"Tiff didn't even tell me! For shit's sake, how could she have Emma and not even tell me?" His face grew red as he continued the rant. "I would've been there for her. I know I was a jerk in the past, but I loved Tiffany. I would've helped her."

Robert came to stand at Beth's side. Emma had relaxed against him, and her eyelids were at half-mast. Soon, she'd be asleep. "Why did you and Tiffany break up?" he asked, his voice whisper soft.

Darren answered in kind. "I told her a long time ago that I didn't want kids. Ever. And I meant it. Even told her I'd made an appointment for a vasectomy. She got... upset."

"Did she know how you felt?" Beth asked. When he shook his head, she sighed. "No wonder she didn't tell you about Emma. She figured you'd think she was trying to trap you or something."

"But she should've told me!" Darren was near to shouting. He glanced at Emma and lowered his voice. "I really would've been there for her."

"I don't doubt that," Beth said. "What's done is done, though. Emma's your daughter." Then she remembered Kelly. "You never had the vasectomy."

"I damn well did," he said with a nod.

"But Kelly is—"

"Pregnant. I know. The baby's not mine."

"Yet you're still marrying her?" Robert asked before Beth could.

"I have to. She needs me. At least, I hope she does."

None of this was making any sense, and she could see the confusion in Robert's eyes as well. "Why don't we all go inside? We can put Emma down for a nap and talk."

* * *

Robert could hear Beth and Darren talking softly as he came down the stairs. He'd been with Emma longer than he'd expected, changing her diaper, holding her, rocking her. He simply hadn't been able to leave her there, no matter how peacefully she was sleeping.

As soon as they figured out what the hell was going on with Darren bringing Emma back, Robert was going to sit his wife down and talk some sense into her.

He nodded to Darren when he sat down beside Beth. When Robert draped his arm over her shoulders, he was pleased that she leaned closer against his side. Whatever catharsis she'd gone through at her sister's grave had brought his wife back to him. *Thank God.*

"Catch me up," Robert said, giving her a quick kiss on the cheek.

"Darren has changed his mind about wanting sole custody of Emma," she said so matter-of-factly he had to blink a few times to let the words sink in.

"Really?"

Darren nodded. "Like I told you outside, I was pissed that Tiff had lied to me. She knew I didn't want to raise a kid."

Robert understood how the guy felt. He hadn't wanted children, either. Not when he was younger. Thankfully, he'd never considered a vasectomy. A scalpel near his balls? He cringed at the mere thought of it.

He couldn't help but ask, "If Kelly's baby isn't yours, why are you two engaged?"

"Kelly didn't know I got snipped." Darren's voice held a note of sadness. "We broke up a while back. She had a one-night stand with her old boyfriend. We were back together before she found out she was knocked up."

And what could he possibly say about that little tidbit of information. "Oh... um... sorry."

Darren shrugged. "My problem, not yours. The guy's a bastard, and I'm not letting him near Kelly or that kid, even if she's not with me now. That's what finally made me understand what you're going through." His gaze wandered to the stairs. "Look, Kelly's kid isn't mine, but it is. And Emma might be my kid, but she's not. Get it?"

"Not really," Robert admitted, even though Beth was nodding.

"You want to know her, but you don't want her to live with you," she said.

Robert stared at her. "You got that from 'Emma might be my kid, but she's not'?"

"I think so."

"Beth's right," Darren said. "All Emma did at my place was cry and ask for you two. At least I think that's what she wanted. She kept saying 'Matka' and 'Bobber.' Not sure what those mean."

"I'm Matka," Beth said. "Her way of saying mom. Robert is Bobber."

Darren nodded. "That's kinda what I thought. Anyway, according to my lawyer, she's happy with you two. I can't turn her life upside down when I don't even want her to be with me full-time. I want to know her, though."

"We totally understand that," Beth said, her whole face lighting up. "We'd never cut you out of her life. Ever. You're her father and—"

"No, I'm not. Not really. But I want to see her from time to time. Okay?"

Robert nodded, squeezing Beth a little tighter. "Absolutely. We'll work something out, I promise."

His heart was singing in happiness. He'd done nothing but worry about Emma, about how the change might cause psychological scars, about whether Darren could be a true father to her. He had to give credit to the man. He was wise enough to know when he'd made a mistake. Now everything could be put back to rights.

Darren stood. "I'll call my lawyer and tell him to drop the custody suit. I won't block your adoption petition, either."

"We can call her Emma Brown, if you'd like," Beth offered.

"Nah. If you're adopting her, let her have the same name as you guys." Darren actually grinned. "If I come see her from time to time, I imagine that'll be confusing enough for her. Some strange man who pops in and out of her life. Give her your name."

They walked Darren to the door, the three of them now quiet in a rather melancholy way. What he was doing took a lot of courage, and Robert was afraid to say anything that might make the man change his mind. Better to stay silent than to accidentally say something stupid.

Beth waved good-bye as Darren backed out of the driveway before shutting the door. Then she turned to stare up at Robert. "We need to talk."

Robert couldn't stop himself from snorting. "B, that is the biggest understatement of the century."

She rose on tiptoes, looped her arms around his neck, and pressed her lips to his. A quick kiss before she eased back, her eyes locked with his. "I love you, Robert Ashford. With all my heart. And I'm never going to let you go."

Chapter 28

Beth was ready to open up to her husband in a way she'd never done before. She was ready to let him in, to stop trying to hold everything together all by herself. And she was ready to explore exactly how he felt about her. Unfortunately, she needed a shower first since she still felt as though she were caked with mud.

As she tried to move away, Robert caught her and pulled her back against him. He tunneled his fingers through her hair and held her head while he ravaged her mouth. Responding in kind, she wrapped her arms around his waist and smoothed her hands down so she could palm his tight backside.

She would've been content to stay that way forever, but his cell phone rang. They eased apart, both sighing as he popped it off his belt and checked the caller ID. "It's Alexis. I was supposed to call her when we found you. She's probably worried sick."

"Then you should answer."

It was difficult being in on only half the conversation. Whatever Alexis was telling him infected Robert until he was practically bouncing on his feet. He'd taken her hand in his and was squeezing it tight enough to cut off the circulation. After telling

Alexis he'd found Beth and that she was fine, he said "yes" and "we know" too many times for Beth to count.

Then he said, "There won't be an annulment." He leveled a hard stare at Beth. "My wife's not going anywhere."

Beth couldn't stop smiling. Robert was right. She wasn't going anywhere. For the first time since she'd moved into this house, it felt like home.

After he ended the call, he kept a tight grip on her hand and dragged her to the couch. He sat before tugging her onto his lap.

"I'm a mess," she protested, trying to stand.

"I don't give a shit." He held her firmly in place. "Damn, I want to make love to you. But we need to talk first."

Since he wasn't disturbed by the dirt, she nuzzled his neck. "I want you, too." Tugging his earlobe with her teeth, she waited for him to tell her whatever it was he thought they needed to discuss. "Well?"

"Well what?"

She traced the edges of his ear with her tongue. "What do you want to talk about?"

"Talk?"

How easy it was to distract him. "Yeah, honey. You said you wanted to talk before we head upstairs and I rip your clothes off." Figuring nothing would get said if she kept teasing him, Beth laid her head against his shoulder.

"Oh yeah. Talk." Wrapping his arms around her, Robert kissed her forehead. "We need to clear the air."

"About?"

"About where we stand. You know, as a couple. Why would you think I'd even consider something as stupid as an annulment?"

Things were so much clearer to her now, as though a thick fog had permeated her thoughts and had now lifted. "I wanted to set you free."

"B..."

She eased back and put her fingertips gently against his lips. "Let me finish. Please."

He nodded as he captured her hand again.

"You told me you loved me, but I couldn't believe you," Beth admitted. "I'd convinced myself you wanted to be Emma's father more than you wanted to be my husband. I thought you were going through, I don't know, some midlife crisis or something."

"Nonsense."

"I realize that now."

He cocked his head. "Do you really?"

"I do." Her teeth tugged on her bottom lip. "At least I *think* I do."

A frustrated growl rose from his chest. He gripped her chin and stared intently into her eyes. "Listen, B, and listen good. I. Love. You. Sure, I love our daughter, too, but I didn't jump into this marriage as a way to be Emma's dad. I let Emma be my excuse."

"I don't understand."

"There's always been a spark between us, even when you first started working at Douglas. I was just a dumbass back then." He shrugged hard enough to jostle her. "I needed to play the field for a while, I guess."

Beth gave his hand a squeeze. "Most guys do."

"Well, then I finally grew up and realized how much I wanted you. I just never found the courage to act on it." Robert gave her a heart-stopping smile. "Then Emma came into your life, and she became a really good reason to hang around you all the time."

"Are you saying you've loved me since I started teaching at Douglas?"

"Not loved," he replied. "It took me spending a lot more time with you to make it grow into love. But I felt something for you, something *strong*. And now it *is* love, B. Even if we didn't have Emma, I'd still want you. I'd still need you. I'd still want us to have our own child, to have a family."

After pressing a quick kiss to his cheek, Beth grinned at him. "I believe you, Robert. I do. And I love you, too."

"So it's settled, then? No more ridiculous talk about annulments?"

She traced an X over her chest. "Cross my heart."

"Good," he said with a decisive nod. "So what do you say we toss out those birth control pills of yours and have one of our own?"

"You want to have a baby? But Emma's home now."

"And she'll make a great older sister."

A smile bloomed on Beth's beautiful face. "A baby..."

Robert gave her a quick, hard kiss. "Yeah, B. A baby. Yours and mine. What do you say?"

"Wow. I just hadn't thought we'd have more kids."

"Of course we will! I was thinking—"

"Seems you've done a lot of that lately. Could become a habit."

He ignored the sarcasm. "Ashford Homes is making really good money. If you want to leave teaching for a while—or forever—to spend time with Emma, and with any babies we have, you could."

After giving her head a small shake, Beth said, "That's enough for now. Please. My head is spinning. You've given me so much to think about."

"Good. So now we need to go see Alexis. She wants to meet

with us after lunch so we can tell her what Darren told us and help plot our next move." His gaze searched hers. "Why are you grinning like the Cheshire cat?"

"Do you realize you haven't stuttered once since Darren left?"

"Really?"

She nodded. "You're not worried anymore, so the stutter disappeared."

"What exactly was I worried about?"

"Me. You thought I might leave you, didn't you? That's why you started stuttering again. You weren't sure I loved you, and you were afraid we'd lose Emma."

He thought it over before he grinned. "I think you're right."

"Well, then…I need a shower if we're going to go see Alexis."

Robert helped her stand, but when she tried to take a step away, he tugged her back into his arms. After a long, lazy, very thorough kiss, he said, "Since we've got plenty of time, how about I join you in the shower?"

Beth laughed, crooked her finger, and ran all the way up the stairs as he chased her.

* * *

When Alexis opened the door to her office and motioned for them to enter, Robert got to his feet, still holding tight to Beth's hand. He couldn't seem to make himself stop touching her.

They'd made love in the shower, fast and furious. After the release that had torn through him, he should've been relaxed and sated. But if his wife so much as batted her eyelashes at him, he'd drag her to someplace private and make love to her all over again. It was as though he couldn't get enough of her, probably because he finally believed deep in his heart that she loved him. Damn good thing, because she held his heart firmly in her hands.

They sat in their customary chairs as Alexis took her seat at her desk. For the first time that Robert could remember, the lawyer had a smile on her face—a genuine, heartfelt smile.

She plucked a paper from the file on her right. "I just received some interesting paperwork that I wanted to share with both of you. Darren Brown is dropping his custody suit and surrendering parental rights to Emma to you two."

"That was fast," Robert said, grinning back at Alexis.

"What do you mean?"

"We only saw him a couple of hours ago."

Her stern frown made him feel bad he hadn't mentioned the visit when Alexis had called. At the time, all Robert could think of was settling things between him and Beth. "I owe you an apology. I should have called when Darren came to visit us."

"He was at your place?"

Robert nodded and told her all they'd discussed.

Beth finished the story. "Between learning about Emma and dealing with Kelly's pregnancy, the poor guy probably felt like the whole world was closing in on him."

Alexis leaned back in her chair. "That explains a lot. Our investigator had discovered he'd had a vasectomy."

"How?" Beth asked. "I mean, shouldn't medical records be private?"

"He told a reporter," Alexis replied. "Last year, the local paper did a story about him starting the new restaurant. When she asked him how he had the time to devote to the place, he told her he wasn't going to have children and admitted to just having had the vasectomy. I was waiting to depose him about it so we could use his reticence to be a father at the custody trial. Seems as if there won't be a trial now."

"Thank God," Beth said, her tone full of relief.

The turn of events still shocked Robert, but he knew better than to question a good thing.

Alexis slapped her palms against her desktop. "Well, then… there's only one thing left to do."

"What's that?" he asked.

"Get that adoption petition to the judge so you can both put all this behind you and focus on the future."

Chapter 29

The gang's all here!" Beth sang out, feeling more like herself than she had in months. The optimism. The positivity. The joy of life. They were all back. "Finally!"

Dani dropped her purse next to a deck chair. "Yeah, yeah. I know. I'm late. *Again.*" She handed Beth the large bowl she carried. "Here's the potato salad, as promised."

"Dandi!" Emma shouted, using her baby talk name for Dani, one they'd all quickly adopted. She kicked her chubby legs and started bouncing against Robert's hip hard enough he had trouble holding on to her.

With a chuckle, Dani went to them. Since she was one of the few people who could coax Emma away from her father, Dani gathered Emma into her arms. "Aunt Dandi's here. Where's my kiss?"

Emma put her hands on either side of Dani's face and gave her a rather sloppy kiss.

Dani shot Robert a conspiratorial smile. "It's ready, Robert."

"Ready? What's ready?" Beth asked as she shifted her gaze

between her husband and her best friend. She knew them both well enough to see right through them.

"The game, as Sherlock Holmes would say, is afoot," Dani teased.

"You'll find out soon enough," Robert replied. "After we eat. Not about to let all this great food go to waste."

Having grown accustomed to his penchant for surprises, she let out a rather fake-sounding resigned sigh. "Which means you'll tell me when you're darn good and ready, right?"

"Exactly." With a chuckle, he pulled her into his arms and planted a kiss on her lips. "You know me too well, B."

Considering the Ladies and their guys were all staring at them, Beth could feel heat bloom on her cheeks. Would she ever become accustomed to showing affection to her husband in front of others?

She'd have to since Robert had a fondness for holding her hand, draping an arm over her shoulder, or giving her a kiss whenever the mood struck.

"Let's eat!" Ben announced from where he stood at Robert's grill, which had been surrendered by Robert because he'd acknowledged Ben's superior chef abilities.

The rest of the crew had supplied the side dishes for the adoption celebration pot luck. Emma was now officially Beth and Robert's daughter. A visitation schedule had been approved by the court so Darren would be a part of Emma's life, but her day-to-day care now rested in the Ashfords' hands.

Everything was finally as it should be.

"Matka!" Emma twisted in Dani's arms, reaching for Beth.

Beth wondered if her heart would ever stop reacting with a surge of happiness whenever her daughter called her. Her gratitude to Darren for putting aside his parental rights and doing the right thing for Emma was boundless. "C'mere, Em."

"I said let's eat," Ben grumbled.

"In a minute, honey," Mallory said as she and Jules joined Beth, Robert, and Dani.

"Did you decide anything about your job yet?" Dani asked Beth.

"Yeah," Mallory said. "I'm dying of curiosity, too. Will you be heading back to school with us in a few weeks, or will Dani and I be the only Ladies who still teach?"

"I'll be back," Beth announced.

Robert jumped into the conversation. "At least for now. Once she's pregnant—"

"Pregnant?" Jules gaped at them. "You're trying to have a baby?"

Beth nodded and smiled as she leaned against her husband. "We are."

Hands on her hips, Jules tried to look angry. The smile belied the body language. "How did I not know this?"

"You missed Ladies' Night Out last week," Mallory teased. "Drama always ensues."

"Flushed the rest of the birth control pills last week," Beth announced.

"We're free, free falling," Robert sang to the tune of the Tom Petty song.

"*Let's. Eat!*" Ben said through a clenched jaw. "Or I'm not going to be held responsible for hamburgers that taste like hockey pucks."

* * *

The sound of a car horn repeatedly honking in a slow, steady rhythm caught Beth's ear.

"Did you hear that?" she asked the Ladies as she put the last plate in the dishwasher and shut the door.

"You mean that annoying neighbor with the stuck car alarm?" Jules asked.

Beth nodded.

"Oh yeah. I hear it."

"Sounds kinda close." Dani went to the back door and opened it. "Like it's coming from the front of *your* house." She shut the door. "You should really go check, Beth."

Since she'd just finished rinsing the sink, Beth dried her hands and set aside the dishcloth. She knit her brows at Mallory and Jules, who'd begun laughing after Dani made her suggestion. They were up to something—something that obviously included Robert. Perhaps Beth could finally find out what they'd all been up to. "Okay…spill."

"Spill?" Dani tossed Beth her faux innocent look, one that had never worked before. "Spill what?"

Rolling her eyes, Beth said, "Fine. I'll play along. How about we all go see whatever it is my husband wants me to see?"

She led the procession to the front door. As she stepped over the threshold and onto the porch, she stopped so abruptly that Dani ran right into her back. "What in the devil…?"

A dark blue Honda CRV sat in the middle of Beth's front lawn, so close she could've stood on the edge of the porch and crawled right into the passenger seat.

Dani gave her a playful push between the shoulder blades. "Go on, silly. Go see for yourself."

Tears stung her eyes as her gaze caught Robert's from where he sat in the driver's seat. "You told me the Beetle was getting new brakes."

A grin lit his handsome face. "I lied."

"I can see that."

"Admit it," Dani said, coming to stand at Beth's side. "You needed something bigger."

"Especially if you're thinking of having another munchkin," Jules added as she and Mallory moved to Beth's other side.

"It's wonderful." Beth would never stop feeling as though she was truly blessed to have such a generous and loving man in her life. "Thank you so much."

Robert kept on grinning. "You like it?"

"I *love* it."

He put the CRV into gear and drove it off the front lawn to park on the driveway. He strode over to the porch, wrapped his arms around Beth's hips, and lifted her. A squeal spilled out as he spun her around in a circle. Then he let her slide down his body until she was in his arms. "You really like it?"

"I told you, I love it. You're so good to me."

"Anything for you, Mrs. Ashford."

Mrs. Ashford. She still had a hard time thinking of herself as anything but Beth Rogers. "I'm not sure I'll ever get used to hearing that name."

Robert gave her a long, lazy kiss. "You're going to have to, B. Good thing you've got a lifetime to learn."

Turn the page for a preview of the next book in the

Ladies Who Lunch

series

Chapter 1

One more day.

That was all Danielle Bradshaw had left. One more day before the school year started and her life would become a routine that made an air traffic controller's schedule seem relaxed.

Up at five in the morning. A three-mile run. Shower and pour some coffee down her throat—maybe finding a moment for some oatmeal or granola—and then get herself dressed and haul her fanny to work. Teach six sophomore English classes, usually with at least thirty kids in each, and head home to do some laundry and try to make a dent in the eternal pile of student papers to grade.

And the next day?

Do it all over again.

"Danielle?" Her principal's call kept her from leaving the main office.

She'd made a quick trip to the heavily guarded supply closet to grab a new gradebook and was going back to her room to get ready to face her new students. Her clean escape had just been thwarted. "Yes?"

"I need your help." He turned to motion to someone in his office. "Nathaniel? Come on out here. I want you to work with Ms. Bradshaw."

Oh no.

She had no doubt what Mr. Reinhardt wanted from her. The department was getting a new teacher. Finally. That would mean some relief for the onerous number of kids the teachers of Stephen Douglas High School faced on a daily basis.

But with that blessing came the need to break in a new teacher. Since she'd been promoted to department head this school year, a position that came with an embarrassingly small raise and a hell of a lot more responsibility, she'd have to be the one to show the newbie the ropes. There was no doubt this was a kid fresh from college, because there was no way the corporation would scare up enough pay for someone with experience. The administrators were too cheap.

Her day was now shot to hell.

Her biggest concern, aside from having to spend every minute of her work day spoon-feeding some barely-old-enough-to-shave guy, was that as department head she should've been included in the decision on which teacher to hire. Since her summer had gone by without a single word from her boss about interviews, she'd simply assumed that the school corporation hadn't scraped together the funds to get a new English instructor.

With a sigh, she tried to paste a smile on her face and welcome the guy who now faced the most challenging nine months of his life. "Hi, I'm—"

The words froze in her throat as she took in the man standing in front of her, flashing her a smile that damn near stopped her heart before sending it slamming against her ribs.

He was blond, his hair cut in a neat, conservative style and slicked back with the right amount of gel. He wore a dark suit and red tie as though a born executive. His eyes were the most fascinating shade of blue, the color of the clearest of the Caribbean waters. And exactly like those waters, Dani could feel herself sinking into them.

"Nathaniel Ryan." He held out his hand. "But I prefer Nate."

Somehow she was able to force herself from her stupor to shake his hand. "Danielle, um, Dani Bradshaw."

Jim Reinhardt cuffed Nate on the shoulder. "Dani will get you introduced and give you a tour of the place." His gaze shifted to her. She knew that look well. It was the same guilty grimace he gave her whenever he'd just given her a nearly impossible task.

Breaking in a new teacher the day before school qualified as a "nearly impossible task." The only thing that kept her from being furious with Jim was the fact that he was the best principal she'd ever worked for.

She found her voice. "What room will he be in?"

"Nate's going to be in the empty room at the end of the English hall."

"Um, okay." The last time anyone had used the room was five years ago. Since then, it had been a place to store all the broken desks. The teachers in her department called it the *Black Hole of Calcutta*.

"Don't worry, Dani," Jim said. "I already had the custodians clear it out. Nate, Dani's going to be your mentor this year. She teaches sophomore English—same thing you'll have. She'll help get you ready for tomorrow, and my office door is always open if you need me. We'll both be observing you a couple of times this year—once the first week or two, so be ready."

On that, he strode back to his office, leaving her with the new teacher.

God, her friends would be laughing at the way she gaped at Nate Ryan. The Ladies Who Lunch, her closest friends, loved to joke about how nonchalant Dani always acted around handsome men. Even though all three of her friends were happily married, they had an eye for good-looking men and ogled any hunk who passed them while Dani rolled her eyes at their brazenness.

If they could only see her now...She couldn't even put together enough words to make a coherent sentence.

She should be talking a blue streak right now, telling this guy—this Nate Ryan—about the ins and outs of Stephen Douglas High School. She should be explaining how to set up his electronic gradebook and attendance file. She should be doing something productive rather than standing there staring at a man who had to be at least nine years younger than her own thirty-one. Thirty-two in a matter of weeks.

The man had a cliché baby face. She'd be amazed if he was more than twenty-one or twenty-two, fresh out of college and full of that naïve enthusiasm for teaching that she lost a little of with each new school year.

A decade ago, she'd been standing where Nate Ryan stood, ready to take on the world. Ready to teach kids and believing she had the power to change the world, to reach each and every student and help them learn to love reading and writing.

Ten years at Douglas High School had seasoned her. She wasn't entirely soured on teaching. Not yet, but that time was on the horizon. One of the Ladies Who Lunch had left teaching only two years ago. Juliana Wilson had been a special education teacher who'd burned out and carved herself a profitable new career as a real estate agent.

Would the Ladies Who Lunch still be the Ladies Who Lunch once they all left the profession? They'd found each other years ago, bonding as they shared their lunch period each day. They'd weathered Juliana jumping ship, still finding time to get together a couple of times a week.

But if Dani left, too?

Who exactly was she fooling? There was no reason even worrying about leaving. As it was, she'd be lucky if she saved enough money to retire at sixty-five.

"So, Ms. Bradshaw..." Nate raked his fingers through his short hair.

Dani got a hold of herself. The poor kid was obviously nervous. "Call me Dani. Please. How about I show you your room? I have no idea what's usable in there, but the department has several sets of classroom books you can use that I can help you carry over. We normally use e-books for our kids because they all have electronic tablets instead of textbooks."

His eyes widened. "Really? Wow. That had to be expensive. I thought schools were pinching pennies like crazy nowadays."

"We are. E-books are cost-effective. They're a helluva lot cheaper than hardcover textbooks. Plus the kids don't get strained backs from carrying them around." She led the way to the big double doors leading to the main office and was pleased when Nate reached past her to pull one open for her.

The man had manners, something sorely lacking in the guys she'd dated the last few years. Not that there'd been that many.

"Follow me," she said, gesturing toward the English hall. "I'll show you to your new home."

* * *

Nate Ryan followed his new boss, trying desperately to keep from staring at her ass.

But *damn*…Her backside was tight and round and begging to be squeezed.

He hadn't expected a department head to be so young. She couldn't be that much older than his own twenty-three. How could she already be the leader of the whole English department? His mother had retired from teaching just last spring. She was barely fifty, but she'd been her school's science department head for only three years.

Maybe Dani was the oldest in the English department. A lot of experienced teachers were leaving the profession. His mother's retirement had all but been forced on her when the school corporation sponsored a buyout for teachers at the top of the pay scale. She'd crunched some numbers based on the money she'd saved over the years and what she'd get for jumping ship and decided that she'd do fine retiring.

His stepfather had joined her mother, taking his thirty-year pension from being a police detective and leaving the force. Now they were working together, writing books and running a blog about traveling in middle age. It was brilliant. Every trip they took was deductible, and they were able to go to the places they'd always dreamed of visiting.

Maybe Danielle Bradshaw had benefited from a mass exodus of older teachers with a promotion. "How old are you?"

Sweet Lord, he'd gone and blurted that out. He forgave himself because his curiosity was killing him.

She stopped and turned to face him. "Did you really just ask me that?"

"I'm afraid I did. Sorry."

"Thirty-one," she replied. "Any particular reason you need to know?"

Not at all surprised his cheeks felt flushed, he shrugged. "I'm really sorry. I was...curious. You seemed kinda young to be department head."

Unlocking the door, she spoke over her shoulder. "I just got the job this year. You'll be my first newbie." She opened the door. "Here you go. Room thirteen."

"Great," he mumbled. Being a new teacher was tough enough. The last thing in the world he needed was to start out with an unlucky room number.

"It's haunted, you know." She tossed him an enigmatic smile.

"My room?"

"Yep. When the school was first built, this was a dressing area for the guys who refereed our basketball games. One of them collapsed during a game in 1976."

"Heart attack?" he asked.

She nodded. "He died in this room."

"Wonderful. Now I've got a ghost *and* an unlucky room number."

Her laugh was as sweet as her voice. Some women had voices that grated on him. High-pitched. Squeaky. Made him want to gnash his teeth.

Dani's voice was a pleasant register, her laugh husky and genuine.

"At least the heat and air-conditioning work in this room," she countered. "My room is like a refrigerator all winter."

"Where's your room? I mean, you're my mentor, right? Shouldn't we be close?"

"I'm in eleven. Right across the hall. Don't worry. If the kids get out of control, I've got a whip and a chair handy. Just scream. I'll come running."

His first classroom, a chance to start his career. Hopes high, Nate flipped on the bank of light switches. The fluorescent lights buzzed and popped, sputtering to life. One look around made him wish they hadn't.

The place was horrible. Desks were lined up in institutional rows, all the seats a boring brown. The walls were what his mother always called "school beige," and there wasn't even a window to bring in any light.

Prisons had to be more inviting.

"Looks like I'm heading to Education Depot at lunch," he said, talking more to himself than his boss. There was a shitload of stuff he'd have to buy. Bulletin board borders. Posters. A desk calendar. He was definitely starting from scratch since his mother had been a science teacher. None of her leftovers would really work with the exception of her YOU CAN'T SCARE ME, I TEACH poster.

"Nope," Dani retorted. "Lunch will be with our department. It's the only chance we get to meet before school starts tomorrow. You'll have to go shopping after school."

He frowned, panic tickling at his nerves.

He shouldn't even be here. Nate had already accepted a job with a department store regional office, writing copy for their advertisements. He was supposed to start tomorrow. All the teaching jobs he'd applied for had been filled during the summer months, so he'd given up hope for this school year. That was as it should be. Teachers should be hired early enough to give them time to plan lessons, decorate classrooms, and gird their loins to face the students.

Instead, he'd received a phone call from Jim Reinhardt yesterday morning. Hoping to put his degree to better use than penning advertisements, he'd interviewed right after lunch and signed his contract first thing this morning. He had not a damn thing ready for the kids who'd be stepping across the threshold of room thirteen tomorrow to greet their new English teacher.

How in the hell am I going to do this?

"I'll help as much as I can." Dani laid her hand on his arm. "I've got your back."

So he'd spoken the question aloud. Not a surprise. His former girlfriend said it was one of his less endearing habits. Of course, she had her own bad habits, one of those being her getting agitated with him easily and often.

Dani drew back her hand and moved toward the bare teacher's desk with the grace of a ballerina. Her hair made him think of a dancer, too. Blond, even a lighter shade than his own. She'd pulled it into a tight bun that accentuated her slender neck.

He suddenly wanted to see how long her hair was, whether it was naturally straight when she let it down. And when she fixed her intense blue eyes on him, every thought he had seemed to fly right out of his brain.

Thirty-one. Eight years older. Nate had always been drawn to older women, probably because girls his age were so damned flighty. His one serious relationship had almost resulted in marriage, but his girlfriend's behavior had changed abruptly after a miscarriage. She'd started going to parties, saying she needed to be young, that losing their baby had made her realize exactly how close she'd come to having to grow up before her time.

They'd broken up after dating less than a year.

Every date he'd gone on since then had left him fearing he'd never have another serious relationship. Did all twentysomething girls think going out and drinking themselves stupid was the only way to celebrate a weekend?

Nate hated going out. Drinking made his head hurt. Besides, he didn't have too many close friends, so a night on the town would be boring. The friends he did have jokingly—or perhaps insultingly?—called him an old fogey. So what? He liked to be in bed by the end of the local news each night, and he was the ultimate creature of habit.

No, girls his age didn't interest him.

But Danielle Bradshaw?

She interested Nate. A lot.

For all he knew, she was happily married with five kids. That, and she was his new boss, the woman who'd be evaluating him to see if this would be his one and only year teaching at Douglas High. He had no business thinking about her as anything but a colleague.

The weight of the world suddenly settled on his shoulders. Tomorrow, six classes of eager new students would be sitting in those stark desks, expecting him to have a syllabus, a set of class rules, and a lesson to teach them.

What he had was jack shit.

Dani stepped over to one of the desks, her gaze sweeping the room. "I don't know about you, but I hate having rows like this. I put my desks in pairs."

"I can move things around?" The only classroom he'd spent time in had been when he student taught, and his supervising teacher hadn't wanted Nate to do anything to personalize the room. That only emphasized the fact that it wasn't Nate's classroom.

She laughed at his question, and he felt his mouth twitch, threatening a grin in response. "It's your room, *Mr. Ryan*. You can move the desks, the bookshelves, the—"

"Should be easy since they're empty," he drawled. "Not sure I'll ever get used to Mr. Ryan, either."

At least she got his dry sense of humor because she chuckled again. "When you hear it a hundred times a day, you will. And no worry on décor. I've got a ton of posters you can use."

"Posters?"

"One of our teachers left a couple of years ago. Went on maternity leave and never came back. She left all of her stuff, and I didn't toss it."

"Typical teacher."

She cocked her head. "Pardon?"

"You're a pack rat."

A smile lit her face. "I resemble that remark. But how do you know that? This is your first job, right?"

He nodded. "My mom was a teacher. I don't think she's ever thrown anything away. Always says she might need it for her classroom."

"If she's anything like me," Dani said, "she never uses any of it. Right?"

"Right."

"Let's go to my room." She herded him toward the door and flipped off the switches. "We'll get you some stuff to brighten up this place."

Although he appreciated her help, he had something more pressing. "I'd rather you hand me a stack of lesson plans for the week. I've got nada, not even a copy of the texts and novels I need to use."

She shut the door behind them. "Don't worry, Nate. I'm the other sophomore-level teacher. We need to sync our lessons, so for now, I'll share all mine with you. As the year goes on, we can start to plan things together."

Surely he'd heard her wrong. Share all her lesson plans? She couldn't mean that. Most teachers seemed to guard their lesson plans as if they were printed on gold tablets. "Really?"

"Really. We've spent the last couple of years aligning curriculum. All of us share so we're teaching the same things at the same time."

"Thank God." Right after the words fell out of his mouth, he realized how desperate he sounded.

"C'mon." She started walking down the hall, the heels of her shoes clicking against the terrazzo floor. "Let's go see what we can scrape up for this nightmare of a classroom."

About the Author

Sandy lives in a quiet suburb of Indianapolis with her husband of thirty years and is a high school social studies teacher. She and her husband own a small stable of harness racehorses and enjoy spending time at the two Indiana racetracks. She has been an Amazon Best Seller and has won numerous writing awards, including two HOLT Medallions.

Please visit her website at sandy-james.com for more information or find her on Twitter or Facebook at sandyjamesbooks.